LAND OF HOPE

Book Three of
THE HUGUENOT CONNECTION
Trilogy

PAUL C. R. MONK

A BLOOMTREE PRESS book.

First published in 2018 by BLOOMTREE PRESS.

ISBN 978-0-9934442-9-6

Copyright © Paul C. R. Monk 2018

www.paulcrmonk.com

Cover design by David Ter-Avanesyan.
Formatting by Polgarus Studio.

BY THE SAME AUTHOR

Strange Metamorphosis

Subterranean Peril

In the Huguenot Connection trilogy:

Merchants of Virtue

Voyage of Malice

Land of Hope

Also in the The Huguenot Connection series:

May Stuart

ONE

'After a number of setbacks, at last I find myself travelling aboard a merchant ship a free man. My only regret, my dear wife, is that I asked you to join me in London, since I am still on the other side of the world.

'As I sail along the North American coast to New York, where I plan to secure my passage to London, I have heard it said many a time that there is great unrest in England.

'I pray that this unrest between the Catholic king and his subjects does not turn to civil war, should William of Orange, as I have heard it suggested, claim the throne of England for himself and his English wife. Should war there be, I pray to God that you, my dear wife, and our children will find refuge, and that it pleaseth God to soon bring us together in this world gone mad.'

IN CADENCE WITH the gentle pitch of the ship, Jacob Delpech lifted his quill off the paper, which he had placed atop a barrel of odorous ginger loaves.

He knew very well that the letter in all probability would not reach Jeanne before he arrived in the English capital.

Nevertheless, setting down on paper his gravest thoughts gave him a vent for his regretted demand. He let the plume tickle the stubble beneath his nose as his cold fingers took refuge inside the sleeve of his fur coat, purchased off Chesapeake Bay, Virginia, from a gentleman travelling south.

The captain's roar above deck interrupted Jacob's train of thought. 'Lay low the mainsails, lads! Keep her easy, keep her well east o' them Oyster Islands!'

The base of the mainmast gave a groan as the crew set his orders into action.

Picking up the thread of his thoughts, Delpech glanced at the young woman opposite him, asleep on the floor in the dim light, her young daughter curled into her body and a cape wrapped around them both. The English ship he had boarded in Nassau had put into port to water and to trade in Carolina, where the woman had pleaded for passage. She had promised the captain that her husband would pay on arrival, he having ventured ahead some months past.

Jacob had since overheard her saying to a neighbouring passenger that she could no longer bear the midges and mosquitoes in Charles Town, having already lost two of her children to fever.

The captain blasted out further orders, and the sleeping huddle began to stir. Clawing her shawl away from her face, the woman found herself locking eyes with the gentleman opposite, and instinctively trying to decipher the meaning of his furrowed brow. Was there a good soul behind that stern, unshaven façade? She had previously decided to believe that there was, so she allowed the corner of her mouth to twitch into a half smile.

Before Jacob realised he was staring at the object of his

inner conversation, he caught the searching, anxious look that accompanied the woman's timid smile. He offered a nod in greeting as he put down his quill and then returned his writing material and letter to his leather pouch. Suppressing his worrying thoughts, he strode to the steps leading to the upper deck, before social convention required that words be exchanged between them. His mind was crowded enough without having to dwell on other people's struggles.

As a man of southern skies, Jacob could never fathom why people had to submit themselves to the rigours of the cold northern winter when there was plenty of room down south. However, there he was, and thankful indeed for his warm overcoat as he stiffly climbed the mid-deck steps and showed his face to the breaking, dingy December morning. Raising a hand to the cold sea spray, he turned his gaze towards the ship's wheel, where there stood a heavily dressed man watching the crew tying back sails.

'New York Bay, Captain?' called Jacob, making an extra effort to articulate through the bitter cold as he climbed the few steps to the quarterdeck.

'Ah, M'sieur Delpech,' belched the captain, hat pulled down tight and greatcoat buttoned to the chin. Flicking his head to starboard, he continued with gruff geniality: 'Aye, Sir, that be Long Island. Gives protection to the harbour, see? And over there, that's Staten.'

Jacob's eyes now followed the captain's nod port side, where, through the thinning swags of mist, he perceived clusters of modest dwellings scattered along the coast, some already smoking from their chimneys.

After a moment's scrutiny, Jacob declared: 'No city walls

there, Captain Stevens, far as I can see.' It was a statement carried forward from a previous conversation which had raised the issue of safety in these northern settlements. They had not only suffered Native Indian raids but, more importantly to Jacob, attacks by French forces from New France, whose leaders were keen to secure fur trade routes. Jacob wondered if he should have waited for passage aboard a ship headed directly to London from the Antilles, rather than jump at his first opportunity to head back to Europe via New York. But he had been impatient to remove himself from the treacherous pirate haven of Nassau, where Captain de Graaf had dropped him off.

''Tis also an island, Sir,' said a loud voice coming from Jacob's right.

Delpech turned from the seascape view to face the large person of Mr van Pel, a Dutchman who had long since settled in the flourishing trading post. He had climbed the mid-deck steps and now joined Jacob at the quarterdeck balustrade. He said: 'Folk of your persuasion have settled and built their homes there in the way of your homeland, you know.'

Where Jacob was from, houses were not made of stone. They were made of peach-pink brick, but he said nothing, just let the fleeting picture of the fertile plain where he was born flash past his mind's eye. He said: 'So they are French Protestants?'

'That they are,' replied the Dutchman, 'and Quakers too. No doubt you'll be able to find a plot there for yourself . . .'

'And a wife to boot, if that be your inclination,' added the captain, having sauntered over to join them.

'Oh, I already have a wife, Captain,' returned Jacob

soberly, 'and my intention is not to stay here. For she and my children await my return in . . .' It suddenly occurred to him that he could not say with certainty where they were—London, Geneva, France? 'In Europe,' he finished.

The Dutch-built merchantman sailed at half sail on an even keel through the placid waters of the natural harbour. Within the hour, she was rounding the small isle that van Pel called Nutten—in reference, according to the Dutchman, to the thriving population of nut trees growing there. At last Jacob began to see through the patchy mist, thicker at this point, to the battery at the tip of the Manhattan trading post.

'New Amsterdam,' said the Dutchman in an ironic tone.

'New York, Sir!' blasted the English captain, placing a heavy, consoling hand on the Dutchman's shoulder before swaggering back up to his command station.

'I wouldn't be surprised if it gets another name change before long, though,' said van Pel to Jacob. Then, as if to plumb the depths of his counterpart's thoughts, he added: 'Or will it go back to being as it was?'

'Haven't the foggiest, my good fellow,' said Jacob, not without some pride in his mastery of the English language, acquired from his travels in the midst of the damnedest devils of the deep blue sea. But he preferred not to enter into a political debate. He did not need to let anyone know his deepest thoughts. Either side of the fence could lead to danger in these times of upheaval, he thought, what with the conflict with New France.

The ship entered smoother waters while Jacob leaned on the balustrade, trying to peer through the dissipating mist at the configuration of New York.

It was composed of a mismatch of Dutch-style buildings made of stone and brick, the windmill that presently stood as still as a sentinel on the west side of the promontory, and an assortment of vessels moored along the eastern side. Jacob thought it more reminiscent of the port of Amsterdam than anything English.

The merchant ship continued her course slowly into the roadstead to the east of the promontory. Leaning with forearms on the bulwark and loosely clasping his hands, Jacob was soon able to more closely make out the influence of visiting cultures and the resulting mix of architectural styles inserted between the crenelated Dutch-built edifices. It was an odd blend, he thought, as odd as the English brick houses built among the white-washed Spanish haciendas and one-storey houses of Port Royale in Jamaica. But this was the New World, after all, a new world he was growing accustomed to. It was a land of many nations where people were thrown together in the mutual hopes of a fresh start and a fair chance of success. He only hoped the sins of the Old World had not washed up on the shores of New York as they had done on the spit of land occupied by Port Royale.

Mr van Pel pointed out City Hall, where the battlement was peopled with stevedores hoisting a winch, market sellers carting their produce, oystermen pushing carts, and small clusters of merchants who Jacob imagined were talking business. But if he could hear their muffled voices through the morning mist, he would find that the dwindling fur and tobacco trade due to border troubles was not the only talk of the New England township. The eighty-tonner lying at the wharf, just in from England, had not only brought linens, woollens, tools, and wine. It had also brought unofficial news of a probable invasion of England by the Prince of Orange and his Dutch army. Would the navigation rights now be reviewed to better suit the colonists' activities? Would New York regain its former status as a province? Would the Catholic king leave England in peace?

But even if he could hear the gossip, it would not have clouded his mind much. His one thought now was to get back to his family; the world could go mad without him. He would take some rest on firm ground, before setting out on another gruelling voyage across the ocean on as solid an ocean-going vessel as he could find. And judging by the size of the English ship at the slip, he was relieved that he had found one that would do the trick.

As he scoured the harbour, it struck him that the colony settlement, though well established, was not exactly as large as Bordeaux or even Marseille. It would surely not be too much of a task, he thought, to locate Daniel Darlington, the Englishman in whose hands he had left Marianne and her grandmother.

He was keen to pay a social visit to the young lady he had watched and cared for during their detention and their escape from Hispaniola. It would tie a loose end in his mind and set him at ease to know that she had found comfort and satisfaction, that neither she nor young Darlington had been accused of involvement in the tragic accident that had caused the death of a drunken soldier, and had forced Delpech to part ways or face trial and execution.

A blast from the captain, followed by the thunderous clanking of running chains, brought the vessel to a timber-creaking halt. The ship came to anchor at a gunshot from Coenties Slip, situated at the mouth of East River. It was, according to van Pel, less prone there to oyster reefs than the Hudson River that flowed along the west side, all the way up to Albany.

The West Indies merchantman—with its delivery of molasses, rum, and ginger—would have to lay in wait for a loading bay to become vacant. But the captain allowed all the passengers to be rowed ashore. All, that is, except for two.

As the travellers excitedly brushed down clothes, straightened hair, and gathered their effects in the dim light of mid-deck, the captain motioned to a lady fastening her daughter's bonnet.

'Madame Blancfort,' he said, standing on the hatch steps. 'With all due respect, I'll have to ask you to remain aboard till yer husband comes to pay your fare.'

Jacob, now standing at the ginger barrel where he had recovered his meagre effects, could not ignore the ball of indignation that surged in his chest. 'But Captain Stevens, Sir,' he protested, placing his leather pouch back down on the barrel of ginger. 'That is wholly unfair. She can hardly run away from the island. Indeed, I will vouch for her and her child.'

'Then I must ask you to do so with coin, Monsieur Delpech,' said the captain affably enough, though standing erect and formal to match the Huguenot's posture.

'It is all right, M'sieur,' said the lady in French. 'I will wait here. We have waited to come to New York for so long, another hour or so will do us no harm.'

'As you wish, Madame,' said Jacob, secretly relieved to opt out of the potentially embarrassing situation, for he did not have the means to spend his money needlessly. He really ought to learn to put the reins on his acute sense of injustice.

'But please, Sir,' continued the woman, 'if you would be so kind as to enquire after my husband. His name is Jeremy Blancfort. Please tell him his wife and daughter are here. He will come immediately, so please do not fret, Sir. What's an hour more compared to a month-long voyage?'

Delpech and the French-speaking wives of the other families aboard assured her they would do as she asked and arranged to meet again in church. Then they proceeded to the upper deck, where they could climb into the boat which would take them to their new lives.

It occurred to Jacob that he would not have left his wife without monies to pay her fare, even if it were to scout for an adequate settlement. Was the husband not conscious of the dangers that could befall a lone woman? At least, he would not have left her entirely without means; for he had seen what became of penniless women in Port Royale. But then, was his situation so very different? Could Jeanne have suffered similarly in Amsterdam, in the hope that her husband would be able to pay her fare on arrival in London?

*

Half an hour later, Jacob Delpech was standing on the timber boardwalk of the cold and foggy wharf with his fellow travellers. These consisted of Irish, Dutch, German, and Huguenot individuals and families who had boarded the ship as it sailed from port to port up the North American coast. Some had relatives in New York. Others spoke of Staten Island, where they planned to purchase land now that their indenture was ended. Jacob glanced around at these hopeful colonists, all looking slightly bewildered. But it was a welcome change from the privateers, pirates, soldiers, and profiteers he had become accustomed to.

The sight of small parties of would-be settlers had long since become an integral part of the New York portscape, and welcoming them had been set up as a procedure. The patrolling town constable who came to greet them invited them to make their presence known in an official capacity, something they would need to do should they wish to apply for denizenship.

'City Hall is over there, Ladies and Gentlemen,' he said in a Dutch accent, pointing across the battery to a fine five-storey brick building. He then waved to a cartman to come and carry their effects while Jacob bade farewell to Mr van Pel.

'Godspeed, and good luck in your endeavours, Sir,' said the Dutchman. Then he sauntered, with stick in hand and sack slung over shoulder, along the wharf and into the busy market street with other returning passengers.

After being at sea for so long, climbing the sturdy stone steps of City Hall without having to counter any pitch or sway brought a secret feeling of security and permanence to more than a few. The petty constable, the cartman, the registration process, and the solidity of the building all enhanced the impression that this township, be it but a speck in the vastness of the American continent, constituted a sure foothold, made to last. However, they pushed the doors into a spacious lobby where furrowed brows and concerned undertones contrasted radically with any feeling of optimism.

They were met by a tall gentleman, in simple but elegant blue attire and a white frilled necktie, who spoke words of welcome in English.

'Sir,' said Jacob, making a slight bow, 'I am sure I will be forgiven if I speak on behalf of my fellow travellers in thanking you for your warm welcome. However, before we begin the process of registering our presence, I have been asked to enquire after a certain Monsieur Blancfort, Jeremy Blancfort.'

The gentleman looked squarely at the somewhat ragged though evidently high-born Huguenot. 'I see,' he said in a subdued tone, as if to prepare the way for some bad news. 'A friend of yours, Sir?'

'No, Sir, I am but a messenger for his wife.'

'Ah, yes,' said the clerk, adjusting his horn-rimmed nose glasses. 'His wife in Carolina, if I am not mistaken. We wrote to her only last week.'

'She *was* in Carolina,' said Jacob. 'She is at present with her daughter on board the merchant ship that brought them here from Charles Town. She is waiting for her husband to liberate her of her debt to the captain, who requires full payment of her fare.'

'Oh,' said the clerk, raising a hand and pinching his chin, 'I am sorry to say, and equally sorry to inform you, that he has met with his maker.'

In truth, having seen so many deaths of late, Jacob was more irked than moved, for who would take responsibility for the poor woman without means now?

In a grave tone befitting the sad news, Jacob said: 'Did he leave any instructions?'

But before the clerk could answer, a red-haired woman stepped forward from the pack and said bluntly: 'Did he leave any money?'

Delpech did not have to turn to his side to recognise the

voice of the Irishwoman who had been Mrs Blancfort's neighbour throughout the sea journey. Jacob was almost embarrassed at his own superfluous question, but relieved that someone else had joined the conversation.

'I regret he did not,' said the clerk. 'The money he had was used towards his burial.'

'If you don't mind me saying,' said the forthright Irishwoman, 'surely to God it would have been put to better use sending it to his family! No use to a dead man, is it now? If you'll beg me pardon.'

The clerk paused a moment for thought, looked towards the wide staircase that resonated with the mutterings of voices and footsteps tripping down the steps. Then, looking back at the woman, he said: 'Well, er, what can I say? I can only hope she finds a new husband, Madam.'

'But she has a child,' said the woman.

'That is not an obstacle in these parts, you'll find,' said the clerk encouragingly. 'We lack children for the future of our colony. She will find a husband soon enough, and all the more so as she has living proof that she is not barren. Provided, of course, that she is not past mothering age . . .'

'No,' said the woman, 'she's certainly got a few more baby-making years in her yet.'

'There we are then,' said the registry agent with a note of triumph, as if he had solved the widow's problems.

The rest of the little group also seemed to be won over by Mrs Blancfort's hypothetical prospects, and let out interjections of relief. It became evident to Jacob that he was not the only one who had neither means nor time for another burden. Nevertheless, looking at the Irish lady, then at the clerk, he said: 'But someone is going to have to break the news to her. And what about her present predicament?'

'I suggest we deal with the matter once we have entered your names into the register,' said the clerk with a winning smile, while moving into step. 'Ladies and Gentlemen, now if you would care to come this way—it won't take long.'

Meanwhile, the approaching footsteps and male voices now resonated more loudly as a cluster of half a dozen men descended into the lobby.

'As I said, Sir,' continued Jacob, walking beside the clerk past the stairway, 'personally, I am only in transit. My plan is to travel to—'

But before Jacob could finish his sentence, a young man broke from the cluster of gentlemen dressed in long, sober cloaks and Brandenburgs. He stopped in front of Jacob and said cheerily: 'Why, it is! Monsieur Delpech, Sir, how good to see you again! I was not expecting you until next week.'

*

'I would personally welcome William as king,' said Daniel Darlington, who had been telling Jacob how he had been summoned that morning to City Hall to discuss the news just in of the possible takeover of England by the Dutch prince.

The two men were walking westward along Pearl Street, and now they crossed Fish Bridge that straddled the narrow canalised river where fishermen brought in their catch. Despite the foul stench of low tide, Jacob felt enlivened by the smell of land air, and by being in the thick of people going about their daily business. Turning to Darlington, he said: 'I only hope it does not end in war.'

'For the moment, I gather this is yet to be confirmed.

And God only knows what has been happening across the ocean. But what really gets my goat is when England sneezes, we catch the flu . . . three months later! And I will add, Monsieur Delpech, that I find it revolting and insulting to be tutored by men who know not an Iroquois from an Abenaki Indian.'

The subject impassioned the young New Yorker, born and bred. But Jacob's polite smile made him see that he was preaching to the choir, and that he was probably guilty of being pedantic to a man who had just walked off a ship from Nassau. 'But here you are, dear Monsieur Delpech,' he said. 'Your presence brings a welcome change. Marianne has been so looking forward to seeing you,' he said as they continued along a narrow street flanked on either side by neatly arranged dwellings of brick, stone, and timber. A fascinating blend of cultures, mused Jacob, though surprised he was to encounter free-roaming poultry and pigs along the way.

However, in truth his thoughts were elsewhere, neither on the high spheres of European leadership nor on the gutter where the pigs foraged. His thoughts were with the woman and child on the ship. How easy it was to fall into debt and ruin, well did he know. But he did his best to tuck the thought away for the time being. 'And I shall be glad to see her!' he said.

'I dare say you will find her somewhat changed, though,' pursued Darlington with a secret smile. Jacob turned away as the young man coloured slightly, the very thought of publicising his intimacy in the street striking him. He touched his ear and let out a puff of vapour with a little cough. 'This is Broadway,' he then said as they turned into a wide thoroughfare. It led past the governor's residence and continued straight past high houses and walled ornamental gardens that had already suffered from the frost. 'Our house is not far from Wall Street,' said Daniel, pointing towards the wall that gave the street its name, 'precisely on the other side of the palisade outside the city gates. Too many rules and regulations to build a house of decent size within.'

They followed the broad thoroughfare through the city gate into a vast countryside that opened with a row of well-kept gardened houses to their right, and a pretty burial ground to their left. The rutted earth road, growing busy with country carters returning from market, rolled on through green pastures to the edge of a distant forest which, according to Darlington, populated the length and breadth of Manhattan. Jacob halted his stride to admire the distant haze of reds, greens, and golds. Sunbeams now shone between purple-bellied clouds onto nearby furrowed fields of dark brown that sloped gently up to a windmill, stationed on higher ground.

From the stillness of a solitary leafless elm tree came the *caaw-caaw* of a crow. A slight variation, thought Jacob, to the call of the ones that used to nest in the lime trees outside his country house in France. But still, the smell of the earth, of mushrooms, of the reinvigorating winter chill, all filled him with the same inner peace he used to experience in <u>Verlhac</u>. It was the smell of the northern hemisphere. It was the smell of home.

'Pleasant, isn't it?' said Darlington, tipping his hat to a carter and his wife as they passed.

'Indeed, Sir, indeed it is,' said Jacob amid the sudden chatter of jays from a cluster of trees in the graveyard. After another beat, Jacob said: 'Do you know how he died? Blancfort, I mean.'

'I do. I believe he contracted an illness,' said Darlington, moving back into step and inviting Jacob to do likewise. 'He was found one day dead in his bed. It was quite the talk of the town. Folk were fearful to know what illness it was that took him away. But it seems to have been a solitary strain.'

Solitary indeed, thought Jacob as they took a right onto a narrow hard-earth track. How cruel the accidents of life could be. 'But his wife and daughter are aboard the ship.'

'I expect the ladies will tell her. Better it be a lady, and I expect the town intendant will see to them. There is nothing you can do to bring the man back. He was buried two weeks ago. Anyway, here we are.'

Before them stood a large stone house, a charming two-storey building with a ground-floor section that jutted out on the right side as the visitor went in. Darlington pushed a wooden gate into the grassy court, where a goat was attached to a piquet to keep the grass trim. Cupping his hand to his mouth, he called out in a sing-song voice. 'Marianne! Madame de Fontenay! We have an important visitor! Marianne . . .'

A face soon appeared at the glazed window that looked out onto the elevated porch. Seconds later, the porch door was pulled open, and Marianne stood on the threshold bearing the bump of pregnancy, her searching eyes showing concern. She was closely followed by her grandmother, who stood as dignified as when Jacob had left her at Cow Island.

*

Marianne sensed Jacob had undergone traumatic experiences in the short time that had separated them.

Even before she had greeted him with open arms and set

him down at the dining-room table, she had noted how gaunt he had become, and that the melancholy in his eyes had grown deeper. And she longed to reach out to him, to return the help he had given her in her times of need. Had he not protected her honour when she had been disarmed? Saved her life from a drunken soldier and put himself at risk of execution? How could she draw him out of his affable carapace?

'Before receiving your message, I expected you to be in Europe by now, my uncle,' she said, placing a cup before him and filling it with hot coffee to go with the fresh bread, goat's butter, and jam to restore him until dinnertime. They kept mostly to English for the benefit of Daniel.

Jacob appreciated her keeping up the uncle-niece act that they had played during their forced exile from France. He knew it stemmed from a genuine affection, but he recognised too her gift for unlocking unsayable secrets from the confines of one's memory.

He had caught her concern at his current physical condition in the pleat of her brow, before her smile broadened in an effort to hide it. It was the same pleat of concern he had seen when, while in confinement in Marseille the previous year, she told him he had only suffered a scratch to his eye when he had collapsed on being told of his daughter's tragic death. But the gash to his eye was deep, and she, with her grandmother, had helped it heal. And she had shined her gentle light when he dreamt of nothing but blackness.

But he was not going to recount to a young mother-to-be, over twenty years his junior, how he had been shipwrecked, taken ill, robbed, and sold to a privateer, and had sided with pirates to capture and ransom a Cuban township.

Turning his gaze from the glowing embers of the wide hearth, he smiled cheerily and said: 'I have had a tumultuous journey to get this far, but do not fret on my account, my dear niece. I am a little fatigued, but well, and I am here in one piece, and very glad to see you looking so well!'

But Marianne, obstinate as ever, said: 'Tumultuous journey, my uncle?'

He would have to concede some ground, so he said: 'Well, in short, I became indentured as a ship's surgeon-barber to a privateer captain, although the term buccaneer would be more appropriate.' He let out a false laugh.

'My goodness!' exclaimed Marianne in an attempt to coax more out of him. But Jacob was not ready to say more.

After a pause for another sip of coffee, Daniel Darlington said: 'What was his name, Sir?'

'Brook, Captain Brook, and I wish never to hear it again.'

'I have heard the name before. I remember de Graaf mentioning it a few times. I have also heard since that he came to a bitter end . . .'

Jacob said nothing of de Graaf, the Dutch-French privateer turned major, who had in fact led the Cuban campaign, but who nevertheless had delivered him from servitude and helped him secure a passage northward from Nassau. But there was one man Jacob did want to know more about. He said: 'Do you know what became of his crew?'

'I do not.'

It was Ducamp who Delpech now wondered about, the faithless, battle-hardened lieutenant who he had left with the hope of redemption. But he feared yet another hope dashed, another fissure in his already weakened faith—not his faith in God, but in humanity. So he said nothing more on it.

Glancing sidelong at her husband, Marianne pressed Jacob's hand and said: 'You must stay here as long as it takes for you to get stronger, my uncle.'

Jacob was not aware that he needed to get stronger. Did he look so worn? He thought not. He just needed to be removed from his immediate past memories and to draw nearer to recovering his family. Was that so difficult to understand?

'There is no need to put yourselves out on my behalf. I shall stay at the tavern we passed in town and be off by the turn of the tide tomorrow, God willing, if not by the end of the week.'

'Ah,' said Darlington, 'the season here has been exceptionally clement so far, but I fear it is about to turn nasty for sea travel. You would do better to hole up until February, Sir. Moreover, I would be surprised if any ship sets out across the ocean before winter's end, Monsieur Delpech. So, please accept our hospitality, not because I owe you the lives of my wife and future child, but because I offer you my friendship, Sir.'

Seeing Jacob still on the fence, Marianne insisted winningly: 'I will not sleep knowing that my only living uncle is alone at a stranger's tavern!'

But it was the old lady, knitting in her chair near the fireplace with a cat on her lap, who at last won him over. Having spent her married life with a French officer, she well knew the look of a man who had been to war. And once all the battle fanfare was over and he was home with his family, she knew of the need to divert thoughts by day and ease nightmares by night, and of the impression of the futility of life, and of disillusionment with God.

'You will stay here, Monsieur Delpech, and nothing more will be said of your piratical adventures!' she said, flitting her eyes at Marianne and Daniel.

Marianne, who had absolute faith in her grandmother's wisdom and was not slow on the uptake, followed up by saying: 'Instead, I will tell you of our plans to build a new house further along the east coast with some French settlers from La Rochelle. Daniel agrees, don't you, darling?'

'The land is good there,' said Darlington, taking up his pipe, 'and if it allows my wife and her grandmother to feel more at home, then that is where we shall live. For I made a promise to a gentleman and a friend, that I would look after them, do you remember, Monsieur Delpech?'

Jacob gave a nod and a smile of approbation. 'I do, Monsieur Darlington, I do.' Marianne, standing between them with a hand on her waist, looked affably cross while her grandmother looked up with a sardonic grin. But before they could say anything, Jacob continued: 'And I believe my dear niece and her grandmother made a promise to look after a certain gifted but impetuous loose cannon in danger of losing his life at sea.'

After a moment's silence for the penny to drop, Daniel burst out into laughter. 'Oh, and they do, and they do,' he said in good fellowship. Then he slung his arm around his wife's waist and brought her to gently perch on his knee. Marianne patted him playfully on the head and topped off his coffee while her grandmother, after an eyebrow raised to Jacob in complicity, continued with her knitting.

'And by the way, I could do with some advice on land management, tobacco to be precise,' continued Darlington as Marianne took away his pipe. 'My guess is there'll be a large market for it, now that His Royal Highness has deprived us of the Delaware country against our wishes.'

He was referring to King James II's order which joined the province of New York to the Dominion of New England. It did not sit well with New Yorkers because it meant depriving them of their constitutional and property rights.

But Jacob was only half listening. His plan was still to leave for Europe at the first opportunity, and never mind the weather. Besides that, with all this talk of promises, a pang of guilt reminded him of one he had made recently. 'I would be glad to be of assistance if I can,' he said. 'But speaking of promises, the lady on the ship . . .' Jacob then explained about the poor woman's predicament to the female company. 'I do hope she has found accommodation,' he concluded.

'She will be cared for, I dare say,' said Marianne.

'You cannot lay down your cloak for every damsel in distress, Monsieur Delpech,' said Darlington.

'No, but I would not want my own wife and child to suffer such humiliation. Would you?'

'Well said!' exclaimed Madame de Fontenay in a confidential voice.

The New Yorker gave a slow, penitent nod of the head. His grey eyes then locked on Jacob's. 'Then I shall enquire after her,' he said with new conviction.

*

Jacob almost regretted watching Darlington—dressed in leathers, beaver hat firmly pulled over his head—mount his steed and canter off amid eddying leaves into the afternoon turned colder and blustery.

'He has to go back to town anyway,' said Marianne a few moments later, turning from the window, 'to meet some French acquaintances whom he promised to introduce to a friend who can assist them with the purchase of land. The land we told you about.'

'Oh, he's always hopping on his horse,' said Madame de Fontenay. 'It is one of the disadvantages of living outside the city walls.' Marianne shook her head in feigned exasperation.

Though far from what Marianne and her grandmother had been used to in her mother country, Jacob could see that the young woman had certainly settled into home life and had made a cosy abode. French dressers, silverware and glasses in a rack, quality furniture, and rugs on the waxed parquet gave the place a positively French appeal that allowed Jacob to feel quite at home.

He sat in an armchair by the fireplace, cracking walnuts. Madame de Fontenay was still seated opposite and still wrestling with another dropped stitch. 'Over the strand and off the needle,' she muttered. It was something she had decided to take up in order to while away the winter evenings, especially now since she had a little someone to knit for. She told Jacob of their voyage from Cow Island, where Delpech had been obliged to leave them with Darlington. 'The last sea voyage I shall endure in this world—knitwise and slide across—and the next, God willing,' she said between stitches, with a mirthful glow in her eyes.

Marianne, meanwhile, anxious to show her command of

home management, proposed to Jacob to set her maid to heating water for the tub, there being no public baths in New York. Jacob, despite the risk of bathing in winter, accepted her offer, remembering the polite turn of her head when they had embraced on the porch, and recalling his wife's heightened sense of smell during her pregnancies. Indeed, he admitted he must stink to high heaven, he said once the black servant girl had positioned the brass tub before the hearth.

'Don't worry, Martha is not a slave, Jacob,' said Marianne, reading his thoughts. 'She gets a wage, food, and a room next to Grandmother's.'

'As you can see, we have moved up in the world!' added Madame de Fontenay with a drop of irony.

'I would not, for a minute, imagine that you could become a supporter of slavery,' said Jacob, flinging a handful of walnut shells into the fire. 'But what about the plantation your husband spoke of?'

'Oh, I will talk him out of it should the notion blossom in his mind, and he will listen to me, have no fear.'

'And he certainly does that, all right,' seconded Madame de Fontenay. 'Why, he will do anything for her, just like my husband used to . . . in the early days. But slaves or no slaves, my dears, what is worrying is being so close to New France. It is bad enough living in the sticks with the wolves!'

'We are not living amid the wolves, Grandmother, rather the squirrels.'

'And the rats! And what if the French invade and capture Manhattan? What will happen to us?'

'That is why those from La Rochelle have chosen the east side, Grandmother. You need not worry, Daniel already told you. And we shall have a splendid house, more land, and people with whom you can speak in French.'

'Oh, I am past worrying about myself, my dear. The French and the Indians wouldn't roast an old timer like me, far too nervy,' said the old woman, as plucky as ever. 'And I am not worried about a splendid house either. I'm quite all right with Martha next door; at least she doesn't keep telling me how to knit properly! I was thinking about you two and the baby.'

'Daniel says there will be a boat moored in the bay in case we need to escape to New York, or to Brooklyn. Besides, if the French attack, which they won't, it would be from the west. They would come down the Hudson River from Albany.'

The old lady gave no answer. Instead, she placed a finger on her lips and nodded towards the opposite armchair.

Perhaps it was the coffee and nuts, or the warmth of the fire, or maybe something else, but Jacob at last had given in to an irrepressible urge to close his eyes. He had fallen into a snorting slumber, stirred only by the intermittent pouring of hot water from a ewer.

*

Half an hour later, he was transported back to his country estate in France, fields golden with wheat and orchards laden with fat fruit. He was standing in the reservoir he had devised for irrigation purposes, where his children and his farmhands sometimes bathed after a long summer day's picking.

He suddenly found himself standing underwater with a crowd of babbling people, fully dressed and having fun, bounding from the shallow lake bed to the surface. He looked around and saw his son Paul kicking away from the stony bottom with a gleeful smile. But as the boy reached the end of his thrust, the water's surface seemed to inch agonisingly further away.

'I need to breathe now,' Jacob heard the boy say calmly after landing back down on the lake bed, eyes beginning to bulge. Jacob seized him by the waist, thrust him upward, but again the boy only broke the surface with his outstretched hands. Jacob propelled the boy upward again with all his might. Again, only the boy's hands reached out of the water.

But suddenly, as the lad began to sink back down, an anonymous hand plunged into the water, clasped the boy's arm, and pulled him out of the lake.

The next instant, Jacob was standing on the grassy shore. Paul was standing, eyes reddened, lips violet with cold, but alive. There came a sudden loud pop, and Jacob, fearing musket fire, threw his arms around his son protectively as a company of dead Spanish cadets came walking, weapons in hands, from out of the black waters of the lake.

'No!' cried Jacob. 'No! Go away!'

Jacob awoke to an insistent knocking at the lounge door.

'Are you all right, Monsieur Delpech?' called the voice of the old lady.

The fire crackled in the grate as he sat up in the bathtub in a cold sweat, burdened by thoughts of his wife stranded in London, burdened by the thought of the woman on the ship drowned in grief and debt.

'All is well, just fell asleep in the tub, ha,' he called out, surprised at the thickness of his voice.

*

25

The following morning, Jacob ached all over and could barely stand, let alone walk. The bone-chilling cold and muffled silence, the bleak light seeping through the window, and the echoey caw of the crow gave an atmosphere of stillness.

Half-frozen and trembling, he managed to slip his arms into his overcoat and stagger from the bedpost to the dresser near the second-floor window. His gaze fell upon a spectacular surprise. A glistening blanket of pure white snow lay over land, rooftops, and trees. He placed an eye to the cold brass telescope mounted on a tripod near the window box and pointed it towards the East River estuary. 'Good God,' he croaked to himself as a cold droplet dripped from his nose. 'The river has frozen over!'

TWO

'My dear sister,

I pray this letter finds you in good health, and that you and my dear nephew have found satisfactory refuge with the good people of Schaffhausen. Your letter gave me much hope for your husband, but both Robert and I are of the opinion that it would be better to rest until the spring, before you travel to London to be reunited with him. Please write back saying you will, my sister. It will reassure me to know you are with friends in wintertime rather than on the roads.

'Elizabeth is becoming a fine young lady and misses you dearly. You must know that she would not follow your guide because, she recently confided, she could not leave her little sister in her grave, even less her baby sister Isabelle. She has indeed become a proper little mother and would make you proud.

'I know it must pain you to be so far from them, but, though Robert has pulled through his illness, I will not pretend that he will ever be strong enough to leave the country. However, a day will come, he is sure, when Lizzy and Isabelle will be able to join you.

'Meanwhile, he has been desperately trying to gather

signatures of trustworthy men so that he may send you a bill of exchange. Although, as you can imagine, given the present climate, almost everyone he has approached would rather wait before committing their names and reputation in case they are discovered financing a Huguenot. It is preposterous, I do concede, but Robert is adamant he will get funds to you eventually. It is merely a question of time.

'I have enclosed a sketch of the girls as they are now. They were drawn last Wednesday 14th December. What merriment we had, and such a job it was to have Isabelle sit still long enough. But she did so when we told her she would be sitting for her mother, the lady in the painting.'

THE SOUND OF children's laughter brought Jeanne's eyes from Suzanne's letter.

She gazed out of her bedroom window at the undulating ice-crusted layers of snow that surrounded the house of her hosts. It sat outside the city walls, a daring decision for sure, but it meant paying fewer taxes and being near the sawmill. And besides, young Etienne Lambrois feared neither villain nor beast.

She watched Paul and a host of rambunctious children guffawing, running and sliding behind horse-drawn sleighs that were being conducted to the frozen lake at the end of the snow-covered track. A steady stream of villagers in boots and furs were cheerily walking or skiing down to join the crowd that had already gathered there. Today was a particularly special day, the last day of the sleigh races. Two of the Huguenots would be racing in the final, and the honour of the seasoned Schaffhausen sleigh drivers was at stake!

Etienne and Jean Fleuret had repaired and made new a number of sleighs, two of which they had purchased for their own winter activities. They were at present driving them down to the lake around which the races had been taking place since yesterday.

Jeanne returned a wave to Paul, who was climbing aboard Jean Fleuret's sleigh, before glancing round at the wall above her pinewood dresser where the sketch of her daughters was pinned. She then reread the lines in her sister's letter that mentioned why Lizzy had refused to join her, and that she missed her mother, which gave Jeanne some consolatory reassurance. But of course, Suzanne could not say the same for her baby daughter, snatched from Jeanne's bosom when she was barely weaned. Isabelle, who would be a walking, talking child by now, would have no recollection of her mother to miss. Jeanne would be *the lady in the painting* at the top of the stairs, that was all. After mulling it over time after time, it now made sense to Jeanne that it could only be God's will for Lizzy to remain in her hometown, where she could watch over her baby sister and at least transmit some of the motherly love Jeanne had given her.

'Jeanne?' called an excited female voice. 'Jeanne? Are you coming?'

'Yes, yes, Claire. Be down in a moment,' returned Jeanne, getting to her feet and reaching for the winter cloak and muff laid out on her bed—her green coat of old no longer sufficing for the rigours of the Swiss winter. They had been given to her by a widowed burgher who had heard of her plight and brutal fall from wealth. But Jeanne had insisted on paying with earnings from her work. She made cloth for a master weaver anxious to learn the techniques taught to her by the French weaver in whose workshop she had been given refuge, before her flight from France.

Without friends, she thought to herself, where would she be now? How would she have survived the harsh northern winter? With a last glimpse through the window at the leaden sky, Jeanne pinned on her flat beaver hat and exited the room, thinking to herself that it would not be easy to give up a roof and her friends when the time came to leave.

*

Down at the lakeside, Jeanne, Claire, and Ginette joined the village folk standing in little clusters —now cheering as the sleighs sped by, now dipping their heads into their shoulders like the subdued crows perched in the tall, bare trees of the nearby copse.

The afternoon rolled on in high spirits, along with hot mulled wine and pleasant chatter, into the final race. Already chimneys on distant farmsteads were letting out wispy ghosts into the purpling sky.

'Beautiful, invigorating, and nose-nippingly cold, Monsieur,' said Jeanne to a burgher who had asked in French how she found their life in the north. Never once had she imagined she would one day experience such a spectacle, born as she was in a warmer clime. Only once had she ever experienced foot-deep snow in her native Quercy. She well remembered how quickly it became the curse of ladies' hems sullied in the ensuing slush.

Yet here in Schaffhausen, where for months on end it fell in places as deep as a maid was tall, folk took it in their stride, fitted as they were with fur-lined clogs to keep toes warm, and *raquettes* tied to shoes to keep them from sinking into the powdery snow. They carted goods on sledges and travelled on rough snow carts that gave a smoother ride than many a luxurious carriage, thought Jeanne, having ridden down to the edge of the frozen lake on one. The racing sleighs, however, were veritable works of art, feasts of the imagination with elaborately carved wooden figureheads of fantastic animals, griffins, naked savages, and wild beasts.

'Come on, Etienne!' cheered Claire as the magnificent pageant of horses and sleighs now approached the bend where the three ladies were standing near the bonfire. Jeanne and Ginette joined in with cheers of encouragement as the sleigh bells grew louder, along with the rumble of hooves and the thunderous swish of the runners. Etienne whooshed by, still holding second place, with dogs yapping at his horses' hooves.

'Go, Jeannot, come on, Paul!' called Ginette as Jean Fleuret's sleigh thundered by, cutting the ice in fifth place. Paul, sitting by his side, threw a wave to his mother as the vehicle flew by at a frightening speed.

The man and the boy had bonded following the loss of Jean's son Pierre, who had been Paul's best friend during their time in Geneva. It was not something Jeanne had wanted to encourage, for she knew how difficult it would be for them both when the time came to depart.

The ladies continued their chatter near the glowing embers of the log fire. Claire's baby, who had been left at the house with the maid, was teething. Ginette was coping with the death of her boy and was glad to be pregnant again. Jeanne spoke of her plans now that she had received a letter from Jacob, telling her where to join him.

'But what if your husband was dead? Where would you go once you got there?' said Ginette Fleuret, round and rosy-cheeked, cradling her large bust with her muff.

'Ginette!' said Claire in feigned reproach, her pretty chin raised, hands held together inside her fur muff. 'I dare say Jeanne has not thought of that eventuality.'

The contrast between the two ladies was almost comical, but Jeanne loved them both equally. If Claire were made of porcelain, refined and fragile, Ginette would be made of potter's clay, robust, rough, and solidly fashioned.

'Well, I think she ought to,' said the seamstress from Marseille, placing her chubby hand on her waist like a handle. 'I mean, if he has gone and popped his clogs, God forbid, where would she go once she got there?'

The question often reverberated through Jeanne's mind like the ever-present sound of carrion birds in the bleakness of winter. What if Jacob had died en route? What if all her prayers had been for nothing? But surely that would be too cruel. Yet, had she not prayed for the safety of her dear three-year-old daughter with the same fervour? Had she not prayed hard for weeks on end, and then seen herself running after Lulu in her dreams, seen her child wriggling from her belly-kisses, and then lying asleep in her arms as per her habit the minute they had begun a carriage journey to their country house? Yet, all the time she had been praying and feeling solace from her prayers, Lulu was dead, her soul long since elevated to heaven. Could her prayers for Jacob be just as much in vain? If they were, then she would rather remain here with her friends, and commit herself to the local language and customs.

'And if he were, my lovey,' pursued Ginette, 'we'd keep

you here with us. I've seen plenty a roving eye glancing sidelong at you, my Jeanne. You're still of marrying age, you know, and there be eligible men even in Schaffhausen!'

'Ginette!' gasped Claire, putting a hand to her mouth.

Ginette went on in a confidential tone. 'Take the widowed burgher . . . nice catch, sensible man . . . you'd bring some refinement to his household, my dear lady. And didn't he say he loves to speak French? A right chatter-mill an' all—'

'Ginette, shhh, you do go on,' said Claire, sensing Jeanne's discomfort.

'I'm only thinking out loud,' said Ginette, who knew, whenever Jeanne let her ramble on, that she was not far from hitting the spot.

'Thank you for your concern, dear Ginette,' said Jeanne good-humouredly, 'but sometimes I'd rather you thought inside your head!' There was no point in denying her deepest doubts that Ginette had a knack of bringing to the fore.

It did sometimes occur to her that it would be easier if her husband had perished. She would bear up to the fact. It would even make her life easier, for she could start over. But there again, who said life was easy? It was not, and Jeanne never had chosen the easy path. If she had, she would have pretended to forsake her faith; she would have kept her children. And Lulu would be alive and well, if she had forsaken her faith.

But what was a person without a soul? An empty vessel navigating life without a destination, without any hope of going somewhere. God was hope, and she hoped, nay, she firmly believed, that the final reunion was in heaven as Jesus had promised. How pointless living would be if there were nothing but blackness, and how terrifying.

'I am sure Jacob is still alive,' said Jeanne with confidence. Once again, she stood proud in the satisfaction that she had beaten down those dreadful demons whose sinful whispers sometimes came to prey on her. 'But you are right, Ginette. I cannot leave my friends again without prior knowledge of Jacob's safe arrival in London. It would not be fair on Paul.'

'No,' said Ginette, 'nor on my Jeannot . . .'

'But he is alive, I am sure!'

Ginette gave Jeanne a squeeze on her arm as the horses drawing the sleighs came cantering back in a thrilling, icy rush. Jeanne's momentary doubts made way for the exhilarating swish of the sleigh blades as Claire clapped and called out her husband's name.

'Come on, Etienne!' shouted Jeanne too as Etienne's horse took the lead coming out of the turn. Jean Fleury and Paul were not far behind as the main pack, closing up the gap, entered the bend.

The fast and massive dogs were racing the horses again, a little too close perhaps for comfort, thought Jeanne, as one of the young dogs, fast and fearless, ran along Etienne's horse as if yapping encouragements at it to go faster. But then the rider just behind, taking advantage of the impetus of the bend, came hurtling fast and furious on the outside.

'How thrilling!' cried Claire, clapping her hands and cheering her man at the top of her voice. 'Come on, Etienne!'

But Jeanne, who had been watching one of the dogs pestering the horses' course, had stopped cheering. An instant later, her fears were confirmed when there came a terrible high-pitched yelp as the dog, who must have slipped on the ice, received a hoof to the head.

'Oh, my goodness!' cried Claire as the animal screeched and rolled across the track.

The Swiss driver close behind skilfully avoided the creature by an inch of its life. But Jeanne now wished he had not. For ten lengths behind, Jean Fleury was also racing out of the bend, taking third place. Jeanne froze in fear, stopping her mouth with her hand. The dog lay in the path of Jean Fleuret's sleigh.

Ginette, standing beside her, let out a loud, guttural cry. Jeannot roared and pulled back the reins, in an effort to steer the horse away from the wounded dog lying in the way of the sleigh runners. But with the pack of racers being so bunched together, there was no place to go. This, after all, was a race of honour. The Swiss drivers, oblivious to the wounded dog immediately ahead, could not be beaten by French novices.

There came a short, appalling squeal, a thud and a horrible crunching sound as Jean's nearside sleigh runner hit the animal full on.

The impetus of the bend and the sudden shift in weight sent the inside sleigh runner flying off the ground. Jeanne saw, as if time were slowed down, the carriage rise up on one side and begin to keel over as the panicked horse continued its course.

Jeannot turned his head to Paul, now clinging to the wooden frame with both hands.

'Jump, Paul! Jump, now!' he screamed, knowing the whole thing would be a death trap should it flip over.

'My God, no!' cried Jeanne as she ran hard, suddenly in

a cold sweat, and with a sickening, pounding fear in her heart.

Jeannot waited until the last moment to jump, until the boy had leapt clear, until the sleigh was almost vertical.

The big man landed solidly in the snow. He quickly got to his feet, while Etienne up ahead managed to take command of the panicked horse that gradually slowed, with the weight of the sleigh now top-side down.

Jeannot Fleuret was already at Paul's side as Jeanne came running up. 'Oh, my God,' he said. 'Paul! Paul, me lad!' With his large, leathery hands, he gently rolled the boy over.

Paul did not answer. The smudge of red snow where his head had lain face down, and the blood streaming down the side of his face from his scalp, bore witness to an unlucky landing.

Jeanne now threw herself into the snow beside her son. She put her head to his mouth. 'Dear God, he is breathing!' she said, trying to remain calm. 'He is breathing!'

Praying to herself that it was not just wishful thinking, she held the boy's head as the group of townsfolk made way for a middle-aged man, panting and puffing, who she recognised as the pharmacist. He was soon on his knees, and bending with gravity over the boy to check his arterial pulse.

THREE

JACOB DID NOT once think he was going to die in New York.

His plan had been to rest with friends a few days, then take the first good ship to Europe. But he had not accounted for the bone-biting cold of the New York winter, which forbade any Europe-bound travel until the thaw.

Neither had he anticipated his sudden illness, though when it struck, he knew from past experience he would just have to resign himself to inactivity until the strain relented. So he kept to his bed in the draughty upper-floor room, heated by a stove that infused the air with the fragrance of thyme.

But his soul remained in torment, caught in a mind-bending vortex of images of his wife and his children, of war and death, of blood-drenched blades and powder and steel. They intermingled like the swirling dance of snowflakes that continued to cover the fields and trees outside his window.

By the fourth day of his illness, he was able to sit up on the edge of his bed and stare at the wall. It provided him with a blank canvas on which to put some order to his crowded thoughts. But how to make any sense of it all with a Christian mind? he wondered.

He clenched his hands together and bowed his head in prayer. But he knew that nothing in earth or heaven could erase the visions of bloody battle, nor take away the grief of losing a child. Consequently, he could not bring himself to pray for the well-being of his family, for he could no longer bear any more disillusionment should tragedy there be. Instead, he prayed to God for his journey to continue, while at the back of his brain, his incessant incantation repeated: *They are all right, of course they are all right, they are all right . . .*

There came a knock at the door. 'Come in,' he said croakily, while the forefront of his mind was still focussed on ending his prayer with *amen.* He turned as the door was pushed open.

'Ah, Monsieur Delpech,' said Madame de Fontenay in her usual sing-song voice. She was followed by Martha, who gave a little curtsy like a proper lady's maid. 'We heard you had come back to the living. How are you?' pursued the old lady. She then turned to take the tray to let Martha make her way to the window, which the girl opened, and then pushed out the shutters set ajar to let in the purple-grey light of a cloud-laden sky.

'We have brought you some warm milk and honey.' Madame de Fontenay placed the tray on the bedside table. Martha, on the other side of the room, closed the windows again, then departed, leaving the door half open. 'She's coming along fine,' said Madame de Fontenay to Jacob, who smiled amusedly at the old lady's determination to keep up Old World standards. 'I used to bring milk and honey to my husband, you know, whenever his nightmares came on. It never failed to bring him a bit of comfort.'

Jacob did not quite know how to respond. Did his terrible dreams provoke shouts in his sleep?

'You mustn't feel ashamed, you know.'

'Oh, I hope my phantoms have not been disturbing you.'

'No, and they will become less tempestuous over time, and perhaps once you have recovered the comfort of your own home.'

'Come, we both know neither you nor I shall ever recover that, Madame,' said Jacob, who was not in the mood for niceties and make-believe.

'Ah, but I wasn't talking about your house, Monsieur Delpech; I was talking about your home. For you can make your home with your loved ones around you anywhere, can you not? Do they not say home is where the heart is?'

'Indeed they do, Madame de Fontenay. Indeed they do,' said Jacob, subdued and slightly guilty at his earlier bluntness. 'I expect you miss your former life, do you not?'

'Oh no, Monsieur Delpech. And there should be no room and no need for pity of things . . . shall we say . . . lost.' It was as if she had peeped into his thoughts.

He had not failed to notice that her attire was now more in keeping with a modest widow than a lady of the aristocracy. How humbling it must be to have fallen from living as a lady to an old settler. But he admired her courage and determination to make something good out of the ruins of her past life.

She went on: 'And to be honest, Monsieur Delpech, I have never been more content, never felt more useful in my entire life! Why, I would much rather be a helpful grandmother than a dead weight in my grand stately home in France. So, please, no pity, neither for me nor for yourself, if I may say so. We just have to get on with it, and start up home again. Don't you agree?'

'I do, Madame de Fontenay. Wise words, well spoken.'

'Bah,' said the lady, swiping her bony hand as though shooing away flies. 'I only wish there were more people around of my generation! And between you, me, and the bedpost, I would have rather preferred to live in a warmer climate, like Madame Odet. She got off the boat in Charles Town, you know. Had people she knew there . . .'

With the evocation of the Carolina colony, Jacob was struck by a thought that had been nagging at the back of his mind, an image of the lady on the ship and her young daughter. She had asked him to find her husband. He had not seen her since then; the news of her husband's death must have broken the poor woman, in debt as she was. 'I was going to ask —' he said.

But footsteps on the stairs, followed by the voice of Marianne, interrupted his train of thought. 'Grandma?' she called out.

'Oh, now look at us!' said the old lady to Jacob, a look of amusement in her eye. 'I would never have thought I would be caught in a gentleman's room by my granddaughter!' Then, calling out, she said: 'Here, my dear, I am with Monsieur Delpech.'

The next moment, standing at the open door with her hand resting on her bump, Marianne said: 'I am so glad you are on the way to full recovery, my uncle. We have made you some broth. Would you like it here or downstairs?'

'Thank you, that is most kind of you. I shall take it

40

downstairs,' said Jacob, who then edged in the nagging question that had not left him since he fell ill. 'By the way, Marianne, do you know what has become of the lady on the ship who lost her husband?'

'Yes, I do. The poor woman is to stand before the tribunal today. They are to decide what to do with her. Her only hope is that a gentleman steps forward to offer to take her as his wife.'

'Oh. Or else?'

'Daniel says her debt will be purchased for her, and she will have to pay back the town treasurer.'

'You mean the poor woman could well end up indentured all over again.'

'I am afraid so.'

'But she has only just finished her four-year term. Is it likely that anyone will step forward?'

'Daniel says nobody will.'

'Why not?' said Jacob, who, in his feeling of injustice, overlooked the non-negligible matter of love and compatibility. 'Are there not enough men seeking a wife and family? I thought that was the crux of the success of any colony.'

'No one will have her yet because of her husband's illness. And she has not been here long enough to be sure she does not carry the disease.'

'But she wasn't even here, and I am willing to vouch for her good nature.'

'But you have been ill, my uncle. It would be as good as a condemned man bearing testimony to a—'

'It would be unfair to send her back into servitude,' interrupted Jacob. 'I must get to the tribunal!'

'You are a good man, my uncle,' said Marianne,

calmingly. 'But you cannot right all the world's wrongs.'

'No, but one should treat people in a Christian manner, and treat them how you would like them to treat you or your family.'

'I do understand, and I would go with you —'

'No, Marianne, I refuse to have you go out in the snow in your condition.'

*

Barely an hour later, Jacob was wading through the glacial morning air, crunching snow under his fur-lined boots despite the country trail having been recently shovelled clear.

Clad in a heavy waxed cloak, he pulled his beaver hat tightly over his forehead to give protection from the gusts of swirling snow as he headed for the city gates. The blustery wind carried the stirring howl of a pack of wolves from the other side of the distant windmill. He slipped and fell over. He picked himself up. He slipped again. He picked himself up again.

'Confounded stuff!' he grumbled under his breath, and wanted to kick himself for bothering about the lady on the ship, and got to thinking he would be better off if he were not a man of his word. But to renounce your true self was like scathing your soul, was it not? His was scathed enough already. Facing the thinning snowfall head-on, he did not hear the muted rumble of hooves behind him. When he saw the pony out of the corner of his eye, he slipped and fell again.

'Jacob, please, get in,' cried a voice from the closed two-person sleigh, driven by a caped and booted black man who tipped his hat.

Jacob scrambled to his feet again and climbed aboard.

'You should not be out in this weather in your condition, my uncle!' said Marianne playfully.

'And neither should you, my niece!' said Jacob. 'I should like to accompany you back.'

'Ha! I am not ill,' returned Marianne, 'and baby is in the warmest place of all.' She called out to the driver: 'To City Hall, Joseph!'

Onwards they sled in the purple snowscape, through the city gate and down the icy thoroughfare Jacob knew now to be called Broad Street. It being weather to be indoors by the fire, they passed only a few handcarts and wagons, and pedestrians wearing native snowshoes, a fascinating invention, thought Jacob.

Within half an hour, he was kicking off snow stuck to his boots before entering with Marianne through the tall doors of City Hall. The lobby was surprisingly crowded with an array of people conversing in clusters. Going to court was visibly as good an activity as any in this weather, deduced Jacob, as he followed Marianne through the crowd, chattering now in Dutch, now in French, with some English thrown into the mix.

Daniel Darlington soon came into view, standing with a small group of gentlemen by the courtroom door. He greeted his wife with playful reproach for venturing out on such a cold day. Turning to Jacob, he said: 'And I was not expecting to see you here, Monsieur Delpech. Are you well?'

'Much better, thank you, Mr Darlington,' said Jacob. 'I was setting out on foot when your wife came along and refused to head back. So here we are. I hope I haven't missed the audience . . .'

Darlington needed no further explanation. He said: 'Actually, you are just in time, Sir. There has been a bidding of indentures and redemptioners this morning, and I believe your lady in question is about to pass. But please, let me introduce you to a good friend of mine.' Darlington turned to his right where there stood a man of wealth, visible by the cut of his cloth rather than ostentatious adornments. In middle age and of average height, he wore a rictus that could have equally been interpreted as a smile or a snarl, depending on one's disposition or circumstance. 'This is Mr Jacob Leisler,' said Darlington. 'He is in the fur trade.' To Leisler, he said: 'Monsieur Jacob Delpech de Castonnet, gentleman notary, landowner, and merchant.'

Both introduced men gave a congenial bow.

'I heard about your tragic plight, Sir,' said Mr Leisler in a faint Germanic accent. 'You must know that here you are among friends.'

'Most kind of you, Sir,' said Jacob, who returned the thin smile, although he was not too keen about his "plight" being talked about in the city hall lobby.

'Indeed, I do believe there are well over a hundred Huguenot families here now, if not two hundred. Many of them originate from a place called La Rochelle. Where might you be from, Mr Delpech? I only ask in case I know of anyone from your hometown.'

'Alas, Monsieur is not from La Rochelle, Mr Leisler,' said Marianne, standing on the other side of her husband.

'I am from Montauban, Sir,' said Jacob, who did not fail to notice that the gentleman had made no hesitation in dropping the particle of his name. But the sound of Jacob's hometown, albeit in his own mouth, fleetingly rekindled his previous life in his mind's eye. That old life seemed like worlds away, standing as he was in a melting pot of cultures, in a fledgling city surrounded by a white wilderness, freezing fog, and wolves.

'No, I am sorry. I know of no one from there. I can, however, introduce you to the Rochelle contingent.'

'Thank you, Sir. However, my intention is not to remain.'

'Pity, because I believe there is a woman in need of a husband.'

It was clear to Jacob that he was speaking to a self-made man, quite possibly a diamond among his peers, but an uncut one at that. Jacob had an instinctive liking for him, though. He said: 'Indeed, I travelled along the coast aboard the same ship as she. And I can vouch for her kindly spirit, although I cannot offer my support in a matrimonial capacity.'

'Then let us see what the "grandees" shall make of the poor young wretch and her daughter from Charles Town!' said Mr Leisler as the crowd began filtering through the doors into the courtroom. 'We are going in.'

*

She stood before the court hopeful, not browbeaten. Her glance caught that of Jacob. Her features, set in defiance, suddenly cracked, and the pleats between her long oval eyes furrowed —a trait that reminded him of his own wife. Then she resumed her resolute pose.

The panelled courtroom of dark-wood partitions and balustrades was spacious and full to the brim, every inch of bench occupied. Aside from the tavern near the fort, the city hall was no doubt the best place for entertainment in town, given the weather, thought Jacob. The dead man's wife was the news of the moment and had attracted feelings of pity, especially as she had a child. Before she passed that morning, a new series of indentured servants and redemptioners off the ship from England had been paraded in to be adjudged. The dead man's lady was the pinnacle for the day's audiences.

'Madame,' said the presiding magistrate, leaning over the bar, 'you have been placed in custody on charges brought against you by Captain Benjamin Stevens, to whom you hold a debt of the price of your fare from Charles Town. After much deliberation, and given the fact that your husband had only recently arrived in the township, the only way out of your predicament will be for the town treasurer to purchase your debt.'

A wave of relief spread over the woman's face as she grasped the shoulder of her child clinging to her leg. The audience let out a sigh of satisfaction.

'However . . . as you have no sustenance, no immediate income, and no relations here in New York, the only way for you to reimburse the town for your debt is through the terms of an indenture contract.'

Groans and muffled protests arose from the benches.

'Your Grace,' beseeched the woman, 'I paid my dues in Charles Town already as an indenture servant for four years. It is that reason that brought us here to New York, to start afresh. My husband wanted to find some land so we could live off our own labours. I beg you, Your Honour, please don't make me go through it all again.'

It was the first time Jacob had heard the woman speak in

English, which he thought she spoke impeccably well after four years of servitude in the English colony.

'Madame,' said the magistrate, 'I see no other means unless your future husband is willing to pay your debt.' The magistrate paused for effect, perhaps in the hope that a gentleman would step forward at the last moment. But no one did. For who would pay the woman's debt when she could come as an indenture? Besides, who was to say she would not bring her late husband's illness with her? Jacob looked on, beset by his inveterate sense of injustice.

Amid whispers and chattering in the audience, a French-accented voice suddenly rose up loud and clear: 'My Lord, Ladies and Gentlemen ... with all due respect, you are asking this poor woman to pay her dues twofold and by the same token to double her burden. If there is any justice in this New World that respects the justice of God, then surely she should be given charity!'

'Hear, hear,' murmured voices from the audience.

The French voice continued: 'Through no fault of her own, her husband has died prematurely. I can personally vouch for her good character and sound bill of health, having voyaged with her all the way from Charles Town. Surely you cannot increase the poor woman's burden!'

The magistrates and the courtroom spectators of New York had just met Jacob Delpech. After a pause to take in both the newcomer and his discourse, a number of courtroom figures voiced their agreement, which led to a free-for-all debate between bench neighbours.

'Order. Order,' called the chief magistrate, who then turned to the newcomer still on his feet. 'Sir, someone has to pay. It is the law of our sovereign.'

The crowd let out unreserved boos.

'Order. Order! Let there be order!' called the magistrate.

The courtroom settled into silence again. The magistrate continued. 'Noises will not advance this young lady's plight. And you, Sir, please be seated,' he said, looking over his spectacle at Jacob. 'Unless you have a firm proposition to make.' Jacob sat back down while the magistrate reasoned: 'As an indentured servant, the lady will enjoy the benefits which include meat, drink, apparel, and lodging. It is the King's law.' The magistrate visibly regretted his last sentence as this time, an even greater roar of discontent rose up on the last two words.

'Down with the Jacobites!'

'Out with the Romans!'

Jacob was about to stand up again when a voice, gruff, confident, and bold, sounded from his left-hand side.

'My Lords . . . My new friend is right,' said the unmistakable voice of Mr Leisler. 'How can we create a new world, free for all, and free from the archaic laws of England, if we cannot even welcome those in their momentary passage of strife? Must we not found our society on equality before God and with the chance for all under His sky to succeed here, no matter what their social condition?'

'Hear, hear!' roared the crowd.

'Order. Order!' called the magistrate. 'Sieur Leisler, would you have the town's treasury pay for everyone's failure?'

'My Lord, the man came here for a month. I remember him well; he was full of courage and ideas. His only failure was his untimely death, and now you ask his spouse to pay?'

'Bend the rules for one, and we will soon be the prime

48

destination for every unskilled labourer and convict from Europe! Is that what you want?' The magistrate, who visibly enjoyed an imposing presence, scanned the audience of spectators from left to right into silence.

Leisler, still standing, flourished a finger and said in a loud and confident voice: 'Then I will pay her fare, Sir!'

The audience gave a roar of approval while the magistrate held up his hand to silence them again. 'That is all very well, but who will pay for her sustenance, Sir? Or would you have her walk the streets with her child? Or work in the tavern?'

The French newcomer then stood up beside the woman's benefactor and said: 'If my friend will pay her debt, I will provide means for her until she is able to gain employment.'

The audience gave another almighty cheer. The woman, bringing her hands to her lips, looked across the room towards Jacob in gratitude.

'Then, Sir,' said the magistrate, 'you would still need to give her monies to see her through the winter, at the least.'

'That is indeed my intention, so help me God,' said Jacob, whose heart secretly sank as he said this. But how could he not practice what he preached?

'So she will find lodgings at the inn until other means become available to her,' said the magistrate with nonchalance.

'No, Sir,' said a woman's voice to Jacob's right. Jacob turned to Marianne beside him. 'The inn is notorious,' she said, rising to her feet, 'notorious for tripping women into sin for the pleasure of the stronger sex! I offer to employ her and give her board and lodging in my home. Provided my husband agrees.'

Daniel Darlington bobbed up in his turn. He said: 'I do, I do that. Whatever my dear wife says . . .'

49

The audience laughed along good-heartedly with Daniel's quip. So old Madame de Fontenay was right, thought Jacob, and what was more, her granddaughter's power of persuasion over her husband was apparently common knowledge.

FOUR

WHAT WITH ALL the brouhaha in the courtroom, Jacob quickly became a familiar figure.

He was pointed at in the snow-clad streets of the town, and singled out with a nudge and a nod in the little French chapel down near the battery, where Huguenots came from all over Manhattan for the Sunday service.

Yet all he really wanted was to make for Europe, which the present winter freeze forbade. He knew deep down that it was just as well, though, weakened as he was by his many misadventures and recent illness. His body would probably not have stood up to the rigours of a gruelling winter voyage in freezing temperatures, should that have been an option.

So he resigned himself to assisting the Darlingtons with drawing up plans to settle around the bay —the bay which the Huguenots from La Rochelle had deemed exceptional enough to start a settlement there. Darlington's intention was to build a farm to cultivate primarily the lucrative tobacco crop that Europeans craved.

In January, Darlington and Delpech decided to take advantage of a window of fresh but cloudless weather.

Having hired two good steeds and a packhorse, the two men rode out northward at the first gleam of dawn, with the intention of getting a look at how the land lay in the dead of winter. It was a twenty-three-mile ride along the Boston post road. After two hours in the saddle, Darlington halted his mount on the hoary crest of another wooded hill. The onward trail descended into an area of gently sloping land that converged into a bay. It was surrounded by a few leafless trees, snow-covered fields, and a litter of log houses with smoking chimneys.

'I give you New Rochelle,' said Darlington with a sweeping motion of his hand. 'You'll see, the land is good and fertile, and the fish are plentiful in the sound beyond.'

Jacob slowly scanned the humble beginnings of the new colony. 'Fine place for a settlement, I should say. Water, high ground for a mill, rich soil, and I wager there is plenty of game in the pantry!' he said, nodding towards the woods.

Onwards they rode, sinking between the fields where green grass and dark-brown earth broke through the thin veil of snow crust. 'As I said, the land was bought up by a lord in London,' said Darlington. 'A Lord Pell. Deceased now, though. So I asked Leisler to negotiate the purchase of six thousand acres on the Huguenots' behalf so they could become owners of their fields rather than leaseholders. He knows the nephew who lives in New York. A certain John Pell.'

'An enterprising fellow, this Leisler.'

'And a good friend. Gave me sound advice when my father and mother died . . . Came to New York as a mercenary soldier, would you believe. Son of a clergyman preacher like myself, and now he is one of the wealthiest merchants in New York.'

'Lady Luck has smiled upon him, then.'

'A little luck and a natural flair for spotting a bargain, I'd say. You may find him brash, unrefined, but he is a good fellow to the marrow, true to his word and as smart as any of the "grandees," as he likes to call them. And he's living proof that here a man can meet with success without a birthright, as I have seen in Europe. Why, pardon me for saying so, but some of your so-called elite are perfect imbeciles, frivolous, and so self-absorbed it is a wonder how folk there put up with them.'

'I will give you no argument there, dear Darlington! Indeed, your ways in these new lands have certainly opened my eyes.'

'Then I'll put it to you again, Sir: come join our ranks. Here a man of your calibre can aspire to great success. My word, you already have the affection of half the population of New York!'

'Ha! It is something I will certainly consider, once I have recovered my family.'

'I urge you to decide quickly, though; the best plots are already being snapped up. But come, there is a tavern where they give a good welcome to riders from Boston and New York, and I will introduce you to a few of the Huguenots. Then I will show you a handsome plot not far from mine. Overlooks the bay. Its south-facing slopes would make for fine farmland, I am sure.'

*

Back at the Darlingtons', the conversation over supper turned to preparations for the spring move and the promise Jacob had made to the Huguenots he had met in New Rochelle.

Learning of Jacob's fluency in English and his former training as a jurist in France, they had asked him if he would assist in linguistic and legal matters. With Jacob's help, they would be able to understand the full purport of Mr Leisler's negotiations for the purchase of the land from John Pell of Pelham Manor.

'I am delighted to hear you accepted,' said Marianne. 'It might sway the balance in favour of your becoming our neighbour . . .'

'Alas, it is not something I am able to contemplate for the time being,' said Jacob, seated across the table. 'I do look forward to making myself useful, however, at least until the thaw, when the first ship is ready to set sail for Europe.'

'If I may say something,' said Mrs Blancfort, looking up from the cauldron in the hearth.

Since her redemption from slavery, she had stepped into her new role as first maid with relish, taking over most of Marianne's activities now that the latter was great with child. All Mrs Blancfort needed now was a husband and a good stepfather for little Françoise, her daughter, who, as usual, was taking her meal in the kitchen with Martha. The notion occurred to her that the Lord may have put Monsieur Delpech in their path for that very reason.

'Yes, you may, Charlotte,' said Marianne, whose poised tone demonstrated her ease in the role of mistress.

'Well, as tragic as it may sound, Monsieur, how do you know your wife's still of this world?'

'Madame Blancfort! Really!' said Marianne, flabbergasted. It was not the way she had been brought up, for servants were not usually permitted to give their opinions unless asked. But this was the New World, and she knew, as did Mrs Blancfort, that relationships were more brazen here, especially since the great majority of wealthy men were recently made.

'No, that is quite all right,' said Jacob, holding up a hand with a complaisant chuckle to show he was not offended. 'I will gladly answer. Indeed, I have oft-times been given to ask myself that very question.' He turned his gaze to Charlotte Blancfort, who smiled candidly back from her place at the hearth. The glowing embers and candlelight gave her complexion a pretty hue and made her large oval eyes glisten attractively. 'I do live in hope that I shall see my wife and children in the very near future. And it is that hope that will carry me across the ocean. There can be no other way.'

'Oh well,' said the first maid, 'it will be a pity to see you go, Monsieur Delpech, a good, strong man of resources such as yourself. A mighty good catch for a lady, if you don't mind me saying so.' She shrugged one shoulder with comic effect, which drew a ripple of laughter from the table, and then went back to dishing out bowls of salted pork and lentil stew.

It was the closest Mrs Blancfort could come to letting Jacob overtly know that she was available and willing, should he ever be inclined to take a new wife.

Jacob took no offense. There was no point in pretending that Charlotte Blancfort was not doing the right thing. If she was here, it was after all while waiting to find a husband.

Jacob said: 'Come, Madame Blancfort, I have no doubt a husband will come along for you soon. You are too young to remain a widow for long, and I am sure that when the fine season comes, the butterflies of love will again flutter in your pretty eyes.'

'Thank you, Monsieur,' said Charlotte.

'Uncle Jacob!' said Marianne, perhaps a little jealous. 'How romantically you sayeth loving things.'

'I have not always been middle-aged, my dear niece!' said Jacob, to which Madame de Fontenay looked up with a glint in her eye.

'Ah, and memory of a full youth is certainly the most comfortable pillow for slumber in old age. So fill it up, I say! Oh, how I used to dance the evening away . . .'

Amid the merriment, Martha marched into the room from the small lobby, nervously wringing her hands. The second maid fixed her eyes on Darlington and said: 'Sir. There's Mr Leisler come knocking at the door, he—'

Before she could finish her sentence, the visitor erupted into the room, with his feathered beaver still on his head. A blustery draught followed him in, making the candles flicker in their lamps and the embers glow redder in the chimney. All heads turned in unison to face him from the dining table that stood before the hearth, the ladies occupying the seats nearest the fire.

'Come in, my dear fellow, and pull up a chair,' said Darlington, standing to greet his friend. Meanwhile, at a nod from Madame de Fontenay, Martha rushed back to the front door to make sure it was properly barred.

After a short greeting all round, Leisler did as suggested, and, swiping his hat from his head, he said: 'Ladies, Gentlemen, please excuse this intrusion. I have important news of further developments in England. We have been given to believe that a Dutch fleet has indeed landed in England!'

'William of Orange at their head . . .' said Darlington.

'Yes, I received the news from a ship's captain, who heard

it from an English merchant who had recently unloaded in Charles Town.'

'If this is true, it is reassuring news,' said Jacob. 'For if he takes the throne, it would mean Louis of France no longer has any sway over England.'

'I agree,' said Leisler, 'but it could also mean war, civil war, if James Stuart tries to resist.'

'What does Lieutenant Governor Nicholls say?' said Darlington.

'He denies any such tidings since no official news has reached his ears.'

'He is in denial!' said Madame de Fontenay, not afraid to vent her thoughts despite her heavy French accent.

'Not quite, Madame. For he has nevertheless given orders for the provincial militias to be on alert to protect the province for the king. King James, that is.'

'But what if James is no longer king?' said Marianne.

'Then the risk is that James will seek support from France,' said Leisler. 'And our trouble is, Jacobites are in power here and in command of our fort.'

'Not to mention our defences are in such a poor state of repair that even the wall would not constitute a major handicap for the French, should they decide to attack.' Darlington was referring to the French stationed in New France, further north.

'I never thought I'd ever hear myself say this of my own countrymen,' said Jacob. 'But if the French attack, then our goose will be cooked!'

'Quite,' seconded Marianne, 'for if they did, I fear we Huguenots would be put to torture before execution.'

'With all due respect, Ladies and Gentlemen, we shall see

to it that French forces will never enter here!' said Leisler. Turning to Darlington and Delpech, he said: 'We must organise a secret safety committee should this news turn out to be true. I have already spoken to Milborne and a few others who would be prepared to take part. Because if New York becomes Catholic, we will all be done for!'

FIVE

IT WAS RUMOURED in taverns and New York homes that the Dutch prince had succeeded in his invasion of England. Bolstered by the feeling of distrust of the Jacobite office holders, Leisler set about secretly planning the defence of the would-be Protestant king's values —values of liberalism and freedom of conscience on par with those of the people of New York.

Due to his knowledge of law and the English language —the go-between language of Dutch and French —Delpech became the ears and mouthpiece of the Huguenot contingent of Manhattan. Little by little, he began to feel a sense of duty towards his co-religionists. In fact, he began to feel in his element, in the faraway land where there was a sense that a new and fairer way of life was not only attainable, but in the making.

But the arctic winds had not yet brought any impartial news from England by way of merchant ships. Only a couple of large Royal Navy vessels had made landfall in the province so far that winter, and only a few droplets of information had leaked through to New York via Boston. What was more, the French were abnormally calm on the New France frontier north of Albany, as if they, too, were awaiting news. What could possibly be happening in Europe?

'Is this state of affairs not ridiculous?' said Darlington late one January afternoon, to a group of prominent New Yorkers brought together in Jacob Leisler's dining room. 'Here we are, waiting for the great powers that be to dispatch crumbs of information to determine our future! I say it is intolerable, Gentlemen. To think they have probably never even set foot on these lands!'

The small committee, which included Darlington, Delpech, Leisler, Milborne, and a few merchants, had gathered in the privacy of Mr Leisler's townhouse, a large and comfortable three-storey stone building veneered with kiln-fired brick and built when the town was under Dutch governance. Decorated with the bold splendour characteristic of Amsterdam merchants, the long, flagstoned dining room where the meeting was being held was adorned with beautifully carved *kasten*, dark-wood panelling, and thick drapes at the window boxes. The party of seven sat around the long dining table on high-backed chairs, a silver tankard in front of each of them.

Delpech had turned up with the intention of asking the ever-busy Leisler if he had made any progress for the Rochelle Huguenots. Sitting before the fire, he could not fail to admire the splendid array of weaponry displayed above the tiled mantel, which tallied with what Darlington had told him of the New Yorker's past in the Dutch army.

'Yes, but we officially belong to the Crown,' said Jacob's neighbour. His name was Jacob Milborne, a methodical Puritan approaching forty who worked as clerk and bookkeeper for a leading merchant. 'And we benefit from its protection. If we did not, then you can be sure that New York would soon be called New Orleans!'

'I do see your point, Sir,' returned Darlington, 'but that also means this town could just as easily be turned over to the French if that be the whim of the so-called elite of England!'

'I think not, my dear Daniel,' said Leisler. The host was sitting slightly back from the dining-room table in his favourite armchair, almost as an observer. He was holding a glowing ember with his pipe tongs, and proceeded to ignite the tobacco in his long-stemmed clay pipe. After drawing upon it twice, he pursued: 'I firmly believe the rumours of King James's demise, and every day I pray for its confirmation.'

'Then we should have to fend off the French anyway,' said Darlington, 'lest they damn us to popery!'

Reaching over to let drop the ember in the hearth and replace the tongs on a brass stand, Leisler said: 'We shall be in better hands if William asserts his wife's right to the throne and becomes king himself.'

'Aye, give me a liberal Dutch Protestant over an English Louis XIV anytime!' said Milborne.

'And we all know William's love for the French king!' The host's ironic remark brought a round of complicit chuckles.

'You can be sure he will send his soldiers to protect our livelihood,' said Nicholas Stuyvesant, the son of the former Dutch governor.

'And his taxes,' added Darlington.

'But if William steps in,' said Milborne, 'at least we shall recover our seal and the independence of our administration.'

'Nonetheless, Gentlemen,' said Leisler, 'Mr Darlington does have a point regarding the remote rule of these lands. As you well know, I am the German-born son of a French Calvinist. You, Sir, are from France. Both of you are of Dutch ancestry. And you, Milborne, are born a subject of His Majesty in Albion. Only Darlington and Stuyvesant here are natives of this city. Yet, I say we are all first and foremost New Yorkers!'

The gentlemen let out hear-hears all round, some lightly tapping the table. Even Darlington gave a nod of acquiescence.

Leisler went on: 'We stand united in our perspective on trade, in our tolerance and love of freedom of worship.' Then, sweeping his head slowly round to include Darlington, he said: 'But the fight for independence from remote powers cannot be for today! First, we must regain our seal and ensure New York will still be our home tomorrow. And for that, we need to be sure the Protestant monarchy will be respected!' Daniel was about to interrupt, but, raising his free hand, Leisler persisted: 'Please, Daniel, hear me out . . . Thank you. For what if our governor, Lieutenant Governor Nicholls, and the military and customs officeholders refuse to acknowledge a Protestant king? What if they side with the enemy, as will James Stuart should he be dethroned?'

'You are right,' conceded Darlington. 'A greater threat looms immediately over us. And I fear, as we stand today, there is no defence set up in case of French attack.'

'One might go so far as to say it could not have been planned better for an invasion,' said Stuyvesant, cocking an insinuating eyebrow.

Darlington said: 'I say we take control of the town. If we do not act—as you say, Milborne—this place may indeed be soon renamed New Orleans . . . I say we act now!'

'The people of New York are vastly behind us,' said Stuyvesant.

'Gentlemen, let us not be hasty, however,' said Leisler, holding his lapel in one hand and the stem of his pipe in the other. 'We must plan this wisely, so that when the time comes, we are able to take over the town without chaos, in the tradition of Stuyvesant senior. And at all costs, I say we await news of an official nature before we take the governor's residence.'

'I agree,' said Milborne, 'or else we risk being tried for treason, no less.'

'Mr Delpech,' said Darlington, looking across the table, 'I know you have come to see Mr Leisler on another matter, and I do not want to drag you into our problems, but what say you?'

What with an Englishman asking a Frenchman what to do in case of French attack, and a Frenchman seeking refuge in an English colony, decidedly, the world really had gone mad, thought Jacob, who, to be truthful, had been enjoying his mulled wine in his silver tankard. The alcohol and the heat from the mulberry-and-white-tiled hearth that crackled peacefully before him had lulled his senses. He now placed his hands composedly upon the table in front of him to give himself a countenance. He said: 'I would say . . . Mr Leisler is right to plan for such an important event, for the French would put any chaos to their advantage. As Mr Leisler's military background will have taught him, if and when the time comes, there must be swift action if we are to stay in control after the takeover. I would humbly suggest that plans be drawn up as soon as possible to prepare actions and designate defence parties, so that the interim commander will know exactly what to implement upon takeover.'

'The fort will have to be manned night and day,' said Darlington.

'We should have to strengthen the city walls,' said Leisler.

'And sufficient warning should be provided to those residing outside the wall should the threat prove imminent,' said Delpech.

'Indeed, we shall have to place sentinels and cannons at strategic outposts,' said Leisler, who then drew again from his pipe.

Seizing the moment, Jacob said: 'Speaking of which, Sir, if I may digress from the discussion just a moment, do we have news from Lord Pell with regards to the land purchase?'

'Ah, I do indeed, Delpech. I have received the first draft of the contract . . .'

'Excellent. I shall set up a meeting with my brethren to finalize land plots and boundaries. I have drawn up a list of no fewer than thirty names . . .'

Delpech said no more on the subject and let the more pressing debate carry on to its conclusion, which was to establish a plan of action by their next meeting.

SIX

JACOB THREW HIMSELF into his new toil. It enabled him to calm his frustrations born of the impossibility of achieving his own goal. His mind thus occupied, he was able to diminish the terrible nightmares that had previously made him restless at night.

He helped translate legal documents; became a go-between to express questions and answers between the Huguenot contingent and Leisler; and was a constant source of knowledge when it came to planning the new settlement, the construction of which would continue in earnest with the thaw. The position of the mill was his specialty, along with land irrigation. It was important to ensure that every plot had access to its own water supply, the value of which could easily have been overlooked in these months of overabundance of ice and snow.

Despite the petty disputes mostly relating to future property boundaries, Delpech found himself playing a pivotal role in the creation of the new township. It gave his life new meaning to be part of something greater than himself, and it was restoring his faith in humanity.

These planning sessions came to a head one day during a meeting after church at the Darlingtons' house. The house was conveniently situated on the track back to New Rochelle. Every Sunday, Huguenots made the hike from their temporary timber country dwellings to New York. A Sunday service was given in the humble French chapel built by French refugees the previous year. For those who had already begun settling in New Rochelle, it meant a forty-six-mile round trek, one which they undertook every Sunday, weather permitting. The men and the heartiest women walked beside the rough oxen-drawn carts that transported children and those not up to the long march. Jacob stood in wonder the first time he saw the caravan wend its way to the gates of New York, singing one of Marot's hymns. The mere sight of them in the nascent light of a Sunday morning never ceased to lighten his own burden and double his desire to assist them in their installation. Though his compensation for his work was not of a tangible nature, it was priceless all the same. They enabled him to recover his bearings and mend his moral compass, damaged in the company of the buccaneers from Port Royal.

'It is but a slight hardship compared to the joy in our hearts of being able to worship God openly,' a man named Bonnefoy had said when Jacob had expressed his admiration after church. 'And what is more,' Bonnefoy had continued, 'what greater joy can there be in the knowledge that we are building the foundations for our children and our children's children, so they may celebrate God's love in a like manner, free from persecution!'

The meeting took place in the dining room after the service, as usual with the would-be councillors of the settlement, some of whom still resided in New York while waiting for the winter to pass. Those who had already begun settling in New Rochelle stayed behind, while the main caravan went on its way back so it would reach home before nightfall.

Marianne sat in for her husband, who was down at the quay, preparing a cargo of tobacco and sugar for the next ship to London. Besides, the meeting being held in French, he preferred his wife to be his ears and his mouthpiece. Madame de Fontenay sat cosily at the hearth with her knitting needles. 'In case things get out of hand!' she had said with a twinkle in her eye. 'Because I am not very good with them for much else.' Then she had given a sigh of despair at the tiny, oddly shaped garment she was trying to knit.

Jacob proceeded to translate a document, showed the settlers a draft of the plots, and noted down any questions for the ensuing exchange with Leisler. The meeting was coming to a close when Monsieur Bonnefoy, a leading tenor of the party in his early forties, popped the question that Jacob suspected would come sooner or later.

'Now, Monsieur Delpech,' he said, resting his clenched hands on the table before him, 'I have been asked unanimously by all those present, if you would care to stand as a member of the new council which, as you know, is to be made up of twelve aldermen.'

It was a heartening proposition for sure, and one that gave Jacob a profound satisfaction. But he knew that it also meant becoming a villager and putting his name down for a plot. Jacob placed his palms down upon the table as if to give himself extra balance. For well he might be tempted to leave his money in this new world, and keep only enough to pay for the voyage back with his family. At last, he said: 'I thank you for the offer, Gentlemen. Alas, as you well know, I cannot stay.'

'We do understand your position, Monsieur Delpech, but once you have recovered your family, you will need a place to settle, will you not?' Monsieur Bonnefoy then opened his arms to embrace the whole table to give more weight to his offer. 'Well, Sir, we should be most honoured if that place be with us.' Amid deep rumblings and hear-hears around the table, Monsieur Bonnefoy persisted: 'This can be your new home with like-minded people who value your moral fibre and your talents. You have given us your expertise freely and without restraint. Your place is among us. What say you, Sir?'

Marianne, sitting opposite Jacob, read the discomfort on his knitted brow. She knew how difficult it would be for him to commit to such an opportunity, and Jacob did not give his word lightly. She knew that leaving Europe indefinitely would mean leaving behind his dead children in their graves, and that two of his daughters might even still be with his sister-in-law, for all he knew. But his modesty forbade him from laying out his personal woes. And now that she had her own child in her belly, she could imagine the pain of having lost one. She glanced towards Madame de Fontenay by the hearth behind her for some tacit guidance. But the old lady simply raised both eyebrows in an expression that Marianne knew well. It told her to act as her heart told her to.

The young woman turned back to the table and, as poised as the men despite her youth, with an indulgent smile in her voice, she said: 'Gentlemen, I pray we show some patience. Perhaps Monsieur Delpech needs to allow the proposition to mature in his mind before committing to an answer.'

Monsieur Bonnefoy, good-natured, said: 'Oh, do not worry yourself, Madame Darlington. We only beg for a preliminary reply so that we can allocate a place.' He then turned back to Jacob. 'What say you, Sir?'

Jacob had gone over the possibility time and time again, and the merchant in him told him he would do far worse than to pledge his return. Sure, it would be an exciting and adventurous new beginning, but could he honestly commit to a plot and a place as councillor? And how safe would this land be in two months, in two years? The threats were numerous: wild animals, Indians allied to the French, the English under King James, invasion from his own countrymen from New France.

'Sir,' he said, 'please do not think me ungrateful if at this minute I do not say *yes*.'

'But you do not say *no* either.'

'I should rather sleep on it and promise to give you my pondered reply when we meet next Sunday.'

It was a fair enough compromise, accepted by all, and one that would buy him time to weight everything correctly in the balance.

*

Later that afternoon, Jacob sat alone with a handful of papers and his pipe in the small sitting room.

The coming events were exciting, and playing a major role in such an adventure as the birth of a township was something he was finding most gratifying. He was acutely aware, too, that a decisive moment in history was about to be played out in New York —that of the defence of the township as a free city.

Of course, he had planned to depart for Europe at the first opportunity, but the merchant vessel, for which Daniel Darlington was preparing a shipment at his warehouse, would set sail for London via Boston, possibly extending the voyage by a week, maybe two. He had also learnt of another ship, albeit smaller, that was due to sail in early March, which was just a few weeks away. Given that this second option was to sail directly from New York to London, it would probably arrive in the English capital only weeks after the Boston ship. Not only would it mean less time at sea, but it would allow him to help tie up any loose ends with regard to the purchase of the land that would harbour New Rochelle. But what should he do about Bonnefoy's offer to buy into the township and take a role as alderman?

His mind was soon swimming again with indecision. 'Get a grip on yourself, man!' he said to himself. He slammed down the documents onto the little round table and gazed into the hearth, elbow on the arm of his armchair, hand cupping his pipe. Little by little —amid the calm of the crackling fire, the purr of the cat kneading the cushion on Madame de Fontenay's chair, and the discreet click of the bracket clock upon the walnut commode —he began to realise to what extent his mind had become overcrowded, submerged in matters that were far away from his initial goal, matters that had nonetheless also become important to him. For was his role not indispensable for a satisfactory outcome? Leisler, after all, was a merchant. Would he not try to price the land so he could make a handsome profit for himself when he sold it on?

But now, sitting with his pipe in the absence of the male party and the cacophony of preparations, he was able at last to put everything into perspective and, hopefully, hear a voice of reason through the commotion of his vagaries . . .

'Are you well, Sir?' said the maid, carrying a pewter tray full of cups, saucers, and a coffee pot.

'Ah, Madame Blancfort,' said Jacob, removing his pipe from his lips. 'Sorry, I was miles away . . .'

'I believe miles away is exactly where you ought to be, Monsieur Delpech,' continued Charlotte Blancfort, brash as ever, 'if you'll pardon me for saying so.' She placed the tray on the low table in front of the fire while Jacob sat agape.

'You know she is right, Monsieur Delpech,' said a lively voice from the doorway. Jacob rose from his seat to face Madame de Fontenay as she hobbled into the room. 'Take no notice,' she said with a nod to her cherry walking stick, 'hip giving me gyp. Good news for you, though. It's a sure sign that milder weather is on its way.'

'You cannot keep fighting everyone else's battles, you know, Sir,' said Charlotte. She then stuck out an arm to help the old lady to her chair.

Madame de Fontenay picked up the cat and dumped it on her lap as she sat down. 'There, lap warmer!' she declared.

'And perhaps, this is not your battle to fight, Jacob!' said the voice of Marianne, who walked in holding her bump with one hand and her lower back with the other. Her belly had grown considerably, and her face had become fuller. It occurred to Jacob how much her life had changed, and how she and her grandmother had taken it in their stride, just like Madame Blancfort, who now only had her daughter left of her family of five. 'At least, not at this time,' pursued

71

Marianne. 'For your true fight is surely elsewhere, my uncle . . . many miles away.'

The ping of the bracket clock announced the time for afternoon coffee, a ritual that the ladies had installed which broke up the monotony of the wintry afternoons. Charlotte Blancfort proceeded to lay out the cups and saucers while Martha and little Françoise brought in the sugar scraped into a bowl from a sugarloaf, and some gingerbread cookies on a pewter plate.

'Did you not say that you lived in hope of seeing your wife and children soon, Monsieur?' said Charlotte. It would have been deemed impertinent of a maid to speak to a guest of her mistress in this fashion. But Marianne knew she would not stay long before she, too, found a new home. Madame de Fontenay just smiled with an amused twinkle in her eye.

'I did indeed,' said Jacob.

'I only mention it,' continued Charlotte, 'because so did I live in hope, Monsieur Delpech. I boarded a ship with no means in the hope of joining my husband. But then I found out that hope alone ain't enough, is it? And truth is, I delayed too. Had I taken the previous ship like I was planning, I would have been able to care for him, and he wouldn't have died alone in his room, and we'd all be together today . . .' Charlotte bit her lip to retain her steely countenance.

'You mustn't let your hope wither away, though, Charlotte,' said Marianne comfortingly.

'Oh, I won't let it, Madame Darlington, thanks to yourselves and all your kindnesses.' Charlotte put on a brave smile that embraced Jacob as well as the old lady.

'You have plenty to hope for, Madame Blancfort,' said Jacob, while Marianne put an arm around her. 'And yes, I do see your point. You have to set your sights and keep to them . . . I admit, I myself . . . seem to have been somewhat swept off my feet.'

'The ship is due to sail in a few days, Jacob,' said Marianne.

'Yes, it has been constantly at the back of my mind. But I have been told there will be another next month, and direct to London, that one.'

'Charlotte is right. I would dally not if I were you, Monsieur Delpech,' said Madame de Fontenay. 'Bring back your family here, if that is your desire. But go and fetch them before it is too late!'

Jacob said: 'I shall weigh up the pros and cons of leaving so soon, I promise.'

Jacob, however, would not have to deliberate for long.

*

The following Tuesday, Jacob was back at Leisler's fine townhouse, going over the plotted map and the adjustments made during Sunday's meeting with the Huguenots.

On the way, he had noted a foretaste of spring: the first white flowers poking through the thin layer of snow on the pretty graveyard near the north gate; the wide sun-splashed thoroughfare in New York, busier than usual; and the animated market near the fort, packed with vendors, animals, and spindled carts. Jacob also noticed the rivers now flowed mostly free of ice.

Only the Huguenots who still resided in New York attended the meeting held in Leisler's dining room.

Marianne, having already spoken with Jacob, had preferred not to attend, given her condition. The party had made good progress: their host was confident that they could get the ball rolling as to the signing of the deed, now that parcels had been drawn and confirmed. All that was required now was for Leisler to make the purchase from John Pell, who had agreed in principle to the sale of the six thousand acres.

The meeting had just come to a close. The attendees were looking through the tall rear window in admiration of Leisler's long garden, bare and hoary but orderly and attractive in the late-morning sunshine, when the manservant announced Daniel Darlington.

Not being one for endless meetings, Daniel had found a pretext to oversee the lading of his cargo down at the wharf at Coenties Slip. He doffed his hat on entering and said: 'Gentlemen, please forgive my intrusion, but I have, if not official news, at least important first-hand news from England.'

All present stared in silent expectation.

'Ah,' said Leisler. 'And what might that be?'

'William of Orange is King of England, Gentlemen!'

There was a short silence before the Huguenots fully took in the announcement, while Leisler stood in stupor, holding his chin.

Monsieur Le Conte, a tall, serious-looking man, taking the initiative, said: 'Zat is good, yes?'

'Indeed it is,' said Jacob. There was a release of tension in the room as the penny dropped.

Leisler, however, remained stern-faced. 'Who told you?' he said.

'A captain just in from Virginia.'

'Then we must act,' said Leisler, now poised for action. 'Gather as many people as you can at the tavern, Daniel.'

Within a few minutes, the Huguenot gentlemen were taking their leave.

Leisler asked Delpech if he could stay behind a minute.

'You know what this means?' said the merchant and former soldier as the door closed behind the last gentleman from New Rochelle.

'Quite possibly war in one form or another, I'm afraid.'

'Yes, I'm afraid you are right, Sir, if it has not already started.'

'Good grief!'

'And knowing your circumstances, Mr Delpech, please do not think me curt if I take it upon myself to offer you some advice.'

'Fear not, Sir, it will be well received.'

'I am sure your compatriots would appreciate your staying to help administer the township, but if you are to leave, I strongly recommend you do so as soon as possible, Sir. You can take the next ship to Boston. From there, it will take you to London. This is my strong advice, Monsieur Delpech, for I fear the French will not be slow in setting up a maritime blockade.'

SEVEN

CLAD IN A waxed travel cloak, Jacob watched the clump of land at the tip of Manhattan become gradually enshrouded in swathes of fog.

Would he return to this New World, clement but cruel, so fragile and yet so resolutely defended by its new populations? It presented a chance indeed to start from a clean slate without all the backlog of centuries of warfare, conflict, and political intrigue. There again, could New York be on the verge of becoming embroiled in imported statutes, mentalities, and traditions?

Standing aft on the quarterdeck of the merchantman, he turned his eyes starboard to the misty shores of Staten Island, where many a Huguenot had braved the journey to make a new life. Another interminable voyage lay ahead of him, he thought while scanning the farmsteads nestled in the slopes, but one nonetheless made sweeter in the knowledge that it would take him to his loved ones. And should England not hold its promise, he might well be driven to risk one more voyage to this land of hope, where he had fellowship and connections, despite the inconveniences which were far from minor. The freezing cold winters were barely tolerable for a man from the Midi of France, and then there was the constant threat of French or native invasion.

The weather remained calm and the going slow for the first days of the ocean crossing. It went without incident until the second week out, when one morning brought the sight of a distant ship. By her colours, she was ascertained to be Dutch, a Dutch fluyt, and she was heading straight into their trajectory. After some debate, the merchant captain, a commanding fellow with a bellowing voice, decided not to change course. If the rumours were true about William of Orange taking the English throne, there would be no call for them to fight off a Dutch attack.

'And if the rumours are not true?' said Jacob, listening in the captain's cabin with the crew.

'If they are not, then she might well blow us out of the water, Sir,' said the captain with a genial chuckle. 'But fear not, if enemies they be, they would aim to take the ship and cargo for the merry sum they would make.'

'What if the flag is a decoy?' said Jacob, calling to mind his buccaneering days. 'What if they are privateers, Sir, or worse, pirates?'

'Ha, then we shall be ready to fly!' said the captain with a heartier laugh. 'And you, Monsieur Delpech, shall stand by the swivel gun ready to fire!'

Jacob did not know the man well enough to determine if it was part of a show of bravery to laugh off the danger, or if his apparent bonhomie indicated that he did not take the threat seriously. Either way, incredible as it seemed, on the whim of a monarch a friend could turn foe and aim to blow you to kingdom come. Surely there must be another way to govern countries?

He pondered Darlington's vision of forming an independent state with no king or aristocracy, where only men of talent were pulled from the rank and file to govern the people for the people. It sounded preposterous, for how could common folk know about international affairs and territorial rights? Yet, would it not be better to lay a country's future with a body of men rather than with just one man designated to rule by birthright?

The Dutch ship had the advantage of coming from Europe with knowledge of the latest developments and what alliances had been made. There again, things could be worse, thought Jacob; the fluyt could have been flying the black flag, or even worse than that, the French *bleu-blanc-rouge*!

By mid-morning, the two ships were just half a nautical mile apart. The sea was calm, the wind fair and in favour of the merchantman from New York should flight be the only option.

'The moment of truth approaches, lads!' called the captain. 'Stand ready to run with the wind!'

Jacob stood at the swivel gun and prayed he would not fail in his mission, that if the time came, he neither found himself with a yellow belly nor one filled with lead.

'The Dutchman still shows no colour for battle, Sir!' called the first mate, looking through his spyglass. It felt to Jacob like the very ship gave a sigh of relief.

Ten minutes later, both ships had reduced sail and hove to so that a brief verbal exchange could be achieved as they passed.

The captains gave a salute as their vessels arrived broadside starboard. With a speaking trumpet held to his lips, the Dutch commander called out. 'News from England.

William of Orange is your new king! William of Orange is King of England!'

'Is there war?' called the English captain, cupping his hands.

'War with France! Beware of French frigates!'

'Is there civil war?'

'There is not,' called the Dutch captain as the ships finished passing each other and sailed onwards into the vastness of the ocean.

*

They were carried along on a favourable wind which made the going fair though the sea became rougher, and the ride more agitated. Jacob found little to do but introspect and try to plan his first steps in London. But then, an unfortunate incident came to drive all introspection away and filled his mind for the remainder of the voyage.

After a day of slack, the wind had picked up again, and the captain gave the command to sail under topsails with a single reef. The crew were in good spirits, and the captain's cat purred comfortably on Jacob's lap while he read his only books, glad to find refuge within his mind. All of a sudden, he heard a cry, a splash, then another voice yelling out: 'Man overboard!'

Delpech promptly brushed the cat aside and ran up the steps to the main deck. Crewmen were striking sails, others running down the length of the ship on the starboard side, their eyes peeled on the water frothing at the ship's timbers.

'There, man!' called a sailor from the rigging. The mate at the aft cast a line over the balustrade so that it landed in the sea, in the trajectory of the young rigger who had slipped from his perch. The drowning sailor threw out an arm in a desperate effort to grasp the cord that would save his life. But agonizingly, he under reached. The captain gave no order to turn back, and it was not expected of him either, for everyone knew that the lad could not swim. He went under once more in the wake of the ship and was seen no more.

The death silenced the crew's merry banter and left Jacob reflecting on the fragility of life, and the sailor's one chance to live or to die.

The sombre spirits were swept aside, however, a few days later, when death also threatened the lives of the bereaved. When the crew were getting to sleep in their hammocks and Jacob had just blown out his candle, there came a great crashing din as the ship became weighed down at the stern and raised at the prow. Seconds later, a deluge came gushing into the lower decks washing the men from their slumber.

It was swiftly determined that they had been hit by a huge wave that had rolled over the stern of the ship, sending great volumes of seawater into the hold. Jacob promptly found himself in a line under lamplight, rapidly passing buckets full of water to the next man while other crew members frantically worked the bilge pumps. All night long, they pumped and baled, fearful of the next great wave that Jacob knew from past experience would certainly sink the vessel. But the gigantic wave must have been a freak of nature, for although the weather was blowy, the sea was not as big as in a storm.

The following morning found the crew fatigued but in cheerier spirits. The drowned sailor was no longer in their forethoughts, thankful as they were not to be joining him in his watery grave.

The voyage continued with fair weather and Godspeed, these two incidents being the only mishaps along the way, but which nonetheless awakened Jacob to the risks of a possible return to the New World.

At the crack of dawn, after eight weeks of ocean travel, they were heartened by the sight of the English coast near Plymouth. But the wind dropped off, and with the current being contrary to travel, they were obliged to lie at anchor near the dunes. They weighed anchor again at nightfall only to have to drop it a day later. It was another ten-day wait before current and wind came favourably together to enable the ship to set sail eastward along the English coast again. She put into port in early April, some seven miles from London, where part of the cargo was due to be unloaded.

By now Jacob's nerves were frayed to the extreme, so close was he to the place that promised to reunite him with his loved ones. He dared not think who of his family he might find in the English capital, and who he might not.

Two days later, unable to wait any longer, he managed to gain passage aboard a small, single-masted fishing boat headed for Billingsgate harbour, which Jacob knew to be a stone's throw away from London Bridge.

*

Should have used small change, thought Jacob as the single-masted fishing boat made its way up the Thames by the light of a half-moon. He had reached into his travel purse and pulled out a silver dollar to pay for his passage to Billingsgate.

The fisherman, mid-forties with a weather-worn face, had peered with alert eyes at the man with a foreign accent.

'From France, Sir?' he had said in a chirpy, matter-of-fact way.

'I am French, indeed, although France is no longer my home.'

'Ah, thought as much,' the fisherman had returned with a satisfied glance to his young mate. 'An 'Uguenot, eh?'

Jacob had answered in the affirmative while the fisherman pocketed the silver dollar and brought out a farthing. Accepting the coin, Jacob had then taken a pew amid the baskets of fish near a heap of netting at the stern. The fisherman had then pushed away with the help of his young mate into the flood tide.

Now Delpech instinctively felt under his cloak for the bulge beneath his waistcoat where he kept his belt purse, of a good deal more consequence than his travel pouch. Turning his collar to the light easterly wind, he set to pondering that these men would be his foes had the King of France not made an enemy of Protestants. How preposterous was that? And he realised the fisherman's fleeting look of suspicion on hearing Jacob's accent was no less justified given that France was now at war with England.

The square sail was rigged close to the prow, and the gentle north-easterly breeze kept it taut while the boatmen steered or heaved with their oars. The star-speckled sky and the glow of the moon were light enough to allow navigation past the looming shadows of moored vessels. The elder fisherman at the helm kept up a running commentary designating the various warships, frigates, and prison ships anchored along the Kentish riverbanks. He also reassured his French passenger, telling him of a great many Huguenots having taken the same river trip to London Town.

'Come in the merchantman, did ya, Sir?' said the fisherman, hand on the rudder.

'Yes, Sir, I did. From New York,' replied Jacob, half turning on the plank seat to face his interlocutor. Why did he have to go as far as to mention the ship's provenance? He wished he had bitten his tongue. But the chirpy fisherman was infectiously sociable and probably knew where it had come from anyway. He was probably only making conversation, thought Jacob; it was the way of city folk.

'There's money in New York, ain't there, Sir?' said the fisherman's mate between two strokes of the oar. Jacob took the young man who was standing at the prow to be the older man's son.

'I believe there is,' said Jacob, then adding, as though to put the record straight: 'That is, if you are in fur or tobacco, and alas, I am in neither. And there is no lack of hardship, not to mention the risk of invasion.'

'And pirates,' said the fisherman's mate with cheeky malice in his voice.

'Speaking of which . . .' said the elder fisherman. Then he pointed in the dark to the north bank foreshore, at the silhouette of a rotting corpse in a cage attached to a post. 'Ole Jim Bailley. Got caught as you can see; then he got tried, tarred, and strung up. Weren't a bad show, though, was it, Wil? We was there, and now there he is. Still sailin' in the wind, ha!' The fisherman doffed his hat. The gruesome cage returned a squeak as it swayed in the wind while the boat slipped by in the smelly black river.

Jacob felt a shudder down the spine as it suddenly occurred to him that the coin he carried could be misconstrued as proof of piracy. For he had no justification as to how he had come by it. Who would believe him if he said that it was reimbursement from the very soldier who had ransacked his home and sold his possessions in France? So he decided it was wiser to simply say, if asked, that the money came from his estate in France. It was just unfortunate, he thought, that the pouch that Lieutenant Ducamp had given him contained more silver dollars and pieces of eight than French ecus.

The nauseating smell of fish was attenuated now by the river sludge, now by the rich bouquet of the spring vegetation—vegetation increasingly interspersed with square silhouettes of buildings as they neared the city.

Barely an hour later, they were passing the Tower of London. It gleamed in the moonlight and stood as proud and square as he remembered it from the time when he spent a season in London with his father. Immediately before him loomed London Bridge, with its frothing waters streaming between the cutwaters below. He looked up at the assortment of towers, turrets, and tall houses, huddled shoulder to shoulder with windows all aglow. He wondered if they still displayed heads of executed criminals on spikes on top of the south bank gatehouse, a sight that had given him nightmares as a young lad, coming as he did from his provincial French town of Montauban.

But at last, here he was, sitting in the main artery of the great sprawling city. Now, he wondered, could he remember the way from the bridge to the French church he attended with his father all those years ago? That church had since burnt to the ground, the district north of the bridge no doubt modified. But he only had to find his way to Threadneedle Street, where, following the great fire of '66, he knew from his father it had been rebuilt on the same spot. The fisherman had not heard of the church, it not being in his parish, but could direct him to the street in question.

They rounded a dung boat from which emanated the nauseating stench of offal and the filth of beasts that grossly overpowered the smell of the fisherman's catch. Fifteen yards further on, the little boat arrived at Billingsgate wharf, where the fisherman's mate cast a line around an oak mooring post. Turning to his wealthy Huguenot traveller, the fisherman said: 'Now, up the stairs and keep going till you come to Thames Street at the top, go left and carry on over the main thoroughfare leading from the bridge. That's still Thames Street. Keep going till you get to the Cock and Bull sign in Dowgate, then go right all the way up, and you'll come to a square where you'll find Threadneedle Street if that's where your church is . . . Place will have changed a lot though since you came 'ere last, Sir, when was it?'

'Sixty-four,' said Jacob, getting up to step onto the wooden boardwalk. Jacob gave thanks and bid farewell to the fishermen.

It was not yet nine o'clock, and there was still a crowd of river folk —merchants, fishwives, and market vendors — collecting and inspecting the last delivery of the tide. Jacob, still with the stench of fish and offal in his nose, was attracted by the savoury smell of pork and roast lamb. The sudden desire to eat, the need to confirm the fisherman's directions, and the proximity of the tavern drove him to push the door into the elegantly named Salutation Tavern. He kept his ears pricked in case he heard French spoken, knowing from the fisherman that many French people had fled across the Channel. But he quickly discerned that most of the patrons quaffing ale at this hour were riverside folk, for what honest gentleman would be out in a tripling house at this hour of the night? Nonetheless, the rush of voices and the warm smells of bodies, ale, and broth filled his senses, made him feel quite heartened by his arrival in London.

Once he had ordered a platter of sausages and oysters, he said to the alewife: 'I am looking for the French church on Threadneedle Street.'

After he repeated his question, partly due to the noise, partly due to his accent, the buxom lady said: 'You wanna cut across Puddin' Lane, my love, up past the butcher's and across into Great Eastcheap.' After further guidance from patrons who knew the area, he was left with a muddled set of directions different from those of the fisherman, which had already slipped his mind anyway. But as long as he was pointed in the right direction, he could always ask along the way.

He stepped back out into the dark and dank street, refreshed and relieved, as the night watchman gave ten of the clock and all well down by the riverside. He followed his feet through the tenement streets of Billingsgate, and through a miserable square that smelled of piss where ladies sang out their compliments in gay, flat tones. He hurried along Pudding Lane where butcher's carts left vile droppings of offal in their wake as they trundled down to the waste barges. The first drops of rain made him pull down his hat and sink his head into his collar as he passed dark alleyways — alleyways where the odd drunkard or vagrant lay crumpled and snoring.

Minutes later, his face glistened in the drizzle, that same fine rain he recalled from his youth when his father had come here to study medicine. But that was back in the '60s, just three years before the great fire that had ravaged the city and rendered this part of it unrecognisable. For where there had been wooden houses and winding lanes, now there were buildings of brick and stone, and straight lanes and narrow alleyways, no doubt, thought Jacob, to reduce the risk of a conflagration spreading should one flare up again.

On turning westward into a narrow side street, he suddenly felt a shadow encroach upon him. As he half turned his upper body, he was violently grabbed from behind. A thick forearm pressed against his larynx, and he was yanked to the entrance of a dark alley.

'Help! Help!' he cried out, struggling for his life. He was thrust further into the alleyway. The next instant, he felt a blow like a cannonball hurled into his gut that forced all breath, all sound, out of his lungs. He doubled over, his lungs taut and burning from the blow and unable to take in air.

His legs were kicked from beneath him, sending him crashing down and hugging the ground. Writhing for air on the hard paving, he then felt an immobilising weight in the small of his back while deft fingers flitted around his waist with a knife.

For the love of Christ, he did not want to draw his last breath here. He spewed out another cry for help with what air he could suck in.

Still wheezing for breath, he heard a baritone voice from a short distance call out: 'Oy! You two! Stop there!'

The weight of a knee was instantly released from his back, and he twisted around, now taking in short, painful gasps, to see the two robbers take flight. Then he heard heavy boots thundering closer.

'You all right, fella?' said the same baritone voice he had just heard.

Now getting to his knees in the light of the watchman's lantern, Jacob instinctively touched the cut over his eye where he had hit the ground. 'Thank you . . .' he said to the big watchman between pants. 'None the worse for wear . . .' The large-boned man helped him to his feet. 'God bless you, Sir,' continued Jacob. 'You may well have . . . have saved my life!'

'That may be, Sir,' said the watchman, 'but I would rather wager they scarpered because they had found what they were after!'

Jacob checked to make sure his travel pouch was still safe in his undercoat pocket. It was. But then he felt for the weighty lump he always carried around his waist. 'Dear God, my purse, they have stolen my purse!'

*

The following morning, in the bleak light of the breaking day, he was greeted by the pastor at the main door of the church.

He had spent the night waiting in the intermittent drizzle, wrapped in his waxed travel cloak which had kept his suit of clothes mostly dry.

After listening to Jacob's account of his origins and his recent encounter, the pastor, a man of advancing years with an academic stoop, took him to the sacristy. He introduced him to a French Londoner, a mild-mannered but forthright gentleman in his late fifties by the name of Samuel Clement. A former merchant, having fled to London when the crackdown on Protestants in France first began, he often acted as warden in these times of abounding refugees, and as a filter to sort the wheat from the chaff. He gave Jacob some water so he could wash the dried blood from his grazed face and hands.

'Had you taken a hackney,' said Mr Clement, handing Jacob some bread and soup, 'London would have reserved you a warmer welcome, Monsieur. It would have set you back one and six, but at least you would have kept your purse!'

'Monsieur, had I known where to get one, I may well have done the very same,' replied Jacob with an affable bow as he took the bowl.

A few hours earlier, he would have been annoyed at the remark that perhaps carried with it a note of scepticism as to the existence of such a large purse. But Jacob had already stamped out his raw anger during the night while waiting for the church to open.

He could have kicked himself for his lack of vigilance, for not taking a bed at an inn, and for having blunted his awareness with one pint of ale too many. That said, the aggressors must surely have known he was carrying Caribbean money, he had surmised, and had passed through his mind all the people with whom he had interacted: the fishermen, the alewife, the patrons of the tavern who might have heard his accent and seen him paying with New World coin; the stevedores who had directed him to the fishing boat in the first place. Or could it have been just a fortuitous encounter? There was little chance he would ever know.

Sitting in the sanctuary of the church as attendants entered to prepare for the Sunday service, he was able to feel at peace and to relativise. At least he no longer carried ill-gotten coin. The lump had literally been cut away from around his belly, like a malignant tumour. And apart from minor cuts and bruises, he had escaped unscathed. Was it not then a blessing in disguise? Not really, he thought to himself, for it left him back in the grips of poverty and starvation.

However, he had escaped with his life, and any sum of money lost would be worth the sight of Jeanne and his children now. He still had his travel pouch, and he would find work; his English had improved no end, thanks to his forced piratic dealings and his time in Jamaica and New York. Moreover, on a more positive note, at least he was rid of the shadow of an accusation of piracy that had loomed over him due to the unjustifiable provenance of his fortune.

'I propose we consult the register after the service,' said the pastor before the service began, 'unless, of course, you find your wife among us this morning.'

The congregation entered. Jacob stood inside the porch with Mr Clement. While the church official perfunctorily checked co-religionists' *méreau* —a token that people showed to prove they belonged to the Protestant faith — Jacob, standing two paces behind him, eagerly watched the faces pass in the hope of seeing his wife.

The church had stood on Threadneedle Street in one shape or another since the first wave of Huguenot immigration to London in the previous century. It had since become a port of call for French Protestants to enable them to establish links for a quicker and more intelligent integration in the capital of Albion, all the more complicated now that England was at war with Louis XIV's France.

The district where it stood had become a traditional place

for Huguenot craftsmen such as watchmakers, silversmiths, and cabinet makers to settle. The immigrant population, who enjoyed a reputation for excellent craftsmanship, had brought with them their habits and customs as well as whatever they had salvaged of their wealth. The sumptuous new buildings in the vicinity of the church—buildings that Jacob had seen in the grey light of morning—attested to their prosperity. Jacob observed a generally well-heeled congregation which made him conscious of how shabby he must look.

His suit of clothes, purchased in New York, was stained; his stockings were mud-splashed, one torn. And his shoes lacked lustre, with one of them missing a buckle that must have come off during the mugging. However, it was plain to most that this man standing by the attendant must be a refugee from France—as many of them had been themselves—and he met not with frowns of disapproval but with sympathetic smiles, and often a handshake of welcome.

But Jeanne was not among them. No one had even heard of her, which was hardly encouraging, given her gregarious nature.

After the service, Jacob followed Pastor Daniel into the sacristy, where the service items were carefully stowed and ledgers diligently filed away on shelves and in simple, dark-wood cabinets.

'I am sorry,' said the pastor, shaking his head dolefully after looking through the register again. 'The name does ring a bell. However, no lady or child by the name of Delpech de Castonnet has declared their presence in London, which does not necessarily mean she is not here.'

'Thank you, Pastor,' said Jacob, 'but I am afraid it does.

For I specifically asked my wife to find her way here.'

Pastor Daniel gave a consoling nod. He moved to a different drawer and began running his fingers over a stack of letters, pulling one out every so often for a closer look, then inserting it back into the pile.

Jacob continued: 'However, that is to some extent a relief. I do not know how she would have sustained herself, as I had given her unsound advice, not thinking I would be held up in New York, and not taking into consideration winter snowfalls in her host country —'

The pastor meanwhile had pulled out another sealed letter. He adjusted his pince-nez on the bridge of his nose. 'Ah,' he said, interrupting Jacob's discourse. 'I knew I had seen the name somewhere.' The pastor then handed Jacob a letter addressed to Jacob Delpech de Castonnet, in care of the French church on Threadneedle Street, London.

With sudden fear in his stomach, Jacob recognised Jeanne's handwriting. He now dreaded the news the letter contained.

'Thank you,' he said, taking a seat while studying the vermilion seal which showed the stamp of Jeanne's signet ring. Was she still in Geneva? Had their children joined her? Had the money he had left been sufficient? And what about Robert, his brother-in-law, who had abjured and remained in Montauban? Had he been able to salvage any of Jacob's wealth? Added to the anxiety, a feeling of guilt now weighed in Jacob's heart. Guilt for not having been able to provide for them, for being caught up in the affairs of New York, for stupidly losing his money to the planter in Jamaica, and now the money he had been given by Lieutenant Ducamp.

He broke the seal, unfolded the letter.

'My dear husband,

'Your letter has given me great hope. However, I am unable to leave Schaffhausen where I have taken refuge, for the snows have fallen in abundance. I am advised to wait for the thaw, indeed until the month of April when it becomes warm enough to travel across country. But do not worry on our account as we are in good company, having found refuge thanks to the friendships we made in Geneva.

'So much has happened that I cannot even begin to tell you, but I am sure your journey has been fraught with incidents, as has ours. I say ours, but I must tell you, it gives me great sorrow to inform you that as yet I have been unable to recover our dear daughters. Only our beloved son has been able to join me, and only thanks to his brave heart and resolute nature, something I am sure will not fail to fill you with pride. Our dear daughter Elizabeth has refused to remove herself from Montauban, preferring to remain with our dear youngest baby.

'Your mother is in prison, Jacob, in Moissac, and your sister also in prison but in Auvillar.

'But bear up, my dear husband, for with the grace of God, we will be together as a family again. So please do not let this news bring you down. But rather look forward to a future date that will bring us at last peace and happiness in each other's company and in our faith in the Lord.

'Your loving wife,

'Jeanne.'

EIGHT

JEANNE HELD HER breath an instant to steel her nerves as the post carriage bore down the towpath.

One side offered the deep greens of hillside pastures, tinged with the tender lime of bourgeoning deciduous trees, the other the spectacular force of the Rhine Falls. An apt image, she thought, of her present situation as she watched the flow of water sliding inexorably nearer to the ledge.

Would she land on the bubbling white foam below, or would she splash onto the rocks? Such was the indecision she felt now, even though there could be no turning back. She had no other choice but to once more exchange the comfort and security of dwelling with friends for the company of strangers and the hazards of the elements, in spite of her apprehension of water travel.

But no matter how strong the temptation of warmth and friendship, she always managed to shoo it away on recalling her prayer to God last December, when her son lay bleeding from his terrible sleigh accident.

As he had lain livid and unconscious in the soft, freezing snow, she realized at that instant that no mortal comfort could rival the desire for the well-being of her children.

She vividly recollected how she had prayed and promised to God that she would relinquish her own comfort for the well-being of her children and the life of her son. Ordinarily, she dismissed such demands on the Almighty —perhaps through a fear of disappointment —but what would her life be without her children? At times like these, she almost regretted not recanting her faith. But there again, she knew that without it, she would be no better than a tree without its heartwood, a hollowed trunk without spiritual fibre, and that would be worse than death, for it would be death without hope.

She turned her eyes from the sliding river waters and levelled them upon her son, wedged between Jeannot and Ginette Fleuret. Though saddened by the departure, he was nonetheless eager to reunite with his father, who had sent a letter confirming his arrival in London. She noted that his hair now covered the patch on his scalp that had been cropped to access the gash to the side of his head, which he had suffered upon his jump from the sleigh. It was Jean Fleuret who had carried the boy —so he would keep warm against his large body —back to the house, where the doctor was able to properly tend to him.

The morning sunshine was dazzling and the cold blue sky uplifting. 'It is as good a day as any to embark on a long journey, I suppose,' said Claire, sitting between her husband, Etienne, and Jeanne. She had finally succumbed to Jeanne's decision to leave with the spring instead of waiting for the more clement season of early summer, when most of the other Huguenots were planning to depart.

'My very thoughts,' said Jeanne, who, with a reassuring smile, removed her hand from her muff and grasped her friend's arm tightly. In times like these, Jeanne knew the younger woman missed her mother. Claire, always the emotive one, fought hard to keep her eyes from filling.

The wagon rolled on down the sloping track, taking them closer to the embarkation point, a stone's throw from the foot of the falls. Etienne Lambrois leaned over to address Jeanne and said: 'I only pray Louis's soldiers do not resume their forays into the Palatinate. Note, if they do, I shall enlist against them . . .'

'And that is another reason why we must depart now if we don't want our road to Amsterdam to be cut off from us,' returned Jeanne, as much to herself as to her friends. They had insisted on travelling the short distance to the river landing stage to wave her and Paul off.

An hour later, Jean Fleuret was carrying Jeanne's waxed linen knapsack onto the flat-bottomed boat. It was an unnecessary action, for it was not that heavy. But Jeanne sensed the rough-cut carpenter needed to vent his tacit emotions this way, to show his care in action rather than in words. He placed the bag carefully under the best seat in the middle of the rough-hewn cabin at the aft of the vessel.

He then joined the others on the wharf, where, behind the clusters of people giving farewells to the half dozen other passengers, stood barrels and packets of merchandise awaiting the next departure. The single-mast boat on which Jeanne and Paul were to embark was already loaded with barrels and parcels tightly bound and secured. The sixty-foot-long vessel was robustly made without finery. Once it had reached its destination, it would be sold for firewood.

'All aboard!' called the master boatman, an affable man of few words by the name of Fandrich.

Jeanne's heart suddenly throbbed with a profound regret at leaving her friends, perhaps never to see them again in this life.

The boom of the falls thirty yards upriver forbade any hushed talk. It was just as well because, at that moment, if a last offer to remain until June was dropped from her friends' lips, she might not have had the heart to refuse. However, neither Claire nor Ginette gave her that opportunity. Instead, they tacitly bolstered her resolve to depart, and let her go despite their longing to keep their merry troop together forever. So, sensing their friend flinch, they emboldened her with brazen words of love and encouragement as they embraced for the last time.

The moment soon passed, and the anguish on Jeanne's face no longer furrowed her brow as Etienne reminded her of the town whence she could take the route to Amsterdam. Yes, she was sure she would not have him ride with her. Of course, she would be fine, she insisted. Moreover, Etienne would be needed at the mill, and quite possibly in the regiments of Prussia, if the French attacked again.

'But a woman travelling alone, my dear Jeanne,' said Claire above the din, again keeping herself from pleading with her friend to stay, albeit for just a few more weeks.

'Worry not, Madame Claire. My mother is not alone,' said Paul in his important voice. 'I will look after her.'

'Well said, and I'm sure ye will, my lad,' said Jean Fleuret, with a large hand on the boy's shoulder. 'But we'll miss ye all the same,' said the carpenter, who had not the strength to resist taking the boy in his arms. 'Remember what I said to ye, my boy. I want you to grow up strong with the goodness in your brave heart intact. You hear me?' The boy gave a nod as the man ticked off moisture from his tear duct. 'You make me proud, Paul, you hear? And I will be proud to call our baby after you, should the baby kicking in Ginette's belly be a boy, that is!'

'And if it ain't, we'll call it Paula, so there!' said Ginette, ready as ever with a quip.

'All aboard, Ladies and Gentlemen, please!' cried the master boatman again. Jeanne and her son took their place amid the cargo, the crew, and the other passengers.

*

The boy sat by his mother, secretly clenching her hand as the rear boatman steered the vessel downstream in the easy-moving waters, the falls now but a distance haze of mist behind them. Just the two of them again, venturing into the unknown, but now their goal was to reach husband and father.

Jeanne had learnt to sit as still as possible, wrapped in her shawls, her hands in her muff, in the most comfortable position so that the pockets of air beneath her clothes remained undisturbed and were constantly warmed by her own body heat. In this way, she could sit like a mother goose, head shrunk into her plumage, offering as little exposure as possible to the elements as the meandering river carried them between forestland and bourgeoning orchards.

By mid-morning, thankfully, the sun was strong enough to warm the timber, which gave off the sweet smell of pitch. Jeanne shared provisions and polite banter with the other passengers, who, it turned out, were all on their way to Berlin. In this spirit, they passed under the covered wooden bridges of Rinaud and Eglisau, continued past Röteln,

Kadelburg, and a quantity of huddled villages. Towards the end of the day, they pulled into the landing stage on the edge of Laufenburg, where they spent the night in a wood cabin on the outskirts of the castle town.

The following morning, as per usage, the three boatmen sent the boat empty of people down the short, impracticable stretch, strewn with rocks. The passengers joined the barque on foot a little further downstream, where they were allowed to take up their places.

Despite Jeanne's initial reluctance of the river journey, only once was there any cause for alarm. They were passing under the covered bridge of Rheinfelden, where the Rhine narrowed into a bend and suddenly became fast-flowing. The boat took a bad furrow of water and soon found itself caught in a swirl. Surprised, the three boatmen found themselves in a spin and hurtling towards the rocks broadside. The master boater roared an order that neither Jeanne nor Paul understood, though the tone indicated the urgency of the situation. Scenes of the horrific shipwreck on Lake Geneva reeled through Jeanne's mind as she found herself scouring the boat with her eyes for something to cling onto, should they capsize. But two of the seasoned navigators dug in their oars in unison to bound off the rock face, while the rear boater steered with his punt to straighten the raft as it rounded the obstacle.

All was re-established, with more fright than hurt, but then a parcel the size of a pillow had become detached and fallen overboard. Paul was nearest the packet. His reflex was to reach for it to save it from being taken with the current. He managed to get both hands on the string that bound it, but on lifting the waterlogged parcel, he was pulled off balance. Jeanne saw the boy about to keel into the water and managed to grab him by his breeches just in time. The lad brought back the packet with commendations from the crew. Jeanne, however, was not in a mood to cheer, and kept the boy within her reach for the rest of the day's journey.

By evening, they made footfall in the beautiful city of Bale, to Jeanne's great relief, for neither she nor Paul could swim if by misfortune they were dumped overboard like the parcel. She was more anxious than ever at the prospect of boarding the barque once again, and the night's sleep in a tavern had not calmed her fears this time. They had not been very fortunate whenever it came to boat travel, and taking no heed of the last episode would be irresponsible if they did not turn to a means of transport more favourable to their capacities. Would going on the water again not be refusing to hear God's warnings?

'But it is the fastest way. Etienne told you, Mother.'

'I know, but certainly not the safest!'

'It is if you consider marauders, wild animals, and soldiers, though. That's why he insisted that we stay with the boat till we reach Worms, where we are to pick up another vessel to Amsterdam.'

'That may be so, but I have had enough frights on the water, thank you very much. It would be different if we knew how to swim, but we do not. And even if we did, it would still be like battling an onslaught of Titans to fight against the current!'

'That is true,' conceded Paul, who understood perfectly well his mother's tacit reference to Pierre's death. Pierre, his best friend, Pierre, who could swim like an eel, and yet who had drowned like a trapped rat.

'We shall go by land the rest of the way to Worms, Sir,' said Jeanne to Herr Fandrich, the master boatman. 'It will take us a good deal longer, I know, but we shall endeavour to catch rides on northbound carts . . .'

She was standing in the nascent light of dawn by the embarkation point; the other passengers were boarding and taking their places of the day before. The half darkness of the spring dawn was quickly growing lighter, and Jeanne could now fully perceive the pleats on the boatman's forehead, and the look of concern under his eyebrows.

He lifted his hat and smoothed back his long, thinning grey hair. 'With all due respect, Madame,' he returned in perfect French, 'I would rather see a lone woman on my boat than think of her walking that road alone. I would not have my lady walk on her own, especially not in days as these, Madame.'

'You are kind, Sir. However, I am afraid I will have to take my chances and feel the earth beneath me with the Lord as my guide.'

'Alas, the Lord will not defend you against villains and soldiers, will he now?' said the boater. 'And what will I say to the gentleman who gave me instructions to make sure you arrive safely in Worms?'

'You will kindly tell him that to arrive safely, I have taken the land route,' said Jeanne, who realised she had painted herself into a corner. For seeing the boater's genuine show of concern, she realised deep inside that the dangers would be far greater travelling without company.

However, the boatman, who had dealt with many a traveller stricken with water fright, took a different approach.

'Madame,' he said, adopting a softer tone, and holding his hat with both hands, 'I was not going to bring the subject up so early in our travels, but news has reached my ears since last night that would give you no choice . . .'

'What news?' said Paul, looking up intently into the man's eyes.

'The French have again entered the Palatinate,' said the boater, with a glance down at the boy before appealing to the lady. 'Even if you kept to this side of the river, it is highly likely that you would encounter French soldiers, or they you, Madame.'

The French entering the Palatinate was what had delayed her journey the previous autumn. Jeanne stood wordless as the boater filled the silence. 'They may well be going further into the Palatinate,' he said, 'but there will still be soldiers patrolling. And with all due respect, a woman with a French accent travelling alone with her boy can only mean one thing, can it not?'

'That we are Huguenots trying to reach the Dutch Republic,' said Paul.

'Believe me, I have seen their work: they have no pity. They will take you back to France if they spare your life at all, I fear, Madame. You may be well aware that soldiers are not tender souls.'

'I am,' said Jeanne.

'Then, please, take your place aboard, Madame. Besides, the worst of the rapid waters is behind us. The Rhine is an old, slow river from now on.'

'I see,' said Jeanne. 'Very well, I see we have no other option, as you say, Herr Fandrich,' she said with a slight bow, and proceeded with Paul to the landing stage, her fear of the soldier a good deal greater than her fear of the elements of God.

'And laddie,' said the boater, glaring at Paul, 'if you see a parcel fall overboard, you leave it for a boater to pluck out, eh?'

'Oh, that he will, all right,' said Jeanne. But her thoughts were already turned to the voyage ahead down the Rhine, where French soldiers were prone to cross.

NINE

PAUL SAT ON deck, eyeing the clutches of French soldiers posted on a bridge and patrolling the quays near Strasbourg.

'It's where the French troops crossed the river to take Philipsburg,' said the master boater in German. It was in response to the boy's question on the river's great width where it meandered past the Alsatian city. By consequence, it was also shallow in places, which made it a crossing point par excellence for French cavaliers to access the regions of the Palatinate.

Continuing in French as he pulled the oar, Herr Fandrich said: 'The scoundrels then advanced on Mannheim further north and razed it to the ground . . . They gave the people a week to get out, but they had no place to go, and right in the middle of winter too. So many of them were given refuge in Worms. Running out of wheat now, though. That's what this lot's for.' He nodded to the cargo of barrels neatly stacked in rows on their sides. 'Strange times these, lad, strange times!'

As the barque slipped along with the current through the slow, meandering river, he told the lad about the sack of the

Palatinate commanded by the French king to burn down towns and villages. Mainz had been razed to the ground, Heidelberg castle partially destroyed.

'Won't we get stopped, though?' said Paul, articulating his mother's fears.

Jeanne was sitting inside on the cabin bench, hidden from view. Crudely built at the aft-most part, the cabin also housed a latrine partitioned by a drape for the convenience of the ladyfolk, of which there was now only one. The others had disembarked to continue their journey by cart to Berlin.

Herr Fandrich said: 'No fear of that. Who would feed the people otherwise? The French might be villains, but they're not stupid. They need folk to pay their taxes, you get me?'

Jeanne felt relief once they had cleared Strasbourg. She could once again sit with her son in admiration of the passing vistas: now of pretty riverside villages and rolling hills of tender-leaved trees and blooming wild flowers; now of cultivated fields and lush green pastures where the land had been deforested.

The barque carried them at a steady pace through the wide and tranquil river that presented no treacherous traps along this stretch to the experienced Rhineland boatmen. They stopped for the night at the only inn of the monastery village of Leimersheim, just five miles short of the Philipsburg fortress which harboured a detachment of French troops. Though Herr Fandrich was authorised to transport wheat for the population, there was no point tempting the devil, so he had decided to travel past the fortified town in the early hours, before the officers were at their posts. He could always bribe a lower-graded guard if need be.

Early next morning, they came into view of the flat fields surrounding the citadel of Philipsburg, situated on the right bank. Jeanne braced herself on seeing neat lines of hundreds of canvas tents. She could hear the distant crackle of the camp kitchen fire and the faint banter of Frenchmen amid the distant bleating of lambs—lambs whose lives would most likely be short, she thought, judging by the number of mouths to feed. It was a wonder that the shepherd had not herded them away from the reach of the soldiers, but then she recalled what Herr Fandrich had said about the French policy of banishing the populace.

Yet it was a strangely picturesque sight to behold as the morning sun shone down on the encampment. Female camp followers were busy cooking in the field or scrubbing down by the river; soldiers were shaving, smoking, cleaning weapons, and tending to horses. Jeanne even felt a guilty pinch of pride at the orderliness of it all.

'Part of your king's army,' uttered Fandrich, seeing Jeanne at the cabin doorway contemplating the activity of the camp.

'Not our king's,' corrected Paul, who sat cross-legged on a warm stack of barrels.

'No, not our king's,' seconded his mother.

'No, of course, otherwise, you wouldn't be on this here boat, would ye?' said the boater with a satisfied smile. 'And besides, we are in conflict with Louis, not France.' She sensed his feeling of revolt. It was right for him to test her partiality, given the affliction her country's army had brought to this land. And she was right to implicitly recall her own predicament as another victim of the Sun King. It cleared the air.

'You are certain our passage shall not be hindered?' she said.

'Like I said, we are authorised to navigate,' said Fandrich. 'The king and his henchmen have no interest in civilians, apart from collecting their taxes.'

'What about the wheat?' said Jeanne.

'They will burn down our homes if by misfortune they deem them in the way of their defences, but it is not their policy to let the king's future taxpayers starve to death. But that said, I suggest you return to the cabin, Madame.'

The boater gave a short, reassuring nod, but Jeanne had been in a similar situation before. It had nearly cost her life in prison and cost her guide his head. But what else was there to do?

'Everything will be all right, with God's grace,' said Frantz, the boater's son, sensing the lady's scepticism. A lean and genial lad in his early twenties, he understood French but spoke mostly in German. Paul translated his words, to which Jeanne responded with a polite but straight smile. She had often said those exact words herself. She had said them before the shipwreck on Lake Geneva. She returned a nod to the boater, then turned to her son.

'Paul, come inside with me, please,' she said in a non-negotiable tone.

As they rounded a kink in the river, they were met with the fortress ramparts that stood before them, firmly implanted into the river bedrock. A little further along, the grim stone walls jutted out, forming a V-shape. The fortification extended at this point to the opposing bank. Jeanne and Paul, peering from behind the drape, did not require any leaps of the imagination to understand the fort's total dominance. The cannons strategically placed on the rampart walls could blast any vessel from the surface of the Rhine.

'Steady as she goes, keep her midstream, boys!' commanded Fandrich in German in a confidential tone, as they slowly passed between the fortifications on either bank.

Jeanne sat back on the rustic bench, and twisted her torso to peer through a knothole in the timber wall to spy the land on the left bank. It was equally occupied by the army of her home country, an army which had become the object of her worst nightmares. She had come so far, and, given the choice, she would rather die on the Rhine than be dragged back to France.

Paul was peeking through the gap between the curtain and the door frame. 'Cannons on either bank,' he said in a low voice, keeping his mother informed. He was about to say something else when a deep voice, calling from the right riverbank, caused Herr Fandrich to shout out a reply.

'What is it?' said Jeanne, moving to the opposite side of the cabin to see through a knothole that Paul had previously punched out in a pinewood plank.

'There are two soldiers on horses,' whispered the boy. 'One's waving to pull us over by the bridge a bit further down.' Paul then kept silent in order to take in the boater's answer and to process it through his brain. Then he said: 'Herr Fandrich is trying to tell them he is carrying wheat, and that his family have been boaters for five generations.'

'Dear God,' said Jeanne, her face suddenly drawn and livid. 'I knew we should have taken the land route!'

The boater stepped to the cabin doorway. 'Stand back,' he said under his breath, then swiped the drape to one side and stood half inside the cabin, reaching for his leather pouch which Jeanne presumed contained his papers. 'Fear not,' he whispered. 'Just stay inside and say nothing. I will tell them you are my wife if need be, but do not speak!'

The helmsman steered the barque in the slow current towards the right bank. The soldiers followed downstream on horseback. Once the barque was ten or fifteen yards from the shore, the boater resumed the exchange in French in a genial manner.

'Ah, vous parlez français!' Jeanne heard one of the soldiers call out. Herr Fandrich gave an affirmative answer and reiterated his purpose and right to travel, saying so in broken French. It was an old trick to flatter the soldier and make himself appear dull and inoffensive.

Jeanne sat, trying to steady her nerves and consider what she might say should she need to play the part of the boater's wife. She knew enough German from her stay in Schaffhausen to deliver short, varied replies. If the Frenchmen did not know she was French, and if they did not speak German, she thought optimistically, there would be no reason to suspect her, would there? It was plausible enough, but what about the boater's son? He was old enough to be her brother. She now wished she could have planned for this eventuality beforehand; if she had, she would have suggested to Fandrich that she was his second wife and that Frantz was born of his first wife, now deceased. But she had succeeded in duping soldiers before. With the grace of God, she could do it again, couldn't she?

The lamb bleats grew louder as they approached the riverbank, and Jeanne could easily make out orders from the camp yonder in French.

'We do not contest your right to navigate, boater,' said

the soldier who had initially called out. 'We have diverted you to warn you that you had better moor at the next landing stage downstream, or it will be at your own risk and peril if you continue on your journey this day.'

'Thank you,' said the boater politely. 'But I not have far to go. Only to Worms, Sir, so with respect, I take that risk.'

'Your cargo can surely wait, can it not?' persisted the soldier.

'I . . . I rather continue,' returned the boater, 'but thank you, Sergeant.'

'Please yourself!' said the soldier, who was not a sergeant but a corporal, which of course the boater knew full well.

'Thank you,' said the boater. 'Good day to you, Sirs!'

Jeanne could hardly believe her ears. She glanced inquisitively at her son, who just shrugged. Had she understood rightly? Were they letting them pass so easily? She placed a finger on her lips to keep Paul from speaking in case, in his enthusiasm, he wanted to explain. Peering through the knothole, she saw the soldiers bring their reins over to steer their mounts away. But then, amid blowing snorts from the horses, she thought she heard a mocking laugh, followed by an ironic comment from the other cavalier, a comment which gave her cause for concern, if not alarm.

'Did he say "enjoy the fireworks"?' she asked Paul.

'I didn't hear,' said the boy.

'I could swear that is what he said . . .'

*

The mention of the comment gave rise to debate, haste, and much concern—concern suddenly amplified when, an hour later, they were navigating towards the city of Speyer.

Built around a magnificent cathedral, the thousand-year-old city was set back from the Rhine by a floodplain and wooded meadowland that rose up gently to the city walls, or rather, what was left of them. Across the field, where squadrons of French soldiers were coming and going, Jeanne could clearly see beyond the tumbledown ramparts straight into the township, which before January would have been screened by stone.

'They wanted to torch the whole city,' said Fandrich as they came level to an inlet used as a river port, 'but the burghers managed to persuade them to limit the demolition to only the fortifications. See?'

'At least people's homes were saved . . .'

'Aye, my fear is they'll try to do the same to Worms—'

Before Fandrich could finish his sentence, Frantz, standing at the prow, let out an exclamation in German.

'God, no!' said Herr Fandrich, twisting his torso to face the east city gate.

Jeanne followed the direction of the young man's index finger with her eyes and instantly saw the reason for their interjections. On the grassy space between the port inlet and the river, horse-drawn cannons were being manoeuvred to line up their barrels towards the city.

'They've come back to finish what they started!' said Georg at the rudder, holding his forehead.

At the same time, Jeanne saw a cluster of men, women, and children near the river's edge, being shoved back from the landing stage.

'They're stopping people from crossing!' said Fandrich. 'Take the boy and crouch down inside the cabin in case they let loose a shot, Madame!' Then, turning to his crew, in the vernacular he said: 'Keep right of midstream, boys!'

They swiftly glided along, keeping their heads down as close to the gunwale as possible. They did not stop at the barks from soldiers who, busy with containing groups of pleading townsfolk, soon gave up trying to hail the boat down. Their ensuing warning shots only served to scatter the townsfolk as the boat continued its course on the far side of the river.

By late morning, they reached the sacked and plundered city of Mannheim, reduced to ruins and rubble. This was the demolished city Herr Fandrich had spoken about, and the reason for his voyage to fetch his cargo of wheat.

If ever Jeanne had felt self-pity during her ordeal, it was now banished from her heart as she envisioned generations of memories blasted out of existence. No longer did she feel that underlying pride on seeing the regiment at their camp in Philipsburg. It was shame and hatred she felt now for her people, so easily subjugated by one king, one law, one religion. She, Paul, and the crew alike stared wordlessly at the sight of total destruction and desolation in the sunny May late morning, now filled with flying insects and tweeting birds. The men had removed their jackets as the boat floated with the current, oars raised out of the water, past the ruins where women were bent over in search of odd pickings of what was left of their homes.

As the men rolled up their sleeves and began to dig into the water again, there came a distant, gut-wrenching, thunderous boom.

'Dear God, they're bombarding Speyer!' said Fandrich, looking southward. It was not long before his supposition was manifested by clouds of black smoke bellowing upward on the horizon behind them. 'I think that fireworks is indeed what you heard, Madame Delpech!'

'Alas!' said Jeanne as other sickening blasts followed.

They all agreed to refrain from halting for lunch and for the men to keep rowing until they reached Worms. While Jeanne cut the oarsmen's bread, cheese, and dried sausage, Paul handed them beakers of beer from a cask. They advanced fast and wordlessly. Could their hometown be on the list too? To be bombed like Speyer or torched like Mannheim? And if it was, what could three unarmed men do to prevent the attack of a whole army bent on methodical destruction? But no one brought that question up. The men only knew they had to get there as quickly as they could to be with their family in their ancestral hometown.

TEN

WHEN JEANNE HAD found out that Herr Fandrich's barque would be travelling to Worms, she could not help feeling that God had meant her to purchase her fare for that boat, rather than a later one.

Worms: the city of the diet where Luther reaffirmed his theses and maintained that salvation was by faith alone; the place where the first Bible was printed in the tongue of the common people. She had imagined herself spending a couple of days strolling with Paul through its lanes and worshipping freely in its churches, savouring the moments to carry with her in her memory. The very mention of the ancient city had given her new encouragement and the assurance that her onward journey would take her to a good place, a land of hope where she could rebuild her life. But her memory of Worms would turn out to be quite different.

It was reassuring to note that, as they approached the great city, there was no trace in the late-afternoon sky of smoke behind the screen of newly leafed trees. But as they emerged from the gentle bend in the river, Jeanne could not help raising her hand to her mouth in horror.

As in Speyer, demolition work had begun on the fortifications that had been blasted or pulled down. Great breaches in the city wall revealed half-timbered dwellings, cobbled streets, and recalcitrant city dwellers who had refused to leave their homes and their possessions unguarded. Troops were assembled at various points: before the east gates between the river and the port inlet, and around the various towers and bridged entries. They were manoeuvring horse-drawn cannons and other machines of destruction.

'Dear God! They are going to torch the whole city!' said Herr Fandrich incredulously. He pointed to the firebombs stacked in a cart, close to the main Rhine entrance where soldiers were preparing their incendiary devices.

As they came broadside to the riverbank, a short distance from the port inlet, winding the rope around the temporary mooring post, Herr Fandrich said: 'Georg, Frantz, take the wheat downstream. We will be needing it now more than ever!' Then, turning to Jeanne, who stood at the cabin door, he said: 'Madame Delpech, once further downstream, you must make for the hills with the boy and join a caravan. The whole stretch of the Rhineland Palatinate will be plagued by the scoundrels! I fear you will have to continue your journey over land.'

'I thank you for getting us this far, Herr Fandrich. I am only sorry we have arrived to such a demonstration of brutality and—' There came an earth-trembling boom that resonated from the north gate. It was immediately followed by a loud, gut-churning chorus of human cries as the tower crumbled to the ground.

'My God! Father, you cannot enter the city now!' said Frantz, whose gestures were eloquent enough for Jeanne to understand his outburst in the vernacular.

'Would you have me leave your grandmother to be buried alive?' said Herr Fandrich, jumping ashore.

'But . . .'

'You know your grandmother, Frantz. She said she would not leave her home if the soldiers came, and you know how mulish she can be.'

'Mother would have persuaded her . . .'

'I hope so, my boy. But I need to be sure! Besides, there is something else I must recover, without which we are unlikely to recover from this tragedy. Now be off,' said Herr Fandrich, releasing the mooring rope from the post. In French, he said: 'Godspeed to you, Madame Delpech . . .'

Just as Fandrich was passing the mooring rope to Georg at the stern, a mounted officer, directing operations forty yards away, turned in his saddle and hailed Fandrich with the only phrase he knew in German: 'Halt! You!' Then, changing to French, he hollered: 'Halt the boat!' He shortened his reins and pulled back, and the horse set forth at a fair canter to the temporary mooring bay.

Realising the boat would never be able to cast off far enough to be out of gunshot, the boater told his crew to hold it and looped the rope back over the mooring post.

'You cannot enter the city,' said the officer, regardless of whether the men aboard could speak French or not.

'Sir, I return just, and I fear my mother still be in there,' said Herr Fandrich.

'Your mother will have been given ample notice, boater. The town is empty, I am telling you, and dangerous . . .'

Neither Jeanne, silently waiting in the cabin with Paul, nor Fandrich was duped. For the city of sixty thousand souls was located sufficiently close to the river for them to have previously seen through the breach in the wall civilians carrying sacks and carting belongings.

The officer persisted: 'And if anyone by obstinacy has remained despite our repeated warnings, then that is down to them, and may they commit their souls to God!' He flicked his eyes over the cargo. 'That wheat you are carrying?' he intoned on his high horse.

'It be that, Sir,' said the boater, despite his son's frown. But Herr Fandrich was also a seasoned trader and knew in his bones there was no point in trying to deny it. His idea from the moment the officer hailed him was to retain as much of it as he could and cast away as quickly as possible.

'For my soldiers?' said the officer.

'To feed the people, Sir,' said Fandrich without irony. There was no point in rubbing the Frenchman the wrong way. 'I . . . I have an authorisation.' Fandrich brought out a paper from his inner pouch and handed it to the officer. He knew the officer would not read it, it being in German, and if he could, he would see that he was reading nothing more than the boater's licence to navigate. 'But please allow me to offer you a couple of barrels. My men will unload them for you here and now, then depart.'

'One-half of what you have!' said the mounted officer.

'This is a town of sixty thousand souls, Sir, but I will give you a quarter.'

'One-third,' insisted the officer, who knew full well he could confiscate all the barrels, but which would also mean making out a report.

'One-third it is, but I will ask you to let me enter the city.'

The officer did not give the second clause much thought. 'Very well,' he said, apparently amused, 'but on your head be it. And bear in mind that the fires will begin shortly. You will have to be quick!'

Fandrich gave instructions to Frantz and Georg to unload and then to continue downstream and keep the cargo hidden at his brother's until the way was clear to Osthofen. Of course, he could not know at this time that the small town had also been sacked. He then stepped to the boat cabin, swiped the drape to one side, and said boldly in German: 'Wife, make haste with the boy. We go now!'

The officer raised an eyebrow on seeing the woman and the boy appear on the open deck and climb out of the barque, but he nonchalantly turned a blind eye. There was nothing to be gained by needlessly bringing complications and other officers into the deal, and the wheat would make a tidy sum for such little fuss.

*

Half turning to Jeanne, Herr Fandrich said: 'I am sorry it turned out this way, Madame Delpech, but I did not think it wise to leave you in the company of soldiers.'

They were passing at a brisk step through the lesser of the northeast gates, unguarded and a stone's throw away from where Frantz and Georg had begun unloading barrels onto the wharfside.

'You need not apologize, Herr Fandrich,' said Jeanne, with her sack strapped to her back, one hand clutching her skirts and the other clasping her son's hand. 'It is rather I who am indebted to you,' she said, while dodging horse muck and a gentleman pushing a handcart.

'Once through the west gate, you must take to the forest, where you'll find others,' continued Fandrich without slowing. 'I will take you across the city. My house is on the way to the gate. But we must hurry!'

Unable to talk for want of controlled breath, Jeanne gave a nod, and, lifting her skirts further, she ran harder behind the boater, with Paul at her side. They hurried down the main thoroughfare of half-timbered houses, past a tavern and shops where shutters had been forced open, windows smashed, and interiors looted. It was surprisingly busy for a town that was supposed to be evacuated, she thought.

They passed countless city-dwellers of every social condition, and even entire families, scurrying towards the west gate, babes in arms and children in tow, belongings stacked and strapped onto handcarts. These were the recalcitrant few, those who had refused to leave their homes. Those who had been hiding in hopes that the soldiers would leave them in peace as they had done back in January, who had refused to believe that their thousand-year-old city would be razed to the ground in a single afternoon, as if its existence had no meaning. Seeing them scuttling through the streets brought back to Jeanne a childhood memory of when, as the River Tarn broke its banks, she saw tens of hundreds of moles scampering from their burrows in the grounds of her father's country house. Of course, it was not fear of water that had brought these people out of their hiding places. It was fear of fire.

Another loud, crashing sound blasted her eardrums from the north wall as another defence tower came down, and a new smell accompanied it. 'Smoke!' cried Paul. 'Look! There!' He pointed with his free hand in the direction of the appalling noise, at flames searing up above the rooftops a few streets away.

'Looks like they've started to torch Jew Lane!' said Fandrich. 'We must hurry!'

They crossed a square where a fountain idly spurted water into a basin. They rounded the church and slowed their pace at a crossroads in the thoroughfare, with the west gate barely a hundred yards in front.

The boater pointed to a street corner, at an abandoned cart that had a broken wheel. 'Wait here,' he said once they had reached it. 'You cannot come any further. My house is too close to the wall they are cannoning. My mother is practically deaf, and if she is inside, she will not have heard the extent of the destruction. If anything happens, you must run straight to the west gate, then to the forest. And stay clear of soldiers!'

In reality, Herr Fandrich suspected his grandmother would have at least felt the vibrations of the crashing towers, and that she had probably fled. But he had something else to recover, something he kept in a secret place that even his wife knew nothing about. It was his hard-earned savings and the gold florins from another age that his father had passed down to him before he died. He kept it all under a floorboard, just like his father had done before him. It was a nest egg for the family, should hard times fall upon them.

Jeanne gave a nod, then placed both hands on the cartwheel to recover her breath. She watched the boater run fifty yards down to the far end of the lane, where he entered a small house that stood in the shadow of a lookout tower.

A dubious place indeed, thought Herr Fandrich, as he entered his home for the last time.

Fanned by the gentle spring breeze, fire was raging higher and faster in the Jewish district and smoke could now be seen rising up in sectors to the south. Jeanne waited with Paul behind the broken-down cart in front of a bakery for what seemed an interminable length of time. Another great belly-churning boom resounded from the north wall while she anxiously watched the last few city dwellers in the thoroughfare running towards the west gate.

But in reality, it must have been no more than a few minutes before Herr Fandrich re-emerged into the narrow street, slinging the strap of a leather pouch over his shoulder. His mother was not with him. Jeanne could have screamed out to him to quicken his step. But to her utter dismay, after a pat to his head and realising he had forgotten his hat, he about-turned and doubled back to his house. 'Now what's he doing?' said Jeanne in exasperation.

He re-emerged thirty seconds later, this time to find a pair of troopers with torches exiting an alleyway a few houses up from Fandrich's. They sauntered cockily towards him.

Jeanne stepped back into the recessed doorway of the bakery, pulling Paul by the collar so he flattened himself likewise against the boarded-up door. Peeping around the edge of the alcove, she saw a quick verbal exchange between Fandrich and one of the soldiers. She could barely hear the sound of their voices in the background of explosions and falling bricks and mortar. But she understood by Herr Fandrich's gesturing that he showed neither anger not exasperation as one of the soldiers passed his torch to his mate.

The trooper then approached Fandrich, pulled out a flintlock from his belt, and reached out with the other hand.

The exchange had brought the soldier, who she could now see was bearded, parallel to Fandrich's front door so that Jeanne's point of view was presented with his right profile. She saw Herr Fandrich instinctively covering his pouch with his right hand, shaking his head and smiling the same genial smile as with the officer at the wharf. But these men were not officers. The bearded soldier now standing three yards from Fandrich pointed the pistol at the boater's chest. There followed a short expletive, then a click and a cracking fizz. Herr Fandrich crumbled to the ground.

Jeanne watched, her eyes wide as Dutch guilders, as the bearded soldier bent down and pulled the leather pouch from Herr Fandrich's shoulder, lifting the limp arm as if he had just slaughtered a goat.

Jeanne placed her hands over her mouth to muffle the sounds of her horror. 'My God, my God!' she murmured with incredulity while the soldiers now entered what looked like a brief wrangle. The other soldier, who sported only whiskers, shook his head, passed back the torch, and walked to the alleyway on the other side of the lane. Looking left and right, the bearded trooper then followed his battle buddy into the alley which led to the Jewish district.

Numbed, trembling, and petrified, she pulled herself from the edge of the alcove and pressed her body back against the bakery front. She let herself sink down the door, her back remaining flat against it, until she was sitting on the heels of her boots. 'Dear God. Where are you?' she murmured, her eyes transfixed in the middle distance. Then she felt a tugging at her shawl, and two small hands alighted upon her shoulders. Paul gently shook her. 'Mother, Mother, come on, Mother. We cannot stay here!'

There came another thunderous crumbling sound, this time of bricks and mortar. A house must have caved in a few streets away. It shook her from her torpor, and she looked squarely at her son as the sound of marching boots filled them both with urgency and a new dread. Advancing a few paces into the main thoroughfare, through the dust and smoke she saw with horror a battery of field artillery filing in through the west gate, in a blurry stream of crimson and fire. Torches in hand, they were turning southward towards the cathedral.

She could not bear the thought of a confrontation with any soldier, let alone with an entire battalion. And what would she say if they were stopped?

But then, glancing in unison with Paul to her right towards what Fandrich had called the Jewish district, they perceived another route out. A narrow side street slanted off the main road to the city wall, or rather, where the wall had stood. For at the end of the backstreet, there was a gaping breach of fallen stone where she could make out the hazy figures of a few city dwellers climbing through it, fleeing for their lives.

The air was growing thicker with smoke blowing in from the houses ablaze at the north wall. But she realised that mixing with the fleeing townsfolk was their only chance of escape. She reached for her son's hand, and needing to reconnect with humanity, brought it to her cheek, cupped and kissed it before striding back to the corner to fetch her sack that she had taken off her back.

She took a last glimpse at Herr Fandrich, lying on the ground at the end of the lane. But to Paul's surprise, she just stopped and stared. 'My God!' she said, unblinking. She could have sworn she saw an arm move. It flexed again from where it had been dumped by the soldier and flopped to the boater's side.

'He must still be alive!' said Paul, looking up at his mother.

'Yes, and we cannot leave him there!'

'But what if they come back?'

Jeanne had grasped the principle of the layout of the city, which consisted of main thoroughfares with lanes running off them. These lanes were also criss-crossed by narrower lanes or alleyways just wide enough for a handcart to pass through. In the boater's lane, Jeanne now noticed two alleys that must give access to side entrances into yards and houses, tucked away within a block of buildings. She pointed to the one a dozen yards down from the crossroads where she and Paul were standing.

'That must run round to the alley further down, where the soldiers first came out,' she said. Then she looked down at her son and gave his hand a squeeze, and they made a dash across the mudded lane, neither seeing nor caring what they were treading in.

They followed the alleyway around the block of humble dwellings to the alley nearest Fandrich's house by the north wall.

The soldiers who had continued into the alleyway on the other side of the street were nowhere in sight. Jeanne and Paul scurried to Fandrich to find him drenched in his own blood, but still breathing. He let out a groan as Jeanne and Paul dragged him by the boots into the dark alley, away from the lookout tower that threatened to crush Fandrich's house at any moment.

'He's badly injured, and he's too heavy for us to carry,' said Jeanne, on her knees, inspecting the wound to the boater's bloody chest. She was back to herself, sharp and practical, and was thinking that, if seen, it would be plausible enough to pass themselves off as the spouse and son of this injured townsman. 'We'll need a handcart or something to carry him . . .' she said, turning back to Paul. But the boy was already running back down the alley. 'Paul, come back!' she called out in a loud whisper.

'Saw a handcart on the way,' said the boy, twisting his torso round to answer in an equally loud whisper. 'Won't be long,' he said, then shot off. She could do nothing else but let him go.

She was wondering how they would carry the boater over piles of tumbledown stone in a handcart when Fandrich half opened his eyes. He turned his head, and, in a faint voice, he said: 'Leave me . . . Madame, save yourselves now . . .'

But Jeanne's attention was elsewhere, and she put a finger to her lips as the sound of boots and French voices drew closer in the lane.

'Where's he bloody gone!' said one of the voices which, she presently ascertained, belonged to the bearded trooper who had shot the boater down and stolen his pouch. 'Told you, man! We shoulda thrown him into his bloody shack and torched it!'

'He's been dragged,' said the other soldier. The pair of them cautiously followed the trail of blood across the cobbles towards the alleyway, a few houses further up.

Jeanne had silently got to her feet, had backtracked down the alley a few yards, then had stopped at a high wooden gate, painted green. She silently tried the latch to find it open, pushed the gate to reveal a boater's yard.

From the entrance of the alley, the soldiers saw the body on the floor, five yards in. They caught a glimpse of a woman's hand as the green gate closed. 'You go through the house!' said the bearded trooper in a low voice to his accomplice before striding to the green wooden gate, where he paused for a moment. He stroked his moustache and lasciviously squeezed his chin with his free hand. Then he booted the gate open to reveal a yard that contained a handcart, ropes, and an array of hooks, short masts, and cordage. He also saw a handsome woman, no doubt the wife of the man he had shot, running to the back door.

Jeanne had her hand on the iron handle when she heard the sound of boots resonating in the corridor inside the house.

The bearded trooper to her rear slowly laid down his torch by the gate as if he did not want to frighten a wild animal.

Jeanne, on turning, noticed Herr Fandrich's leather satchel slung over the trooper's shoulder, and another larger, bulging bag as she eased her way slowly back into the court.

'You'll do, my pretty German maid!' said the trooper, moving slowly towards the handcart that stood between them. 'Don't be shy now . . .'

Knowing what he had done, knowing what he was about to attempt, Jeanne stood erect, superior, no longer wanting to hide behind a false identity. And in a controlled, fierce, and forceful voice, she said: 'You should be ashamed of yourself, young man!'

The trooper, momentarily taken aback by the woman's outburst in French, glanced over to his fellow looter, now standing on the step of the back door.

'Bet she's a Huguenot toff,' said the fellow looter.

'Are ya?' said the bearded trooper, looping the syllables in the direction of Jeanne, who stood, steely-eyed, in anticipation of an attack from both sides.

But the accomplice looter just chortled and said: 'We all know what happens to Huguenots, don't we? One good thing, though, she ain't likely to tell tales on us, is she?'

'What d'ya mean?'

'Come on, man, now's not the time. We got Jew Street to do before it burns. And she's hardly gonna be running into the arms of the captain, is she!'

'Oh, I ain't letting this one pass, colleague. I'll catch you up in a mo'. . .'

'Suit yourself, man,' said the fellow soldier, leaving his mate alone in the yard with the Huguenot toff.

The bearded soldier, with one sly eye on the dame, placed his musket against the wall, unstrapped his cumbersome bag, and let it drop to the ground. He could see her trying to figure out which way to run, her eyes flitting this way and that, but there was no chance of getting out; he had her cornered. It was cute, though, and all the raunchier given the fact he had never had the pleasure of a toff, let alone a Huguenot toff.

'You stay away from me!' growled Jeanne, and tried to think of something better to say to get him talking, to delay the inevitable. If she could make him turn around the cart, she could grab his musket. But then what? How did it work? Did you just pull the trigger? What if it wasn't loaded?

But the soldier was in no mood for playing cat and mouse. He had much to do, many houses to plunder, and he was not going to waste any more time. He just wanted to shoot his bolt and be done. So he feigned to approach slowly; then, in a surge of brute strength, he rammed the handcart against the fence, cutting off her escape route. He grasped her, pulled her towards him.

She struggled, beat his chest, scratched his beard as he spun her round like a puppet and forced her face down onto the handcart deck.

He clenched her from behind, squeezed her pleasing bust, and latched onto her by the hips. Then, keeping a strong, firm weight in the small of her back with a forearm, he began lifting up her skirts.

She roared with rage, managed to wriggle free, twist herself round, and pull him to her so he could not get a swing in. She felt for his side, gripped his knife, pulled it out of its sheath. But he smiled a mischievous, lubricous smile, wrapped his hand around her slender wrist, and directed the knife to her throat.

'Just relax, duchess,' he said in a low, menacing voice, 'and everything will be all right . . .' He pushed her flat against the cart deck, nudged her thighs apart with his knees. But then, he keeled over.

She looked up at the space previously occupied by the bearded face and saw the butt of the soldier's musket, then the intense brow of Frantz as she dropped the knife onto the cart.

Frantz reached out a hand to her, fetched her up off the handcart deck.

'Thank you,' she said, brushing her skirts down. Bending over the soldier lying unconscious on the ground, she wrenched the leather satchel from over his shoulder. 'Your father's,' she said, handing it to Frantz. 'He is still alive . . .'

'I saw,' said Frantz, urgently turning back towards the yard gate where Paul was now standing. There was no time for awkwardness. After Jeanne persuaded Frantz to refrain from finishing off the soldier with his own flintlock, they directed their steps through the alleyways and backstreet to the north wall.

Frantz transported Herr Fandrich, still barely conscious, in the handcart. Within ten minutes, they were at the breach in the wall by the Jewish district. Frantz carried his father in his arms while Jeanne and Paul dragged the cart over the rubble to the other side.

By now, French troopers were torching the houses in all districts, throwing firebombs onto thatches and detonating mines. Townsfolk who had refused to leave were pleading with soldiers on foot and officers on horseback. But it was clear these men had a job to do and, ignoring the protestations, went about it in a businesslike fashion, no doubt to distance themselves from the calamity of their acts. A few who did answer the protestations more often than not did so in jeers and scorn, then set light to cloth and thatch, like they were taking pleasure in braving the forbidden but exquisite act of destruction.

Frantz, gritted teeth and bare arms hard as brass, wheeled his father behind Jeanne and Paul as they melded into the stream of townsfolk fleeing to the high ground among the trees. These were the ones who had not wanted to abandon their homes until the last moment. Now they marched onwards in silence, their ancestral city all ablaze behind them.

*

The appalling clamour of crumbling mortar, followed by the dreadful cries of people losing their heritage, had intermittently broken Jeanne's slumber that night under the trees.

Now the skyline over the city of Worms was paling. In an hour, it would be day. In an hour, the full horror of the destructive binge would no longer be an incredible nightmare: it would be a reality etched in their memories. Already some folk were stirring; men stoking fires, women heating broth with whatever edibles they had been able to take with them.

As Jeanne sat back against a pine tree, Paul's head on her lap, she glanced round at Frantz, sitting by his father who was laid stretched out on rags. 'How is he now?' she said in a soft voice.

'Not different since the doctor dug out the bullet,' said Frantz, keeping his voice down so as not to wake the boy. He spoke in French, with scatterings of German when the French words eluded him.

'What did the doctor say?' said Jeanne. 'If he makes it through the night, he might recover, didn't he?'

'Yes.'

'He lost a lot of blood, though.'

'And he would be dead by now if it was not for you.'

'And so would I be if it weren't for you, Frantz,' said Jeanne, touching his forearm.

'You can thank your boy for that, ein gescheiter Bursche! He hailed us down as we were putting out, ran along the wharf yelling out till we heard him . . .'

'What will you do now?'

'Take him to my uncle's, where I think my family are. If he dies, I want him to be with family . . .'

'What can I do?'

'There's nothing more; this is not your war. You must continue westward as you started, Madame Delpech. I heard some folk will be heading that way on foot. Go with them to Bingen. Once past Bingen, you'll be safe. That is where the Rhine narrows into a deep gorge, and you will be able to travel safely by river the rest of the way.'

ELEVEN

THREE DAYS AFTER the torching of Worms, Jeanne and the boy sat with blistered feet on the high ground overlooking the port town of Bingen.

It lay huddled around a knoll upon which stood a run-down medieval castle. Down by the riverbank, she could easily make out a horde clustered around the landing stage. A handful of French soldiers were supervising the Palatinate exiles who were queuing to embark on the next rivercraft.

She took a moment to contemplate the beautiful spring morning. Wild flowers stood all abloom in the meadow around her. Only the hum of flying insects and the distant clonk of cowbells interrupted the peace.

The previous days had not been too unkind either. Whenever it showered, at least she and Paul had been able to find shelter in a barn or among wide-leafed trees with the rest of the contingent they were travelling with. And being able to answer calls of nature in a timely fashion—without the embarrassment of having to hold oneself over a latrine at the stern of a moving vessel—by far made up for her aching feet.

She had a thought for Herr Fandrich. He had made it through the night. After sunrise, he had opened his eyes and, like Frantz, bid her and the boy farewell. She had insisted on helping them in their onward journey to their relation's house. But Frantz had urged them to move on with the group of folk who were taking to the road. And if experience had taught Jeanne one thing, it was to travel in company, the more the merrier, although of course there was nothing merry about these bedraggled exiles.

A great many of the townsfolk of Worms had remained in the vicinity with the intention of rebuilding their homes from the ruins of the inferno. But a whole host of them had decided they could no longer bring themselves to return to a charred home in the knowledge that, even if they rebuilt it like in '77, it stood a fair chance of being burnt down again. Such was the fate of those living in the Palatinate, straddled as it was across the contested river Rhine.

They had trekked across the hills of the Palatinate, passing haymakers agog and shepherds agape. Oft-times, they were able to shelter in barns where, since heifers and cows now stayed out at night, they had the good fortune to put their heads down on straw. Time and again, they witnessed the horrors of the French King's scorched earth policy. It left standing no building that could serve the armies of the League of Augsburg, and forced more devastated people to join the ranks of the exiled. And yet, the war had not officially begun.

It put Jeanne's own predicament into perspective. And now, as the vast majority of the forty or fifty fellow travellers had done, she put it to the far reaches of her mind and focussed on the present moment, the lovely and precious present, no longer giving a thought for the future.

Having kicked off her boots, she was now rubbing her swollen feet. 'I can no longer put one foot in front of the other,' she said.

'Neither can I,' said Paul, who was sinking his bare toes into a lush patch of clover while resting his chin on his knees.

Jeanne looked down again at the Palatinate exiles that she had let go ahead. Word had got out that civilians were allowed to get away to the Low Countries. And sure enough, she had observed the crimson-and-blue-uniformed French soldiers letting the leading batch board a previous vessel.

'What do we do now, Mum?' said Paul, following her gaze. She turned back to him with a smile, a youthful smile. It always melted her heart whenever he called her "Mum" instead of "Mother," as convention dictated by his breeding. But here in the open countryside, there were no conventions, just the living, breathing, lazy air of burgeoning summer all around them.

'We have a choice,' she said, tightening her smile. 'Either we walk to Amsterdam, which means another fifteen days' trek. Or we risk taking the next boat.' Jeanne nodded back towards the port below them, where a large rivercraft was coming to moor.

'But there are French soldiers down there,' he retorted.

'Yes, but they will take us for civilians from the Palatinate. I don't think they will be much bothered about catching Huguenots.'

'But we can hardly show our papers, can we?'

'Neither can many of those we travelled with. We can say they were lost to fire.' Then, glancing down at Paul's feet, she said: 'Careful of the bees, darling. You don't want to get stung.'

*

134

The flat-bottomed rivercraft could carry at least fifty passengers, thought Jeanne. So it should be able to carry her, Paul, and the remaining folk waiting at the landing stage, where people from Bingen had provided food and drink.

They shuffled along with the queue. Jeanne counted five French soldiers controlling the embarkation. Two were barring the access to the gangway so people could pay and board in an orderly manner. They had set up a table behind which one of them was seated. Two more were keeping the queue in order. And another one was servilely assisting with loading bags and young children, and collecting tips. Though the latter had his back to her, his gait seemed strangely familiar. But in the anxiety of the imminent departure, she brushed the notion aside, put it down to nerves or coincidence. For who could she possibly know in the French army?

The uplifting babble and children's laughter from the crowd came as an antidote to the gloomy drudgery of the previous days. It was a cheerful interlude, a suspension of sadness, bathed in the comforting warmth of the sun. Psalms were sung in German, adding to the comfort and excitement of the "excursion" into the lowlands, to a new life. But Jeanne knew it would not be just plain sailing and, just as she had experienced before them, these Palatines would soon hit upon the harsh realities of integrating a new culture and language.

However, living life in the present enabled Jeanne to experience the benefit of these moments of solace. They helped her to keep going, thankful in the knowledge that the river would soon take them away from persecution for good. While standing in the queue, she had observed up front a number of Palatinate women alone with young children, passing without papers. It was confirmation that they would not require a passport as long as they paid the tithe.

She looked down at Paul, standing brave and ready to play his part. He had inherited her ear for accents, she mused. As he was so young, his brain had worked like a sponge in Schaffhausen, absorbing the new language with his comrades of play, a language of which she had only gained a rudimentary grasp. But at least they looked like any other Palatine traveller; their clothes, though of quality fabric, presented no finery. Paul wore a brimmed hat, and Jeanne had pulled her shawl over her head as had many of the women to hide against unwanted glances and the sun, though gentle it was.

'Der nächste, bitte!'

The syllables struck like a hammer, flattening her musings as the previous passengers, having paid, advanced up the gangway to board the riverboat.

She steeled her nerves, threaded her arm through the strap of her knapsack, and advanced with her hand on her son's shoulder to the landing stage gate. The soldier in a blue frock coat flipped his hand to prompt her to move more quickly. 'Schnell, schnell!' he snapped, in the assumption that this lady was a German Palatine like all the rest.

The other soldier, a young sergeant with a benevolent, moustached face, smiled upon her approach from the camp table behind which he was seated. But it was the older fellow, standing six feet tall with stubble on his chin, who quick-fired the questions in a gruff voice in German.

'For two?'

Jeanne nodded.

'Where you from?'

'Worms,' returned the boy in German.

The balmy-faced soldier noted the information in a logbook open on the table, while the older man told her the price to pay to board. She well knew this was illegal and unethical, but at least it meant these soldiers were more preoccupied with financial gain than with catching Huguenots. A lesser evil, perhaps, that would enable them to move on. She lowered her eyes to conceal her look of scorn as she placed the silver thalers she had previously prepared on the table.

'Papers?' continued the tall soldier in German. But his question, alarming though it was at first, quickly allayed any anxiety, for it was indeed a question. It was not an order to hand over a passport. Like some of the ladies she had observed before her, she simply shook her head.

'Lost in the fire,' said Paul in German.

'Can't she speak for herself?'

'Not since the fire,' returned the boy.

The soldier stared at them for an instant, then acknowledged the statement with a curt nod and told them the price for travelling without papers. This, too, was an abuse of power, scornful and illegal. Jeanne nevertheless unshouldered her sack and dug for the extra coin.

But as she lowered her head, in the corner of her eye, she caught sight of the servile soldier lumbering up the gangway. He was striding back in a syncopated gait to fetch another bag for which the previous family had paid a surcharge. A sudden surge of blood sent her heart pounding as she raised her hand to her mouth. The man had a mutilated thumb.

She flashed a glance at the other hand, only to see it also

had suffered the thumbscrew. She now recognised the laboured gait of Monsieur Crespin. Céphas Crespin, who was also known to her as the pauper. The pauper who had gained her trust with the intent to rob her. The pauper who had abandoned drowning people at the shipwreck on Lake Geneva. The man who had attacked her, beaten her, and left her for dead. What should she do?

Buying time, with her back to the gangway, she made as if she was scouring her sack. She brought out an empty hand, looked the tall man in the eye, and shook her head. She grabbed her son's hand and prepared to leave, pressing Paul's shoulder for him to make haste. But the boy did not need a cue, for he had followed his mother's look of panic and also had seen the mutilated thumbs of Crespin.

'Hey, lady!' called out the balmy-faced sergeant. He pushed away from the camp table and hopped round to intercept her. 'Where you going?' he continued in French. Jeanne did not answer. Instead, she gave a curt shake of the head and continued onwards, back towards the queue.

The tall man by now had stepped over to translate into German. The sergeant affably insisted, 'Tell her she can pay in food, sausage, or whatever takes her fancy.'

Taking care to at least let the translation begin, she shook her head resolutely.

The boy looked up at the soldiers with purpose. 'We will see later,' he said.

'In that case,' said the sergeant to his subordinate, 'tell her she can take back her fare. We are not thieves, are we, lads?'

'What's up?' called out an oily, smiling voice before the translator could finish. 'Little lady got cold feet, has she?'

Jeanne recognised the all-too-familiar voice of Céphas Crespin, and he was lumbering up towards her.

She dared not turn around. Keeping one hand on Paul's shoulder in front of her, she pulled her shawl more tightly around her bust and head with the other hand.

'Where she from?' said Céphas Crespin, now standing between the table and the remaining queue of a dozen people.

'Worms,' said the translator.

At that moment, Jeanne felt a hand claw the top of her shawl and rip it from over her head to reveal her swan-like neck and her fine brown hair tied up in a chignon.

They might have been able to outrun the decrepit pauper, but there was no chance of escaping these young men, who were now joined by one of the troopers previously positioned to watch the queue.

She swung round. Her hairpin fell out and let tumble her miniature Bible. But it was no big deal; here, everyone was a Protestant. The soldiers let it lie where it was.

Jeanne looked Crespin squarely in the eyes. He had a full beard now that covered half his face, which explained why she had not made the connection on seeing him from a distance. She recognised his pockmarked cheeks all right, though, and the snarl on his upper lip as he smiled at her vacantly, without emotion or recognition.

'Can't pay the surcharge,' said the sergeant.

'Where she say she's from?' said Crespin, who was by far the oldest of the soldiers.

'Can't talk, but the boy says they're from Worms,' said the tall translator.

Céphas Crespin turned back to the lady. He then smiled

his deliberate fawning smile of old, the smile he had perfected to gain her trust when carrying fabrics for her at the church in Geneva. Now it only filled her with disgust and scorn. And she loathed him all the more for pretending to give her hope that he had somehow not recognised her.

"Course she ain't paid,' said Crespin, keeping his eyes dotingly fixed upon her. 'She's a rotten, stingy Hugo!'

With a self-satisfied smile, he bent down to retrieve her miniature Bible, while the sergeant gave the nod to his subordinates to arrest her.

But Jeanne's hatred of this man bending down at her feet was all-consuming—this man who would have slit her son's throat for a bagful of booty. She was oblivious now to the men attending her as she screamed out, 'You evil wretch! You evil, obnoxious wretch!'

Slipping her arms free from the soldiers' hold, and mustering all her might, she delivered her boot into the pauper's smarmy face, into the scoundrel who would rather loot dead bodies than attempt to save drowning people. As he rose up, cupping his nose, she then kicked him between the legs. And again she kicked him as he staggered in agony until the soldiers, hampered by the boy and protestations of injustice from some of the exiles, at last managed to pin back her flailing arms and drag her away.

*

An hour after the riverboat had departed, Jeanne and the boy arrived by packhorse at a field encampment.

After enquiry, the sergeant was directed to the top of the camp, where the commander was inspecting the field guns. Young Sergeant David suddenly realised how ridiculous he and his crew must seem, escorting a woman and a boy. Camp followers looked on with amusement amid catcalls and hoots from soldiers cleaning their arms and playing dominoes. The escort seemed excessive. It reminded him of a time when he was out hunting for game one day and found himself with five other huntsmen, beating about a single bush to get a pheasant to come out and take flight. But he could hardly double back now.

He was beginning to loathe Crespin's influence, the easy coin made by cashing in on the exiles' desperation, and now the arrest of a Huguenot lady on foreign turf. It was not as if they could put her in prison. What would they do with her?

It gave Jeanne no joy either to hear the softer consonants and vowel sounds of her mother tongue as she marched along the alley of bivouacs, where soldiers and their ladies eyed her speculatively. How could her journey of escape end here after so much hardship? Paul would be taken from her. He would be brought up by Jesuits, who would end up hammering their dogma into his skull until they had cracked it like a nut. He would be broken, brought up to fight for the king, and die a young man on one of his battlefields.

The commander was in discussion with his artillery man where the field camp met a meadow of long grass and wild flowers. Sergeant David approached with his cortège. It comprised three soldiers, a corporal with a bloodstained nose, a young boy, and a fine-looking lady of noble carriage. The commander's curiosity was piqued enough for him to suspend his conversation. With a flourish of the hand, he granted permission for the young sergeant to speak.

'Monsieur le Marquis de Boufflers, Sir,' said the sergeant.

'We encountered no enemy, the only encounter being of a religious nature more than anything else, Sir.' Sergeant David then glanced over his shoulder to where Jeanne had been told to halt with the boy. They were flanked by two soldiers on either side.

With his foot on the carriage wheel of a twelve-pounder, de Boufflers placed an elbow on his knee and his chin on his fist. But before he could respond, the corporal with the blood-splashed nose stepped forward from the right flank of the female prisoner. 'Permission to speak, Sir,' said Corporal Cortege eagerly. He was not going to let this squirt of a sergeant fifteen years his junior get all the credit. 'I recognised the lady from my surveillance days in Geneva, Sir.'

'That is true, Sir,' said Sergeant David generously. 'There would have been no call to arrest her otherwise.'

'She is a Huguenot,' added Crespin, in case the allusion had escaped the marquis. He handed him the miniature Bible in support of his statement.

'Name?' said de Boufflers.

'Delpech, Sir,' said Crespin, 'Jeanne Delpech.'

'Countess Delpech de Castonnet,' corrected the lady, standing erect. Inside, however, she was submerged in mixed emotions of fear and fury. For she realised she was standing before the very man who had caused the loss of her social position, the death of her child, the imprisonment of her husband, and the estrangement of her baby and eldest daughter.

She recalled her sister relating to her how he looked when he had first entered her hometown of Montauban. He had shown then, too, the characteristic arrogance and nonchalant flick of the wrist that pertained to the generation bred in the manners of Versailles.

'Where are you from, Madame?' he said in a polite fashion.

Jeanne stood proud but speechless before the architect of her sufferance.

'Come, speak up, Madame, we have not got all day!'

But still she stood tongue-tied. Then she felt a hand clasp the bun of her chignon, and heard the voice of Crespin. 'You've been asked a question —owww!' The last word was punctuated by a sudden cry of pain as the boy placed his boot in the shin of his mother's aggressor. The pauper turned and clobbered the lad, who promptly fell to the ground.

'Don't you dare!' said Jeanne, who was held at either elbow by the soldiers who flanked her. She shook herself free, then reached for the boy, who had picked himself up off the floor and was rubbing his cheek.

'Where are you from, Madame?' said the marquis more firmly, which made everyone remember their places.

'I am from Montauban,' said Jeanne, at last, having released her vocal inhibition. 'A place you know well, Sir.'

'Indeed, Madame. Wonderful town, too hot in the summer, though. But the people are understanding and most welcoming!'

Jeanne no longer saw the illustrious commander in uniform, but a churl being ironic in the most callous and unchristian way. She was suddenly inhabited by a rush of fury.

'You, you scoundrel!' she said. 'You take yourself for an honourable gentleman, but you, Sir, are no more a gentleman than this leech here!' She gave a flick of the head towards Corporal Crespin on her right and persisted, narrowing her eyes, in restrained wrath. 'You have ruined my family, invaded my home, taken my children, and sent my husband across the world. In the name of what saint or devil, I ask you!'

'In the name of political and religious unity, Madame,' said de Boufflers, quick to follow up and removing his foot from the carriage.

'I am a Christian, Sir, and I am French!'

'But you are a Huguenot, Madame!'

'And proud to be so, Sir, like all the Protestants of this land. And know, Sir, you will never break my spirit; you will not break that of my son either. I would rather die and face my Lord and judge!' She felt herself succumbing to her anger, sliding dangerously out of control. So, standing firm, she shut her mouth, not because de Boufflers had held up a hand as if to stop an onslaught, but because she knew she must find a valid reason for this man of war and strategy not to send her back to France. He would be more irritated than moved by an appeal founded on emotion alone.

'That may be so, Madame,' he said with superior calmness. 'However, as you can imagine, I have other preoccupations than self-righteous Huguenots to think about . . .' He made a discreet gesture to encompass the line of cannons parked on the edge of the field camp.

'Then let us go,' said Jeanne levelly. 'You cannot take me back to France! Moreover, this is not French soil. You have no right to hold me here!'

'Sir,' said Crespin, slipping in with his insistent, droning tone, feeling that his revenge was slipping from his grasp. 'Shall I put them somewhere, Sir?'

'What, and mobilise three soldiers, Corporal?' said de Boufflers.

He was in a lethargic mood that afternoon. And he was weary of the scorched earth campaign, fatigued by the company of soldiers. He turned his head away towards the meadow of long grass and wild flowers, bathed in late-afternoon sunshine.

Although this lady did not look particularly fashionable in her modest garb, she did have breeding. She had character, too, and he liked a lady with character. It was what had attracted him to Madame de Maintenon. The lady was right; this was not officially French soil . . . at least, not yet. He could not argue with that.

He turned back to her. 'Countess . . .' he said with a nod, and tossed her Bible to her. But to everyone's astonishment, she visibly took this as a cue to leave. She grabbed the boy's hand and stomped clean off into the meadow.

'Sir? What shall I do?' said a baffled Sergeant David.

De Boufflers was gazing wordlessly across the meadow where the sunlight was lending the long grass a golden tinge, as the lady and the boy made a trail through it. *Delpech*. He had heard the name before; now he remembered. Delpech, of course, the merchant gentleman who would not renounce his faith, and neither could he shut his mouth for the life of him. He had sent the man packing to God knew where and used the little family as an example to those who might be tempted to convert back. And for all intents and purposes, it had been a success. At least, it had done the job during his appointment as colonel-general of the dragonnades. Anything else no longer mattered, for unity had been forged in France.

'Halt or I'll fire!' called out Crespin. He had understood from de Boufflers's previous remark that there could be no prisoners. In other words, some things in wartime were better done differently, and he had primed his matchlock musket with powder.

Jeanne, resolute, did not break her stride. She would not go back to France to spend the rest of her life in prison. And she would not allow her son to be broken. She clenched Paul's hand tightly as she heard the sound of a charge being rammed into the barrel of a musket. But she strode on through the lush green grass, amid the late-afternoon sunshine and insects all abuzz. She now locked eyes with Paul, who smiled back with a look of determination that told her he understood and accepted the risk. He reciprocated her squeeze of the hand.

The pauper cocked his match while de Boufflers still stood in contemplation of the lady and her boy. So this is where her destiny has led her, he thought, back into the wolf's mouth; how strange. Of course, he had experienced similar coincidences, and he knew that they meant nothing. This one, though, would make for excellent conversation material at court.

'Halt, I say!' called Corporal Crespin, who then blew upon the match cord to kindle the embers, and opened the pan, giving the smouldering cord access to the gunpowder.

'Sir?' said an anxious Sergeant David, who knew that Crespin rarely missed a target.

At last, de Boufflers raised his hand to hold the fire. But Crespin had pulled his arm sharply to his shoulder and had the boy nicely in his sights. The proud lady would live the rest of her life in remorse for the death of her son. It would teach her to play with a Crespin. And besides, he was only interpreting orders. So he squeezed the trigger nice and smoothly without the slightest jerk. But the instant he did so, a downward blow stuck the barrel of the musket.

'Leave it, soldier!' said de Boufflers, letting go of the barrel as the countess swiftly yanked the boy into her path. She glanced back over her shoulder, then strode onwards with her son in front of her. 'She will not be broken,' said de Boufflers.

'But, Sir . . .'

'Let her go, man. Instead, pray for your own rotten soul lest you die on the field. Your section will be fronting the action in the morning!'

TWELVE

IN BEAUTIFUL AMSTERDAM, Jeanne was relieved to experience life without the constant threat of being pounced upon by French soldiers.

And the wait in the bustling merchant city par excellence had the advantage of allowing her and Paul to rest their sore and weary feet. They were staying at the tall canal-side house of a Huguenot who had made a new life there as a clockmaker. The Dutch, though austere in appearance, loved to spend their money on non-wearable luxuries, and his timepieces were much prized.

A methodical, clever, and neat man with a spiritual understanding of the universe, Monsieur François Barandon no longer regretted the fortune he had lost to the French royal coffers. He had moved on, and besides, his former wealth had certainly already been spent by the war-hungry king, whereas his new fortune, born of his own hard work and talent, was growing. The narrow house built over four storeys, its lavish furnishings, its well-stocked basement and loft, proved it.

'Dear Madame Delpech, I am certain that your husband,

resourceful as he has previously proven to be, will no doubt turn his talent into silver again,' said Monsieur Barandon to Jeanne one day. They were seated at table in the high-ceilinged dining room whose walls were beautifully painted with bucolic scenes and pictures of trees laden with fruit.

'The problem is not his lack of talent,' returned Jeanne, lowering her pewter fork, 'or his hard-earned knowledge, but the fact that laws learnt in France cannot be applied to foreign cultures as can techniques of time craft.'

'That is true, François,' said his wife, an impeccably dressed and robust lady in her mid-thirties with her fair hair drawn back into a coif. 'We should count ourselves lucky and thank God for the choices you have been given to make.'

'Does that mean that God has not helped my father, then?' said Paul, who should not really have spoken at all. But as his young mind evolved precociously due to events, he had begun to take liberties. The Barandons' young daughters, just a year or two younger, sniggered at his gall.

'Paul, dear!' said Jeanne, though finding it difficult to justify reprimanding him. He had been her travel companion, and she had come to treat him almost as an equal despite his age.

'The boy is quite welcome to speak his mind in this house, Madame Delpech,' said Monsieur Barandon with a reassuring smile. 'Come, lad, now's your chance to develop your argument, and we shall see if we can answer it.'

'Well, otherwise, he would have made Father choose a trade that would bring him prosperity in adversity, wouldn't he?'

'An interesting point,' said Monsieur Barandon, lost for words. Jeanne came to the rescue.

'No, Paul, dear,' she began in a condescending tone, 'it does not mean that at all. God has given us the liberty to make our own way through life, and sometimes life deals blows that cannot be anticipated. Otherwise, we would have left the country many years ago, as your father used to say we should. But what God has given us is the ability to strive on in adversity, and strive on we must if we love him, and we will be rewarded in life as befits our expectations. And for the time being, it is for our family to be reunited under the same roof.'

So I was right after all, then, thought Paul, who had begun to suspect that God was not playing fair at all. But he kept these thoughts to himself, for fear of upsetting his mother.

'Amen,' said Monsieur Barandon. 'And let us pray that your father will remain strong in faith to strive forward despite the odds life and the devil throw at him. And let us in the same way give thanks to God that I have the blessing here today of your company to remind me how the cards of life are not evenly dealt.'

That evening, Jeanne lay awake in the large feather bed, wondering how in the world Jacob could weave a livelihood in London.

*

Two hundred and sixty miles across the Channel, Jacob lay wondering how he could have fallen from grace so quickly.

He was forty-five today —forty-five and no place to call his own after having worked hard all his life. He had overcome hurdles of oppression time and again. Time and again, he had picked himself up, dusted himself off, and set forth on his battle horse, all to end up in middle age living in two rooms in a lowly district outside London. And to top it off, with no talent for the manual trades that Huguenots so often excelled at, he saw his remaining monies dwindling at an alarming rate in the horribly expensive English capital.

It was unfair, but to dwell on it would be to give in to self-pity. In the sallow light of a candle lamp, with a hand on the twinge in his back, he sat up on the edge of his rope bed that sagged in the middle. His eyes fell upon the little acorn faces—each representing a member of his family— lined up in a row on the straw seat of a wooden chair that he used as a bedside table. No, actually, he had not lost everything, he reminded himself.

He stood up and removed the straw tick mattress. Then he got down on his knees on the rough floorboards and reached for the straining wrench, a mallet, and a couple of pegs which he kept under the bed. These were the tools for tightening the rope that was threaded the length and width through the holes in the oak bedframe. Next, picking up the slack with the wrench and wedging the taut side with a peg, he began methodically tightening the rope that formed the bed base, pulling it hole by hole on alternate sides so that he could at least sleep tight. Then he put back the mattress and made his bed.

Feeling better for the exercise, he sat back on the edge of his tightened bed and picked up the book lying on top of his Bible on the chair. Monsieur de Sève had handed it to him the previous week at the coffeehouse behind the Exchange.

Jacob had met Philippe de Sève at the French church. A Huguenot from Berne, ten years Jacob's junior, he had lost his wife and their child in France during childbirth. He had arrived in the English capital a few weeks before Jacob. Both being of southern stock, they had formed a solid friendship from the start and rendezvoused every day at the coffeehouse on Birchin Lane, a five-minute walk from the church, where they could catch up on events in France and in England. They kept up each other's spirits, and made plans for a later date that would see them in partnership to take advantage of their Huguenot connections inside France.

Jacob flicked through the book. It was titled *The Compleat Soldier, or expert artillery-man*. On handing it to Jacob, Philippe de Sève had told him of Marshal Schomberg's defection from the French army, having refused, like so many veteran soldiers of his generation, to recant his faith. The duke may have been one of France's greatest generals, but he was too close to the grave to risk losing the way to eternal peace in heaven.

'Schomberg has laid down his sword to William and Mary,' de Sève had told Delpech that late morning in the crowded coffeehouse. It being pleasant and balmy, Jacob recalled the place being alive with chatter, laughter, and shouted greetings. The doors and windows had been flung open, though the sweltering air was still heavy with the fragrance of roasting coffee and tobacco smoke. Jacob and Philippe had sat head to head in a walnut booth so they could hear themselves speak, their hats and frock coats hung up on a wall peg above them. 'The king has commissioned him with raising an army, my dear Delpech.'

'Good Lord, is he going to fight against his king?'

'No, an English one. James Stewart is in Ireland, preparing to retake the English throne . . .'

'Not good. That would mean a Catholic king in England!'

'Precisely. That is where we come in, my good fellow, us

and thousands of Huguenots like us. Schomberg is keen to enlist good cavaliers and men of quality. There is no reason why we cannot both put ourselves forward. I am told by Monsieur Despierre that we would receive a lieutenant's salary. As much as seven pounds two shillings, my word!'

Jacob remembered choking on his pipe at this point during the conversation. He had spent many a restless night torturing himself over how to regain what he had lost, nay, how to provide for his family and pay his rent in the coming months. 'I should say any salary would be welcome,' he had said, wiping a moist eye and lowering his pipe.

'It is a godsend, Delpech. It stands to reason,' de Sève had returned with cheer.

Looking back on the scene now as he flicked through the pages of the soldier's guidebook, Jacob realised the pay was very attractive indeed when you considered that a carpenter only got one-seventh the amount. The new English king must be very keen to keep his new throne, and Parliament just as adamant to stave off a Catholic return, he thought. However, he did not think, as did his friend, that it was a godsend to send men to the battlefield, rather the work of the devil or higher powers on earth. But he had kept the notion to himself in the coffeehouse, there being many other Huguenots elated to fight against any allied forces of the French king—a king who had banished them from their own homes and confiscated their lands.

A leaf inside the guidebook fell from between the pages to the floor. Jacob bent down and picked it up. On it was printed a ballad titled "The Protestant Courage." Jacob read the first verse:

'Sound up the trumpet, beat up the drum,
Let not a soul be subject to fear,
Since the true pride of all Christendom,
Does against France in valour appear,
The courageous worthy seamen,
Does from all parts to London advance,
For England's promotion, they'll fight on the Ocean,
Against all the strength and power of France.'

The *power of France* could well be thought of as the dethroned English king, Jacob thought, as de Sève had argued. For was not King James financed by the coffers of Louis XIV, who was providing men and arms?

Jacob did not want to go to war against his own country, though. Neither did he want to kill or be killed. But Philippe de Sève had reassured him that they would not be on the front lines. And besides, it was out of the question to let a cousin of the despotic king plague the lands of refuge.

Jacob slid his legs onto the bed, now taut, glanced at the acorn faces on the straw chair, then snuffed out the candle, condemned as he was to go to war.

*

Philippe de Sève also rented a room in the timber-framed tenement building on the narrow, unpaved street east of Brick Lane. In fact, it was de Sève who had advised Delpech to take the second-floor rooms before they were snapped up, given the continuing influx of Protestant refugees.

The digs were spartan, the plaster between struts and beams was cracked in places, and the coarse timber floorboards at first made Jacob almost lose his balance. But the two rooms, one street-facing, the other looking out onto back yards of the new constructions, were spacious, cheap, and, being on the second floor, relatively well-lit.

It did not take long for him to spruce the place up and give it a godly sheen, knowing Jeanne could arrive at any moment. It was bad enough asking her to reside in the poor district outside the city walls; he could not expect her to live without the bare necessities as well. So, thanks to church contacts and the travel money which had not been stolen, for a good price he was able to purchase simple but sturdy furnishings: an unpretentious four-poster which came with a trundle bed underneath, a dining table and straw-seated chairs, an upholstered two-seater, a wardrobe with a glace, appropriate bathing equipment, and a three-panel screen for privacy. The church supplied him with crockery, covers, and bed linen.

It was cheap, and the area rough, but it meant he would not have to ask for alms from the Huguenot church to pay the rent. Like this, at least there would be one place where he could hold up his head, and keep up the pretence of bourgeois etiquette.

Jacob had paid his rent that morning to his landlady, a top-heavy, large-hipped lady in midlife who occupied the first floor with her cat and memories of her late husbands.

Mrs Smythe was far from being the pleasantest of Londoners Jacob had met. As de Sève put it, she was a paradox unto herself. She took their rent money with one hand and with the other was ready to shoo away all the aliens back to where they came from, to *fight their battles on their own turf,* as she liked to say. By *aliens,* she especially meant the French, who had brought with them their fancy dressmaking skills and silk- weaving techniques. 'Bless my soul, London is not the place it was!' she would blurt out whenever her eye caught sight of a passer-by in the Frenchified fashion.

Mrs Smythe owned the weaving workshop on the ground floor, which she had taken over after the death of her first husband, a weaver by trade of Flemish descent. She was beginning to feel the pinch of the influx of French weavers whose unparalleled mastery and extravagant variety could only previously be procured at much expense from the famous looms of Lyons. Lustring, velvet, brocade, satin, *peau de soie*, fine ladies' mantuas, corded silk called ducape, and fabric of mingled silk and cotton—all of the highest excellence—were becoming the new norm. By consequence, Mrs Smythe's plainer fabrics were fast going out of fashion, and she had reduced her workforce to just an aging part-time journeyman called Alf, an accommodating man of few words who ran errands, fixed the loom, and delivered the cloth to clients; Nelly, a seventeen-year-old seamstress whose parents had placed her with the childless widow of her second uncle once removed; and her good self.

Thankfully, she was able to rent out her upper-floor rooms for increasingly higher prices, paradoxically thanks to the workforce from across the Channel, which enabled her to balance her books. Like Jacob, having been driven out of home and country with little or nothing, these skilled refugees craved work and vied for lodgings in the cheap parish east of the city walls, currently under development for their accommodation. The allotted area was known as Spitalfields. And it was a stone's throw away from Mrs Smythe's house.

156

Jacob sat in the comfortable, albeit worn, upholstered armchair he had retrieved from a church acquaintance. He had put on the shoes he had waxed a moment earlier, and now sat staring at the wooden cross he had nailed to a support timber. He was feeling pretty low, wondering how on earth he could escape from the infernal spiral that had time and time again relieved him of his wealth. It was moments like these, when his mind was empty, that he found himself prey to his inherent bourgeois fear of becoming destitute.

But a familiar knock on the door brought him back from his thoughts and put a brighter tempo into his heart. He pulled himself up and stepped to the door, which he opened knowing full well who he would find on the other side.

Philippe de Sève was dressed in a black suit, a white lace collar, and white stockings despite the season. A black felt hat crowned his head, from which his natural cavalier locks cascaded onto his shoulders.

'Good day to you, dear fellow,' said Philippe, standing before the door. 'Magnificent start to the day!'

'A fair morning indeed,' said Jacob cheerily, closing his front door behind him.

'Let us hope it will bring us as fair news,' returned Philippe. They stepped to the narrow stairwell, so narrow in fact that Jacob had been obliged to use a long rope cast from the window to hoist his furniture inside.

Jacob knew full well what his friend was referring to. But Jacob's hopes were not at all focussed on the imminent announcement of their mobilisation. He hoped, as every morning, to receive news of Jeanne via the church on Threadneedle Street.

'I was wondering,' said de Sève as they continued down the rickety wooden staircase, 'do you think we are to wear our uniforms on the way there?'

'You mean to join the regiment?'

'Yes, bearing in mind that we are permitted to join them as we see fit. We are not obliged to leave with them from London.'

'Well, I suppose it would make us rather conspicuous,' said Jacob. 'On the other hand, it would make for a lighter pack if we did.'

'Fair point,' said Philippe. 'I must remember to enquire while you are at church. It will make a change from this suit I purchased from that Dutch puritan I told you about. Why, I verily feel like a condemned man.'

'Ha, wait till you get your first pay, my dear friend, though take guard not to overindulge in the colour such as myself. I do feel such a pillicock in this bright blue . . .'

Whenever they walked down the narrow and uneven staircase to the first floor, they normally hushed and trod carefully. But in the exuberance of the sunny morning after a week of summer showers, they both overlooked their habit until it was too late.

The landlady's front door cracked open. Then Mrs Smythe, dressed in her grey overdress, beige bodice, and white apron and bonnet, appeared overtly industrious with an old birch broom that had seen better days.

It was still early in the morning, and Mrs Smythe would not be down to the workshop for another hour. She looked haggard, her hair as lustreless as dried broomcorn. She had spent another sleepless night wondering how long she could hold on to Nelly, who was also her first husband's second niece once removed. Maybe she could let her go two days a week until more orders came in; it would not be long before the autumn winds reminded ladies of their winter wardrobe. But then, the girl might go and find work with the enemy.

On the other hand, why did she not just give up the ghost and rent out the workshop to the Frenchies? She would if she could, but she knew deep down that it was beyond her. It made her cringe and toss and turn in her sheets at the mere thought of it. The small outfit had been started by her first husband when they were young, her husband whom she had loved.

The two Frenchmen gave her good day as they made footfall upon the landing.

'Why can't you talk in English?' she said with her usual frankness and sardonic smile.

'We do, Madam,' said Jacob, smiling politely, 'but is it not normal to speak the language of one's homeland with a fellow countryman?'

'Get away with you,' she said, giving half a sweep, then stopping again as the gentlemen tried to edge their way past her. 'And how does anyone know you're not popish spies plotting against the king, then? We're not daft over here, you know,' she said with a fearsome glare.

Jacob paused a moment on the landing. With his arms crossed, he peered down into Mrs Smythe's clever but anxious eyes. Standing erect, he said: 'Then I invite you to follow us now, and you will see where we go every morning.'

'And where's that in English, then, if it isn't the coffeehouse?' challenged the landlady.

'To the French church, Madam, the Protestant church!'

'To the blimmin' church? Ha, why, bless my soul,' said

Mrs Smythe, shaking her head incredulously. 'If my first husband could hear you now, he'd soon talk some virility into youse, all right. I mean, aren't you gentlemen supposed to be looking for work? Church is for Sunday, for heaven's sake!'

Did he really have to listen to this? He had remained as polite as humanly possible. Were he in a stronger position, he would give her a piece of his mind. But besides the fact that this was not his country of birth, he felt all the weaker because he had no revenue and therefore was not paying taxes. He had little doubt that Mrs Smythe suspected that it irked him not to be pulling his own weight. Or perhaps he was just being overly sensitive.

Refusing to enter into a fruitless debate, Jacob bowed his head and gave the woman a stern farewell. She swept after them as if to shoo them away, as they went bundling the rest of the way down the stairwell. She knew as well as they did that she could easily find other lodgers should the need arise, and fetch a higher price for the rooms given the increasing demand.

Philippe de Sève's riled glance to Jacob needed no words as they stepped into the street. Delpech pursed his lips and chased away a fat bluebottle. The city stench rising with the heat of the morning sun made Philippe turn his nose into his scented lapel. But at least the lane was dry, littered with splashes and turds thrown from chamber pots, but mostly dry. They passed by the open square of land, the tenterground, where already women were laying out their cloth tautly on the tenters. Philippe tipped his hat politely to one of the young ladies.

'Good day, Mademoiselle,' he said in French, which was no

less common an occurrence nowadays than giving good day to an acquaintance in the streets of Pau. Indeed, the jabber that arose from such gatherings of ladies often resounded in French. The young lady gave a coy smile and a bow as she continued hooking her woven fabric tautly on the wooden frames, to keep it square and prevent it from shrinking.

'Would you have a twinkle in your eye for an apprentice weaver, de Sève?' said Jacob in a surprised voice, as they entered an alleyway where cats were lounging half in the sun, half in the shade.

'Are you afraid she might be below me, Jacob?' said Philippe in jest.

In fact, Jacob's surprise was only a half measure. He had experienced a similar egalitarian feeling of excitement in the new colonies. For the new refugees, London was a place where the usual social fences had not yet been erected and the customary exterior signs of wealth not established. Everyone was more or less in the same boat.

'In fact, I do fancy I might take a wife on my return, actually,' continued Philippe.

'And good for you, Sir!' said Jacob brightly. He had seen his friend on the wretched days when his loneliness made him haggard. For unlike Jacob, Philippe had no family reunion to look forward to; his loved ones were all dead, his solitude all-consuming. 'And would you be planning on becoming a rag merchant?' said Jacob in banter.

'Oh no, my dear fellow. We have our master plan.' Philippe said it in jest, but Jacob was nonetheless secretly reassured to hear it. Philippe went on. 'I dare say in a few years' time, Londoners will have as much choice of home-made fabric as in France!'

'And not only fabrics, my good fellow,' said Jacob, recalling the respected watchmakers and silversmiths he had met through the church. 'I dare say that soon, the only French merchandise that we shall be able to ship exclusively from France will be crops and wine!'

'And that is where we come in, Messieurs Delpech and de Sève, Merchants of London!' said Philippe with a flourish of the hand.

'And lucky it is for us that planters cannot bring with them our clement skies of southern France!'

At the end of a narrow alleyway, they came to the busy thoroughfare that met with Whitechapel Street from Hare Street and the open fields east of Shoreditch. This was the appropriately named Brick Lane, where cartloads of bricks were trundled into the city from the kilns in the fields.

'It will be an avenue from London all the way to the village of Hackney, according to some,' said de Sève as they crossed the rutted road, still unpaved at that end.

'I have no doubt it will,' said Jacob, 'considering the number of brick carts I have seen passing through here every day of the week; it is truly phenomenal. The city seems to gobble them up at an astounding rate! I am given to believe, too, that Spittle Fields will no longer be what its name suggests.'

'Spittle Court, they should rename it,' said Philippe, 'if the building petition goes through.'

There was business indeed in building houses made of brick, thought Jacob, amazed at the multiple opportunities that the monstrous city offered a man of means. But means is what he and de Sève lacked. So they had agreed to pool their earnings once they were decommissioned, with the aim of entering into business together.

'Bonjour, Messieurs,' said a gentleman, walking with his wife who Jacob recognised from the French Church. Both Philippe and Jacob gave a polite bow to the acquaintance and continued on their way westward. They took the route past the modest, pretty weavers' dwellings of Fashion Street, then along the old artillery garden until they arrived at Bishop's Gate Street. The wide thoroughfare was already heaving with streams of horse-drawn traffic, mostly headed cityward, and hawkers crying out their wares.

It was not long before they found themselves at their usual parting point under the sign of the Flying Horse Inn, near Bishop's Gate. A carthorse was drinking at the trough, others were lined up to carry their passengers into the city, and sedan bearers stood ready with their black chairs to carry their fares through the alleyways and backstreets where horse travel was forbidden.

'I shall meet you at the usual place, I hope with news of our leaving date, my dear Delpech,' said Philippe.

'It is a fine season to be going on a journey,' said Jacob. 'It will be a welcome change to get out into the fresh air of the countryside, I must say. Meet you at the coffeehouse later!'

The two men set out on their separate ways, de Sève heading westward towards the new artillery ground. Jacob continued through Bishop's Gate, down the wide and traffic-choked avenue towards Threadneedle Street as he had done every day since settling in Albion.

'Prithee . . . make way!' came a deep shout from behind as he entered the street in question. He niftily stepped aside to let strong-armed bearers carrying a sedan chair scurry by. Jacob watched it glide past him, no doubt on its way to the

Exchange. It reminded him of his brother-in-law's account of how his wife was forced by brutes of the French army to spend the night with her newborn baby in one such chair. It was during the month of August, four years ago almost to the day. While she was in labour at her sister's, Jacob had been forced to serve soldiers who had taken over his own home. Had he known she would be thrown into the streets just two nights after the baby was born, he would have thrown down his life to relieve her. But by the grace of God she had endured, and escaped to the country. She had found a winter sanctuary in one of his brother-in-law's farmsteads. But come spring, her baby and children were wrenched away from her when she was forced into hiding to avoid imprisonment. Having since travelled across the world, would he have rather chosen to recant, now knowing the suffering and destitution his allegiance to his Protestant faith would bring to him and his family? He could not say.

The peal of church bells chiming in the hour and another hawker's cry prompted him to instead contemplate the city's awakening, to distract his mind from thoughts of his family and how they had been able to manage without him. He continued to remind himself that God had given him such trials for a reason, saved him from others perhaps to live to fight another day. Nevertheless, he had not expected to enlist one day to fight on a battlefield.

It was eight o'clock. The shuffle of people on the pavements thickened: well-heeled gentlemen heading for the Royal Exchange, labourers in working attire, and ladies with baskets on their way to Wool Church market. He was glad for the daily pretext for a foray into these more sumptuous streets, rebuilt after the great fire, a welcome respite from the district where he now resided. It was a well-hooved district and a testimony to the wealth of opportunity the city had to offer. If he could muster enough funds with de Sève to create a decent investment pot, he might well be able to build up his fortune again. He might well one day be walking with those merchants to the great temple of commerce, the Royal Exchange.

There was much to do beforehand, though. For starters, there was a war to be won, and then there were the restrictions imposed on non-natives to be tackled.

At last he came to the new French church. The early-morning service being over, it was virtually empty. No sooner had he entered the cool brick building and bowed in reverence than he was greeted by the pastor.

'Monsieur Delpech, I was expecting you.'

Jacob's heart leapt—the pastor was hobbling excitedly towards him from the vestry, and he was brandishing a letter.

A note from Robert might bring him news of monies recovered; one from Jeanne would bring him the love he needed right now to go on.

Jacob took the letter. 'Thank you, Pastor,' he said. 'Thank you very much.' The old man gave a wordless bow and left him to the discretion of a rear pew.

Jacob sat forward, half closing his eyes. But he could not bring himself to pray that the contents would be good tidings. The news it contained was already written, and there was nothing any prayers could do to alter the facts.

He recognised Jeanne's elegant handwriting. At last he broke the crimson seal. Anxiously, he unfolded the letter. In the hunger for information, his eyes could not track whole sentences from start to finish, but singled out key words.

They picked out 'Palatinate,' 'refugees,' 'Amsterdam,' 'ship,' 'London,' 'soon,' 'Paul,' 'August.'

'Dear God. Thank you, thank you!' he whispered as he sat back, the sheet trembling in his hand. He swallowed, steadied his nerves, then read the letter again sentence by sentence from start to finish.

*

Philippe could hardly wait for Jacob to take a seat opposite him.

'Schomberg wants to leave in early August while the weather holds,' he said excitedly. 'We are to attend training in uniform from tomorrow morning until we head for Wales for the crossing to Ireland.'

They were sitting in their usual haunt on Birchin Lane off Cornhill. Jacob had just paid his penny and ordered a bowl of the black, gritty drink that he took with a pipe to take away the bitterness. The exuberant chatter and chink of crockery made any discreet conversation impossible. But Jacob did not mind; he had his own news that he wanted to shout to the world.

'Yes, I heard. Bumped into Monsieur Lafont, who was on the way to the chophouse,' he said while the serving boy nonchalantly filled his bowl, pouring the thick coffee from considerable height. 'I only hope I see my wife beforehand!' Jacob's boyish grin broadened irresistibly into a wide smile.

Philippe, who sported a pointy beard, brought his pipe from his mouth. Wide-eyed, he said: 'Why, my dear fellow! Is she due in?'

Jacob gave a curt nod which allowed him time to quash the surge of emotion. 'Yes,' he said at last as the boy moved on to another table with his jug of coffee. 'I received a letter, says she's in Amsterdam, that she's getting the next ship to London.'

'Do you know when?'

'She says they are to embark once enough passengers have been accounted for. I imagine they could even be here in a matter of days . . .'

'Or weeks,' said Philippe, grasping the tail of his goatee. 'The only thing is, Jacob, we are to join up with the regiment in Wales in ten days.'

'Then we shall try to hold back as long as possible. Are you with me?'

'I am, Sir!' said Philippe, raising his cup.

'Good, then we shall go to the chophouse for lunch to celebrate!'

*

The following morning, Lieutenants Delpech and de Sève walked down the staircase of the Smythe tenement building, their boots falling heavily on the steps. Mrs Smythe, broom in hand, stood agape at her door upon seeing two dazzling soldiers dressed in pearl-grey frock coats and breeches, and white neck scarves and sashes. It was a uniform she did not recognise, for it was the uniform of the Huguenot regiments of King William of England.

'Madam,' said Jacob, tipping his felt hat as Mrs Smythe scuttled backwards through her door.

THIRTEEN

JEANNE AWOKE TO the insistent tugging at the hood of her cloak and the strident cries of gulls.

She cracked open an eye to see the dawning day filtering into the gun deck through the hatches, bringing colour to the huddle of fellow passengers. She turned her head to the caress on her cheek. 'We're in London, Mother,' said Paul in a low, excited voice. He had returned from above, where Jeanne could now hear shipmen scurrying about the deck in response to the orders heartily hailed in Dutch.

'Klaar voor de kaapstander!'

'We are coming to anchor,' continued Paul, his eyes bright and shining like two silver shillings as the folk around them—some propped up against posts and barrels, others lying willy-nilly upon the deck timbers—groaned into consciousness.

Blurry-eyed, the passengers began to gather their meagre belongings, some their yawning offspring, while bundled babies suckled at their mothers' breasts. People began looking around like alert stoats, wondering whether to abandon their places and make a move to the upper deck where the air, though chilly, was at least free of the foul smell of bilge water and the like. But their choice for the time being seemed to favour the latter, inured as they were to the stench of unwashed bodies, and sick and pisspots.

For Jeanne, the immediate relief was that of arriving safely to port, for the crossing had been rough at times, causing people to puke in unison. She had never travelled in a cargo ship over the open sea, and never had she been so fearful as when the boat had rocked and swayed far more than the craft on which she had travelled on Lake Geneva.

However, the general feeling of deliverance that accompanied the end of any seafaring voyage lay largely muffled under the anxiety of now facing the unknown, in a different language, and in a nation presently at war with their country of origin.

The clomping of boots descending steps diverted the voyagers' attention to the hatch, where a stout Dutch gentleman—the same who had shepherded them onto the ship in Amsterdam—hummed and clapped his hands together. 'Ladies and Gentlemen,' he said in accented French, standing on the second step from the bottom. 'Welcome to London Town. Please make your way above deck in order to board the wherries that will ferry you ashore.'

Jeanne shouldered the sack she had used as a pillow. Then, holding onto her son's hand, she followed the queue of passengers up to the main deck, where they were met by the soft, golden light of early morning.

Even the nauseating stench of river sludge and city offal did not quell Jeanne's amazement at finding herself suddenly in the middle of a great sprawling metropolis. Awestruck, she stood with Paul at the starboard balustrade. Her gaze passed along the north bank, where tall, shabby timber-framed dwellings and riverside warehouses touched shoulders with palatial buildings in the shimmering light of morning. 'That's the Tower of London,' said Paul, pointing to the white tower on their right. 'It's where they keep traitors before they are executed,' he continued, proud to impart knowledge recently acquired from a rigger as they had sailed up the Thames at dawn.

Jeanne slowly scanned the riverbank from the Tower, past Custom House to Billingsgate wharf, wondering how on earth they could fit into such a jungle of stone, bricks, and mortar.

'And that,' said the boy, motioning to his left as though he were announcing a theatre act at a fair, 'that is London Bridge!'

It was an extraordinary sight for a provincial lady to behold. What a pageant of light and fantasy, she thought, facing what seemed like a thousand windows reflecting the first rays of the sun. 'Why, it's a whole village on a bridge!' she said as her eyes followed the roofline. She marvelled at the hotchpotch of gables, turrets, and cupolas atop houses, many of whose first floors extended thrillingly over the water.

The boy pointed towards the south bank gatehouse. 'That end is where Papa said he saw heads on spikes when he came here with Grandpa,' he said, amused at the look of disgust on his mother's face. But thinking about it, she remembered that Jacob had indeed stayed in London as a young man, and probably could still speak the language. Her heart pulsated with a new ray of hope. Could this truly be the land of opportunity Jacob had spoken of?

The Dutch merchantman lay at anchor amid a flotilla of tall ships and small craft, waiting for a landing dock to be able to unload. Meanwhile, the refugees were brought by wherry to the north bank by the dozen. Jeanne and her son descended unsteadily into one such rowboat—used ordinarily to ferry Londoners the length and breadth of the Thames—and were soon being given a hand up the slippery stone steps before Custom House. It was August 14th.

Some of the passengers were met in an effusion of joy by friends or relations, who stepped out from the crowd waiting twenty paces back from the steps. They had been tipped off as to the arrival of the long-awaited ship by a church messenger, who had received the news that the vessel had entered the Thames estuary. Jeanne and Paul scanned the dock in the hope that their eyes would meet those of their husband and father.

A welcome committee of ladies and gentlemen stood to one side, ready to direct those without relations to temporary accommodation. Behind them, Jeanne recognised the faces of passengers who had been ferried ashore in a previous wherry. However, she was about to find out that she would not be joining them, that she would not need to count on the kindness of yet another stranger.

A white-haired pastor with a Genevan accent, holding a notebook and a graphite stick, opened his arms in welcome. He gave instructions in French that those without prior arrangements would be catered for and should wait with their fellow passengers until the wherries had transported everyone from the ship.

'But before you do,' said Pastor Daniel, 'please step

forward if your name is on my list here.' The little party stood in expectation, with their effects at their feet. Both Jeanne and Paul continued to scan the crowd for late arrivals. In fact, they had not stopped scouring the scene since they descended from the ship into the wherry. But their eyes had still not found what they were looking for as the pastor's croaky voice read out his list of names.

'Monsieur Brocard . . . Madame Cazenave . . . Monsieur Dalençon . . .' he said, leaving a pause between each name for the owner to step forward. As of yet, no one had. He went on. 'Madame Delpech de Castonnet.' Again he paused and looked up. But lost in the search for her husband, Jeanne was not sure she had heard right. Paul, who had not missed a syllable, tugged her hand, and they both stepped forward.

The priest gave a brief smile and motioned to them to stand next to him, then continued with his short list. After a few more names, it turned out that, of all the passengers, Jeanne's name was the only one on it.

As she stood by the pastor, she dwelt on why her name had been singled out, why Jacob had not come to meet them. Was he ill, or worse? She turned to Paul, whom she sensed was trying to decipher the pleat in her brow. She touched his cheek in a gesture of mutual comfort.

'Madame Delpech,' said the pastor some minutes later in French, having introduced himself as the pastor of the French church on Threadneedle Street. 'I have a letter for you from your husband.'

'Oh?' said Jeanne. 'Is there anything wrong?'

'Rest assured, Madame, nothing wrong, no.'

'Then why could he not meet us himself?'

'He had to depart, Madame. However, he has left you a

key to your accommodation, which I will be only too glad to accompany you to, once you have registered and taken refreshment at the church.' Jeanne thanked him and tried not to let her disappointment show. But the pastor nonetheless sensed her confusion. He said: 'He was obliged to leave four days ago with his regiment, Madame.'

'His regiment?' said Jeanne, somewhat taken aback.

'Yes, Madame, he is a lieutenant in King William's army. I would not be surprised if he had already made landfall on Irish soil by now.'

FOURTEEN

STANDING BY THE campfire with his bowl of beef-and-pea soup, Jacob contemplated the lough, its calm waters shimmering in the dawn.

The stench of mudflats—populated with wading fowl—mingled with a hint of heather that wafted down from the emerald hills. And the acrid tang of black powder floated over the port town of Carrickfergus.

Jacob, like ten thousand other Huguenots would do, had answered the call to join King William's army. It gave the Huguenots honourable employment and allowed them to potentially cross swords with their persecutors. For word had got out that James II's army in Ireland was to be supplemented by Louis XIV's soldiers. The first challenge was to oust the deposed Catholic king's forces from the Protestant towns captured in the north. As the Jacobites retreated, they plundered settlements and villages, burning everything they could not take with them. It was the same scorched earth policy Louis of France had resorted to in the Palatinate.

It was August 28th. Jacob and Philippe were among the

two-hundred-strong cavalry regiment that had disembarked six days earlier at White House, located between Belfast and Carrickfergus. The former had been relieved of Jacobites, who had retreated southward upon the arrival of Marshall Schomberg's main army. The latter was still occupied by a pro-Catholic Irish garrison composed of one battalion and nine companies. Their mission was to slow the English army under Schomberg as much as possible to allow James time to rebuild his depleted army after his failed attempt to take Derry. Before retreating within the town walls, they had put flame to any building that might serve the Williamites.

Jacob took another sip of his savoury soup. Then he turned his gaze to the web of masts that stood like a hundred Protestant steeples upon the smooth and peaceful lough. Peaceful, that is, since Schomberg had ordered the royal ships to menacingly train their guns on the besieged castle, and since the Jacobites had raised the white flag.

But despite the surrender, it was clear to Jacob that the Catholic commanders had accomplished their mission. Not only had they delayed Schomberg's march south, they had managed to negotiate favourable conditions of surrender. The terms allowed the defeated garrison to "march out with flying Colours, Arms, lighted Matches, and their own Baggage . . ." What was more, the Jacobite invaders were to "be conducted by a Squadron of Horse to the nearest Garrison of the Enemy." In other words, until they were out of harm's reach of the Protestant inhabitants who might not like to see the instigators of their recent torment get away scot-free.

Jacob was among the horsemen selected to accompany the Jacobites the first few miles out of town. He gulped down the last dregs of his broth, then lit a pipe, thinking how odd it was that he missed his awful bowl of coffee at the coffeehouse in London. He was soon puffing away in protection against the smell of the last cartload of bodies that had rolled by. The last count was over one hundred and fifty men killed on each side, plus a handful of cows.

Around him, tents were being dismantled by gentlemen's valets. Through the gaping hole in the north wall, he could see the devastated town, strewn with debris and rubble, the tops of buildings blown off, and smoke still coiling into the balmy sky. He now gazed at the cloud of flies above the festering carcasses of the lead-peppered cows. They had been herded atop the rubble of the breach by the besieged soldiers in a desperate bid to prevent the besiegers from entering the town.

'Damn waste of good meat,' said Philippe, holding the reins of two horses as he came strolling up. He handed the reins of one to Jacob, who, not in the mood for banter, gave a thick grunt. It occurred to him that the same could be said of the cartload of dead men, who looked no less morbid and spiritless than the dead bovines. It was frightening.

Two hours later, Jacob and Philippe were waiting in their saddles outside the east gate with their cavalry squadron. Three hundred and fifty battle-worn Jacobites were marching from the castle with their wives, children, and camp followers in tow. To the beat of their drum, they marched up the ravaged street that was flanked by Schomberg's foot soldiers. Jacob saw haggard-looking townsfolk watching in dismay and anger. After sizing up the instigators of their living nightmare, many of them now hurled insults between the shoulders of Schomberg's troopers, who were letting the invaders get away with their flags flying.

At last, the dishevelled column of Irish Catholic soldiers approached the gate where the Williamite cavalry squadron were to take up their escort mission. Jacob looked around dubiously at his English captain, Sir William Russel.

Having delayed their departure from London in the hope of seeing Jeanne before leaving for Ireland, Jacob and de Sève had embarked from Highlake with an English cavalry regiment. It had been agreed that the two French lieutenants would join their Huguenot regiment in Belfast once the siege of Carrickfergus was over.

The captain gave orders for the detachment to split into two so that twenty-five horsemen rode on either flank of the Irish garrison. It all suddenly seemed to Jacob like a very tall order. Not the task of keeping the garrison in line, but the more delicate challenge of keeping the townsfolk from taking their revenge. It quickly became clear the population would carry their verbal attacks much further than the city gate.

'They should expect a rough quarter of an hour,' called Jacob in French to de Sève.

Philippe, a few lengths in front, turned in his saddle. 'Aye, they say you only reap what you sow, my friend! And I'd rather be up here than down there right now!'

The swelling crowd was clearly curious to find out what was going to happen to their former captors.

No sooner had they left the gate than the most vocal womenfolk marched up to the Jacobite column with verbal digs and hard pokes to provoke a reaction, until a horseman closed the gap and established order.

'Cavaliers, keep tight!' ordered the captain, cantering up and down the file of enemy soldiers. But gaps were inevitable along the line of horses, and the forays of verbal aggression continued.

The file continued their march to the beat of their drum past the first houses, charred and gutted, that lined the road south outside the town wall.

Old Mrs O'Leary in a grey peasant's bodice and skirt, hair bound in cloth, was collecting her thoughts inside her roofless, burnt-out home where she had raised her sons. Gareth had died from the fever, and Edward was killed as he strove to protect their hometown from the invading Jacobite force. She was not prone to tears, old Mrs O'Leary. She was hard as toenails and not one to make waves either; ripples, rather, was the philosophy handed down to her from her French grandfather. *Little by little the bird builds his nest*, she used to say to her boys, who were hampered with the impetuosity of youth and lacking the guiding hand of their father, missing at sea.

In the void of her loss, she was thankful that Gareth had fathered a son. The toddler had been taken north with his mother to their Scottish cousin's in Ballymena. She was thinking that she might join them; the child looked so much like her Gareth. But her ears pricked on hearing the march of boots. And the accompanying outbursts suddenly pierced the bubble of her grief.

She turned from the blackened room where her kitchen had been, and looked through the burnt-out window. She then scurried to the threshold, where the wooden door was still half-hinged and open.

There she stood, hawkeyed, as though picking out her

prey. A minute later, eyes all aglare, Mrs O'Leary stomped across the dozen or so yards that separated her from the passing Jacobite file. Mad-eyed and with a primal rage, she let out a visceral cry that made even the townsfolk start with horror. It did not form decipherable words, though the appalling sound was eloquent in itself. It expressed all the grief, pain, and anger of a mother who had lost her babies and the home she had brought them up in. It was a cry that needed no words, a cry that many understood, including Delpech and de Sève, between whose horses she had lunged towards the Jacobite column. They both searched in alarm for the source of such soul-wrenching sorrow.

Fingers curled into rigid dart-like claws, she charged at the soldier who had flamed her house. She reached for his face but only managed to scratch his neck and latch hold of his long hair. Turning sharply, he shook her off, clamped her upper arms and then flung her to the ground like a bundle of sticks. Two women came to her aid as, on her knees, she belched out her pain in a woeful wail, holding her belly like she was giving birth.

An eruption of voices and indignation rose up as a group of womenfolk broke into the file in a single body. They swooped upon the soldier like vultures, tore at his face, pulled him down. They then dragged him from the rank and covered him in blows from pounding knuckles and rough brogues on feet.

Philippe and Jacob managed to coordinate their mounts to push back the assailants. Meanwhile, the soldier was pulled back from the ground into the Jacobite line by his brothers in arms, visibly none too keen for a fight.

But the soldier made a sign that did nothing to lessen the

tension. Instead, it spread the feeling of indignation as fast as the flames that had ravaged Mrs O'Leary's house. The crowd called for justice to be done, that the Jacobites be led away to be massacred, each and every one of them. But they were not. It soon became clear to them that their enemies were merely being conducted away from the scene of their crimes, as if they were on a church parade.

By the time they had marched a mile out of the township, the townsfolk had measured the cavaliers' willingness to intervene. It was clearly less fervent than the crowd's visceral desire for bloody justice. Justice for their destroyed homes, their dead husbands and sons, their diminished health through privation of food, and the disease-ridden tots that might not see the end of day.

Wild kicks began to hit home and isolated punches to fly. Jacob sensed as well as the Jacobite officers that just one spark of fury from the column would ignite an explosive reaction. Captain Russel sent one of the French cavaliers for reinforcements, telling him to leave discreetly and then fly like the wind.

The inevitable happened soon after Philippe's departure.

A soldier's wife reacted viciously as a Protestant fishwife stepped up and tugged her chignon from behind. Had the soldier's wife let herself suffer the dishonour and let the woman have her moment of satisfaction, then maybe she would have lost nothing more than a bit of face. But ferocious as a wildcat, she turned: 'Get off me, ya filthy faggot!' she screamed, twisting and clawing the air as her assailant went on pulling the chignon back, forcing the soldier's wife to her knees.

'Let her go or I'll let fly!' shouted her husband, holding

his musket by the barrel as if he was about to use it as a bat.

But the fishwife sneered and pulled the woman's bun harder, making wide circles which made her scream louder and the onlookers laugh harder. The husband swung back his musket, but a burly Protestant stepped forward and snatched it from the soldier's grasp. The Jacobite let loose a punch. The Protestant whacked the butt of the musket handsomely round the soldier's ear. The Jacobite tumbled, a corpus of townsfolk surged forward as if on cue, and the fighting began.

The soldiers were better equipped to fight, but the townsfolk were angrier, their raw fury quadrupling their strength and desire for instant, bloody justice. They easily wrested the firearms from their former captors' hands. The Catholic commanders ordered their men not to draw their sabres, knowing that if they did, their own massacre would be inevitable.

The soldier's wife was now a plaything. Townsfolk of both sexes clawed voraciously at her shawl, bodice, and skirt, tearing them to shreds. Within minutes, she was on her hands and knees in the mud in nothing but her shift, trembling like a frightened bitch. Then her face was pushed down into the mud and the rest of her clothing ripped off in seconds, her body groped, her blood-stained bloomers held high.

The women went on the rampage against their adversaries of the same sex, to tear off their clothes, and give them back some of the medicine that the Catholic wives had dealt them in their own homes.

Sporadic fighting erupted all along the file. Even high-grade officers were set upon. The horsemen, unable to intervene with their arms, could only endeavour to separate the brawlers with their mounts. After another intervention, Delpech saw a soldier step out from the column and start making for the woods across the bog.

Damon Laverty had joined King James's army not just because everyone else had. In truth, he couldn't care less about who was in charge across the Irish Sea. All he cared about was pretty Maddy O'Flanerty, the baker's daughter, and getting some decent pay in order to fetch her hand. But he was not prepared to give his life for the sake of a king's throne. It was a good crack at first, but now he had had enough. And what was he going to say to his best mate's ma about her son Danny getting his head shot off by a cannonball?

He put it all to the side for the moment. The woods were close by, and if he could just sneak off while no one was looking, just like Jerry his other pal had done before the siege began, then he could be home in less than three days. Then he would do as his old man had told him to do: he would take to the oar and bring the fish to market like his forebears had done.

'Where you off to, laddie?'

Damon looked up. He saw two angry-looking men facing him. One of them was holding a dense, knotted stick that he was tapping into the palm of his hand. Damon turned to his right, only to face a woman standing impassively between two other men. He recognised her. She was the one he had to pull away from Danny while her husband was being held for clobbering a sergeant. The sergeant then had the man shot and his house torched.

'L-Look, listen,' Damon blurted out, sensing his life was

in danger. 'I didn't shoot your husband . . . I . . . I could have aimed to kill, but I did not. I swear to God I aimed aside.' But his plea made no difference. This was not a tribunal. It was going to be an execution.

The sound of cantering hooves made the party turn in unison. A chestnut-brown horse came through the middle of the pack, carrying a soldier in grey uniform.

'Stand back!' cried out Lieutenant Delpech to the assailants.

'He's ours!' roared one of the men.

'Is retaliation what the Lord taught you?' returned Jacob sternly.

'Is plundering and burning and killing what the Lord taught them?' said the woman virulently. 'He killed my husband!'

'I didn't, I swear to God, I aimed aside!' said Damon desperately.

'Aye, we'll pay our dues in heaven or hell, as long as these bastards get what they deserve!' said one of the men.

'For the love of Christ,' said Jacob, maintaining a loud, commanding tone of voice, 'has there not been enough of killing?'

But since they were blinded by grief, humiliation, and anger, Jacob was sure these people would not let the man live. Turning and bending down to the soldier, he said sharply: 'Give me your hand now!' It was the only way of saving him from execution and the townsfolk from mortal sin.

Damon did not think twice. He seized the cavalier's hand and climbed behind him sharpish. In her hunger for revenge, the woman ran behind the horse for a few yards while shouting out: 'You dirty, filthy scumbag! Come back here and yer dead!'

Jacob cantered back to the main file where horses were screening the Jacobites from the furious, madding crowd.

Damon descended, back among his regiment.

Another woman cried out in indignation: 'You should be executing the bastards!'

'Whose side are you on, anyway?' shouted a man.

Trying to keep control of his shying horse, Jacob said in a loud but controlled voice: 'I am on the side of God!'

But the townsfolk were not impressed; they were not ready for a moral lecture. They had already seen too many men and women die through turning the other cheek.

The jostling crowd began surging like the ebb and flow of a swelling sea, and more and more Jacobites were being set upon, some dragged from their column to receive a beating. Jacob realised that someone was about to be killed, and that the first death would lead to a massacre, one way or the other, and he was in the thick of it.

But then a rapid movement entered the corner of his eye. He turned to see a scarlet coat, a blue sash, and a hand holding up a pistol midway down the line. A deep, gravelly voice called for order, but to no effect. Then a tremendous blast rent the air, sending birds from the surrounding woods into flight. The clamour died down as quickly as when Mrs O'Leary had let out her primal cry. Officers being manhandled were able to shake themselves from the grips of their assailants as an instance of total calm followed.

It was the old duke in person, Schomberg, sitting high and mighty on his large horse, a picture of dignity and conviction in his grey periwig and tricorne hat. He was holding up his smoking gun. Raising his accented voice, the marshal endeavoured to talk sense into the townsfolk. But the voice of the crowd soon rose up again, calling for executions, and protesting against the Jacobites being marched off without so much as being called to account for their dastardly actions.

Damon Laverty sensed that things were about to turn nasty again. The townsfolk had become a sinister mob. He had been saved once by a greycoat, but he knew that none of the other Protestant horsemen had much heart to impose order upon their fellow Protestants.

So, eyeing his previous pursuers and the vindictive woman now calling for immediate justice, again he decided to slip away. Taking advantage of the distraction caused by Schomberg, he backtracked discreetly through the file of soldiers. Then he dashed back the short distance to the approaching battalion of Williamites on foot.

Meanwhile, midway back up the line, Schomberg intoned with finality: 'Get back to your town, or face the consequences!'

At the tail end of the column, Jacob noticed other Jacobite troops following Laverty's lead, preferring to find refuge among their Williamite counterparts than to risk facing the mob.

But now fully aware of the battalion of redcoats on foot coming up the rear, the townsfolk stood back, some unclenching their fists, others lowering the arms they had snatched from their former gaolers.

Under the duke's command, the battalion on foot swiftly took control. They pushed the dishevelled Jacobites back into line, and forced the battered and bruised to limp onwards. Denuded wives were clad in coats to cover up.

In this way, the Jacobite column was conducted to a safe distance from Carrickfergus, the pretty port town they had left in ruin and desolation.

On leaving the Jacobites to their fate on their march south through the hills to Newry, Delpech turned to de Sève, who had ridden up to his flank. 'I wonder if any of those men will be held to account,' he said.

'God's justice will prevail,' said Philippe. Jacob still hoped it would. Philippe went on: 'I just wonder why we are letting them go only to return our fire another day!'

Jacob then saw the young soldier he had saved. He was marching in file with Schomberg's men. 'The world is an unfathomable mess,' said Jacob, and took refuge in his pipe.

*

Some hours later, on marching upon Belfast bay with his new brothers in arms, Damon Laverty got to thinking that he might even be able to find a way to join a ship and sail to the New World, where he had heard fortunes were made.

FIFTEEN

SITTING ON HIS chestnut-brown mount, Jacob said a silent prayer for the souls of the men whose bodies were being released from the hangman's noose.

Jacob sometimes wondered if Protestants and Catholics had forgotten they were Christian. But he knew the men's souls would be with God if they had faith, be they Protestant or Catholic. They would be judged on their life's deeds, not their desertion from the English army.

They had left Belfast the day before. Marshall Schomberg had recovered all of his army and had set the whole train of twelve thousand foot soldiers and two thousand on horseback on the road to Dublin. That was where James Stuart had set up his government, and where the bulk of the Catholic king's army was encamped.

The bodies were swung onto a cart waiting on the roadside outside the fort of Hillsborough. Jacob clicked his horse onwards.

Private Laverty continued to stare for a full minute after watching the grim fate of the Protestant deserters. He knew it was what awaited him should he get caught by his former brothers in arms.

For the time being, he had let go of his hopes of finding a ship to take him to the New World where fortunes were made. Instead, he thumbed the rosary deep inside the pocket of his new jacket that had belonged to a dead Williamite. It was what his mother had taught him to do as a boy, to pray to the Virgin Mary in times of trouble. He had seen men dangle before without giving it a second thought. But perhaps the unsettling sensation in his stomach was due to his feeling under the weather. It always made him feel down whenever he got a sniffle. He should have learnt to smoke a pipe like a sailor, he thought to himself; it settled the nerves, apparently, cleared away foul smells, and staved off hunger.

On horseback, Delpech discovered a beautiful land made up of lush green glens, wooded mounds, and pretty villages. But the further southward he rode, the more devastated the landscape became, Jacobite invaders having looted and torched entire townlands that were now empty of people.

With such a large army, the going was slow. They spent the night outside the deserted market town of Dromore. By the end of the next day, they had reached Loughbrickland, where they encamped on the side of a hill. The Huguenot cavalry regiments were allocated their own area so as not to stir up inherent rivalries between English and French troops.

Jacob was getting used to hearing French spoken all around him. It still seemed odd, though, to hear a Huguenot rejoice upon finding an old acquaintance or a distant cousin in the fields of Ireland. The main topic of conversation since leaving Dromore was the latest intelligence regarding the township of Newry. A key position on the road to Dublin, Newry was the last stop before the Slieve Gullion mountain that separated Ulster from Leinster and the plains of Meath.

'Berwick?' said Jacob to Monsieur de Bostaquet, an affable and forthright middle-aged gentleman turned soldier. Having fled France and relinquished his fortune rather than his faith, he had joined the Dutch provinces and crossed the Channel to England in King William's army. They were standing around the campfire, having just left their horses to pasture. De Bostaquet knew the ropes, gave guidance to the many gentlemen merchants who swelled the Huguenot ranks so they were more battle-savvy than they would have been. Jacob and Philippe appreciated his company.

'The Duke of Berwick,' said de Bostaquet, 'King James' natural son, from a second bed, but his natural son all the same, Sir.'

'I heard he has a reputation, this Berwick,' said Philippe.

'Indeed, already, one so young too. Not yet twenty if my memory does not fail me, and already given with passion to the practice of pillage and torching. One to watch, you might say,' added de Bostaquet with a hint of irony, 'and now the blighter is in Newry!'

On the news of Berwick's occupation of Newry, Schomberg pushed his army southward through the increasingly ravaged glenscape. The rare farmsteads Jacob passed had all been pillaged and torched. And with no one about to harvest it, the corn stood rotting in the fields. But worst of all, the weather turned bad: now a fine drizzle, now torrential rain.

By the time they reached the foothills of the Morne Mountains north of Newry, Berwick had retreated with his army, leaving a town in flames in his wake.

'Dear God,' said Jacob, looking down from the hills at the

coils of smoke rising above the walled township. The place was clearly still ablaze. 'Why such gratuitous destruction?'

'It is exactly the tactic Louis's commanders employed in the Palatinate,' said Monsieur de Bostaquet, riding by Jacob's left flank. 'It is so we find nothing we can use.'

They clicked at their mounts and rode down into the town, where a few townsfolk were still fighting the fire with buckets. Only a handful of houses were still standing.

Schomberg was both moved and furious over the dastardly acts that Berwick continued to perpetrate. The marshal ordered a corps of horse to press onwards in an attempt to surprise the young scoundrel before he destroyed the township of Dundalk.

*

Damon Laverty's morale was in his boots. The weather was atrocious, the soup as clear as cabbage water, and the high winds kept blowing down his tent, which he would have to pitch all over again tomorrow. He should have stayed with his garrison and marched south; at least they were fed properly with solid portions of meat and a decent clump of bread to soak up the broth juice. He never seemed to make the right choice, though, either jumping in too early or not holding out long enough to reap the fruit of steadfastness. Was he really so fickle? That was what his mother often called him, fickle as the wind, and he was beginning to think she was right.

A troop on horseback passed by him. Soaked to the skin, he looked up from the stake he was hammering into the sodden ground, angling it so that it would stay in. He caught sight of the French cavalier who had saved him from a summary execution. He stood upright and gave a salute, for you never knew when you might need a friend. Then a treacherous gust kicked into camp, blowing a wet canvas flap into his face. It was all bloody unfair.

*

No sooner had they been served their bowl of watered-down broth than Jacob's party were called to saddle up.

Jacob's backside still ached from the previous stint in the saddle as he rode past the infantry camp, where he caught sight of the young soldier he had rescued. He had visibly defected, or deserted, depending from which side of the fence you looked at it. Delpech gave a nod to the soldier's salute. The lad looked so young, thought Jacob, or was it he who was getting old? He had noticed that people seemed to be looking younger these days, quite frightening to think about. Or could it be that, given the nature of the context in which he found himself, he was surrounded by an abnormally young population compared to normal everyday life? At any rate, he was consequently all the more glad for Isaac de Bostaquet's company. Hale and hearty in his mid-fifties, de Bostaquet was a tour de force and served as a source of hope—hope that it was not too late for Jacob to endure life's battles and raise his children to his family's former station.

The party rode on to the assembly point south of the town at the foot of Slieve Gullion mountain. There they joined Count Mesnart, Schomberg's third son, who was in charge of leading the detachment of officers to Dundalk.

*

Jacob, like every other cavalier, kept his aches and pains to himself. For they all knew that an epidemic could be looming on the horizon. Even as they rode past the infantry camp, Jacob had noted the chorus of splutterings and groans.

'In a word, camp fever,' said Isaac to Jacob as the cavalry train rode two abreast into the hilly terrain. 'You don't want to stay in camp too long, my good fellow. Avoid it like the plague!'

But Jacob soon found there were inconveniences that counterbalanced the benefits of being out on a mission. Lashing rain and gale-force winds constantly assailed the party in their arduous trek through the tricky, boggy tracks of Slieve Gullion. Neither Jacob nor Philippe had a cape. Their unwaxed jackets became heavy sopping weights on their shoulders. To add to the hindrance, the retreating Jacobite soldiers had taken care to smash river fords, which meant the horses had to wade through the cold mountain waters.

Philippe cursed the clap of thunder and the rain that now came down even harder as they crossed a mountain stream.

'There is one consolation, though,' said Isaac as they rode on through the night between the dark wooded slopes. 'Means there is less likelihood of musket attack.'

'That's true, because of the rain?' said Philippe.

'Ha, of course, a musket will not fire in the wet,' added Jacob.

'Indeed,' said Isaac. 'Gunpowder does not like water any more than we do!'

He was right, of course. For although Jacobite scouts were certainly following their progress, the Williamite detachment encountered no enemy vedettes, and they breached the hill of Faughart as the sun cracked through the violet clouds over Dundalk Bay. Jacob scrutinised the sky, as did others of the detachment. Then, with satisfaction, he said: 'There is no smoke!'

The cavaliers had battled hard against fatigue and the elements, but it had paid off. Now they rode into Dundalk town, saved from destruction and without a shot being fired. Young Berwick, having got wind of the cavaliers' approach, had given the order to flee during the night.

*

The unwalled town consisted of one long street that ran north to south from the tip of the Kilcurry estuary. The first task was to scour both town and surrounding country in search of provisions for the men and forage for the horses. Jacob and Philippe searched the deserted houses, but Berwick's army had already helped themselves. The two men could gather but a beggarly store of corn, hardly of any consequence for the cavalry detachment, let alone the main bulk of the army soon to arrive.

Thankfully, some hours later, as the main army marched down the hill, sopping and caked in mud, a patrol turned up with two thousand sheep, and the slaughter began.

Meanwhile, Delpech and de Sève dried their clothes and stole forty winks in a vacant house, relieved to find a bed, a hearth, and shelter from the howling wind and the rain. But barely had any notion of rudimentary comfort seeped into their tired minds and limbs than the call was raised again. This time, it was for officers to double back through the mountain to Moyry Pass to help retrieve the soldiers who had collapsed from hunger, fatigue, or illness.

Jacob saddled up with Philippe, Isaac, and the rest of the task force. Though the rain had ceased, eight thousand hooves and twenty thousand marching boots had turned the mountain trail into a quagmire in places. But within the hour, they had reached Moyry Castle, a rudimentary three-storey tower house that guarded the pass, and which at present gave refuge to the lame men.

*

Even though his limbs were as stiff as an old maid's, Damon Laverty could have kicked himself for joining their stupid war in the first place. And he had no inclination to leave the tower house, especially so late in the day. It was more than he could bear to pull his aching body away now from the drowsy heat of the fire crackling in the hearth on the second floor. The dry logs piled at the side of the fire had been a constant source of comfort. He had been looking forward to a nice warm night with a solid roof over his head, away from the relentless wind and dampness of camp life.

'Up you get if you want food tonight, soldier!' said the sergeant, a man chosen to stick with the stragglers for his stern but indulgent temperament, uncommon for a man of his station. A seasoned soldier, Sergeant Tatlock had seen many a comrade fall in the line of duty, and he knew most of this untidy lot would probably not live to tell their tales. Even so, his mission was to shepherd them into camp.

Damon now preferred to keep his own company, especially since the recent talk of Roman Catholics needing to be purged from the Williamite rank and file. It had filtered down to him that Schomberg had become increasingly wary of Jacobite sympathizers. Faced with a growing lack of resources, recruiters had not been overly cautious as to their recruits' religious backgrounds. Catholic soldiers had been told to show themselves. Those who had done so had not been ill-treated, for they were still soldiers of the English army. Many had been wrongly sent to Ireland and so were shipped off to fight against the French in northern Europe. Damon would have stood up likewise, but what if he was sent packing back to his garrison instead? He would dance at the end of a noose just like those Protestant deserters. Besides, he did not want to fight the French on the flats of Flanders. So he had curled up and kept himself to himself.

'Ow!' he croaked, on feeling a sharp dig in his butt.

'You're taking the piss, soldier! ON. YOUR. BLOODY. FEET! NOW!' roared Tatlock, which sent shock waves through the lad's skull. Not wanting another boot in his crack, Damon climbed slowly to his feet. He gathered his overclothes, hung out near the fire. He put on his breeches, jacket, and boots. Then he followed the line of fatigued and ailing men down the ladder to the chilly ground floor.

Twenty minutes later, they were assembled in the grey light of the afternoon in the cattle enclosure that surrounded the stone keep. From here, the feeblest were given transport, while the walking sick were met by their mounted escort, waiting to lead them to Dundalk.

It was a two-hour march to camp that would take three. Because of the deep, slippery mud left in the wake of the main army, the caravan took a different route where the ground would be firmer. But they came upon a swollen stream where the ford required a quick fix for the marchers to pass over.

Damon hardly had the force to stand in the chain, let alone pass on the broken stones for the next soldier to place. At one point, he lost his footing and found himself thigh-deep in cold, rushing water. The sergeant boomed his discontent. Then he said: 'Now you're in the bloody drink, soldier, you might as well wade to the other side and wait under the trees!'

Half an hour later, the men were marching over the stepping stones. Damon got up to join the line, staggering onwards in the muddy path in his sodden boots and breeches as if he were dragging nine-pound cannonballs attached to his ankles.

'Close up the rear, soldier!' roared the sergeant. But, unable to carry himself any faster, Damon lagged behind. Then he saw one of the horses up ahead swing round. The next moment, a hand was thrust before him.

'Give me your hand!' said the horseman to the foot soldier.

Damon recognised the French lieutenant.

'Yes, Sir, thank you, Sir,' said Damon, his foot in the vacated stirrup, quite chuffed that his salute back at Newry camp had borne its fruit. The saddle was warm, and the horse's hide made excellent leg warmers.

'Your name?' said Jacob.

'Private Laverty, Sir.'

'Well, Laverty, do not drop off, do not fall off, and we will be in camp an hour before sundown. A bowl of mutton stew will be waiting for you.'

'Thank you, Sir,' said Damon, heartened by the prospect of meat.

They spoke briefly about the terrain, the uncommonly

wet season, and what the Irish soldier's father did for a living.

'How old are you, Laverty?'

'Eighteen and a half, Sir.'

'Oh,' said Jacob, taken aback at such a young age.

'Aye, same age as the Duke of Berwick, I am told, Sir,' added Damon in as virile a voice as he could muster, which was not difficult given its croakiness.

'What would your mother say about you being in the English army?'

'That I'm a heathen, Sir,' said the lad spontaneously; he regretted it the moment it came out. So he hastened to add: 'But I'm not, Sir. I believe in God as much as the next man.'

'That is good,' said Jacob. He did not ask if the lad was of Protestant or Catholic ancestry.

On they rode, falling silent the rest of the way, Damon fighting against the desire to sleep. He was a stocky lad, and normally resistant to the elements, having spent many a rough day on the water fishing with his da. But it was different out at sea. For a start, there was always something to do to keep your mind alert. And his da never went out twice, only once every day, except in stormy weather and on the day of the Lord. 'Otherwise, you'll not give your body time to flush out all the chill,' his da would say to his mates, who were sometimes tempted to go out on a second tide.

And then there was always the reward of the catch, and the thought of his ma's stew and a blazing fire to chase away the damp inside. Damon could hear her nightly refrain: 'Remember to thank the Lord and his Mother for your safe return!'

'Here we are,' said the French lieutenant, pulling on the reins of his mount. Jacob was glad they had arrived, what with the lad's coughing in his back.

Evening was encroaching. Fires were lit amid the clusters of men, bivouacked in a field dotted with trees that looked over Dundalk Bay. It lay before Kilcurry River and was strewn with soldiers' clothes hung out to dry on trees and on lines. Not all the tents had been erected, which Jacob took to mean that they would not be staying long.

'Grab yourself some stew,' said Delpech, pointing towards the camp mess, where camp followers were dishing out food to a swarm of men.

Damon roused himself from thoughts of his soft feather bed as he let go of the rosary buried in his pocket. Groggy-headed, he thanked the Frenchman and climbed down. He had forgotten his body was stiff, his ankles still weak, as he swung his right leg back over the horse's rump. On hitting the ground, he stumbled backwards and fell on his butt.

'You all right?' said the French lieutenant.

'Aye,' said the lad, 'I'll not fall any further!'

Getting to his feet, he instinctively felt his jacket pocket. A look of alarm spread across his face.

Jacob saw, in the half light, at the same time as the soldier, a wooden rosary lying in the mud where the lad had fallen.

'I'm not a spy, Sir,' said Damon.

'I don't doubt you,' said Jacob, who thought the lad to be sincere. He had spoken of his home like any homesick soldier. Not an ounce of disdain against Protestants came out of his mouth, even though Jacob had laid a few rhetorical traps. 'But keep it inside your pocket, eh?'

Jacob was not against Catholics, and he appreciated that some people needed material rituals to connect with the Lord. He rode off to put his horse to pasture, and to let the lad recover his rosary. He thought nothing more of it.

SIXTEEN

JEANNE WAS DRAINED after trudging with Paul from the spinning wheel maker's shop in the late summer sunshine.

They had hiked through the interminable streets of Whitechapel and up Brick Lane. In her life, she had never seen so many people in one day. It made her wonder where they all lived. It was also both surprising and reassuring to hear French so often spoken as they had approached the weaver district where she had her digs.

Back in her rooms, the excitement of her purchase was such that she found the strength to laugh and dance around it with her son, and at the risk of making the floorboards creak. The spinning wheel would bring in enough revenue to sustain them, even if it meant long hours of repetitive wrist-aching activity. But it was a price she was willing to pay if it rendered her free from the alms. And through the church, she had already met tailors and dressmakers who would be willing to take her yarn.

She poured two glasses of lemon water from an earthenware jug while Paul eagerly put the spinning wheel together. But then, as she contemplated how the light fell in the room, a cloud darkened her brow at the recollection of the landlady's glare on the first-floor landing. Mrs Smythe had opened her door as they had passed. Standing with her back arched on her threshold, arms cradling her large bosom, she had looked frowningly upon them as they carried a stool and spinning wheel parts.

'Bonjour, Madame,' Jeanne had said, holding the stool and the spoked wheel. She could have kicked herself for not remembering how to address a person in English. The landlady had knitted her eyebrows, tutted, then stepped back into her rooms and closed her door.

Jeanne had only spoken to her once before, just over a week earlier, through the old pastor who had translated the rules of the house upon her arrival. Those rules made no mention of a spinning wheel, though perhaps she ought to have at least informed the landlady first. Jeanne remembered the look of disapproval when she had expressed that she did not know English yet. She did not see herself now fumbling like a child for words she could not translate and trying to mime out an explanation. So she had not said anything. She realised, however, she would have to learn the fundamentals of the language quickly if she was to get by.

It wasn't as if she had purchased a cumbersome loom that might require a licence, though. And besides, she had learnt her lesson in Geneva, and could not afford to pay for a loom only for it to be smashed. But a spinning wheel: every home had a spinning wheel . . .

*

Next morning, Jeanne rose with the lark and went to fetch water from the well.

She went early, while Paul was still sleeping, so she would not have to queue. Not because she was pressed for time or did not want to see people. No, by going early, at least she would not have to foolishly avert eye contact. For she felt embarrassed at not being able to even fumble for a greeting in the vernacular. Of course, she had spoken with people at the church a number of times, but everyone there spoke to her in French. Moreover, having lost all her capacity to communicate in her usual simple elegance, she was now totally bereft of her standing and dignity. Snobbishly, perhaps, she did not want people to think she was inferior, and she could hardly wear a sign on her back telling people she was born a countess.

The night had been stifling, and now the wind had picked up, blowing thick, dingy clouds from the east. It felt like it was going to rain. She passed by a square where linen was blowing in the wind on the tenterhooks. The way was familiar to her now, and she had previously seen that this was where cloth was stretched and hung out to dry. As she approached the well, her heart sank on seeing two ladies, one short and pudgy in middle age, the other a young maiden, slim and lithe. The young maiden gave the older lady good day as Jeanne arrived. Jeanne smiled and nodded.

Marie-Anne Chaumet was a spirited maiden, born in Lyons with a natural smile. She had arrived in London with her aunt and uncle and was apprenticed to a French weaving house whose owner also originated from Lyons. Her youth allowed her to take life one day at a time and worry neither about the past nor the future.

'I hope it's not the end of summer already,' she said to the lady in her naturally perky voice as she looked up at the heavens.

'Oh, you are French!' responded Jeanne, in her normal, restrained bourgeois voice, though not without a note of cheeriness. She was nonetheless glad to set the tone.

'Marie-Anne,' said the younger woman, neither impressed nor put out by the bourgeois accent. She knew that most Huguenots were no better off than she was, and this lady was no exception. Otherwise, why would she be fetching water herself? She went on. 'But they call me Mary around here, though,' she said.

Jeanne presented herself with her nobiliary particle, something she usually dropped, it being overly long. But here, alone as she was, she might only get one chance to make known her identity and true station. Then, fearing class isolation, with a smile she said: 'But Jeanne Delpech will do.'

Marie-Anne spoke of her learning to become a weaver at the house of Dublanc, once a fine house with a solid reputation for quality work in Lyons.

'I have just purchased a spinning wheel myself,' said Jeanne, before realising how lowly it must appear she had fallen.

'You, Madame?' said Marie-Anne.

'My . . . my husband is at war,' said Jeanne, which was explanation enough.

'It has taken the best of them,' said Marie-Anne, with a momentary droop in the mouth as she recalled the young man who used to give her the eye. But it soon passed, and, smiling, she said: 'Anyway, there's always a demand for cloth, but weaving is where the money is, Madame, and that's what I want to be. Then I shall marry a weaver. Can you weave?'

'I can, actually. My speciality is thick cloth.'

'That's good; it'll soon be the season for it. I'm sure you could get employment.'

That was precisely what Jeanne wanted to hear, and it confirmed her decision to purchase a small loom. She would put it by the south-facing window that overlooked the back yards. But would she be within legality if she got one? She would ask at the church. If the maiden's employer was allowed to ply his trade, then why couldn't she? She would specialise in the cloth of Montauban and perhaps a few fineries. She would be no match for the master silk weavers, but at least she could earn a better living than from spinning.

'I was actually thinking of getting my own loom.' Jeanne wondered if she had said too much to this infectious young maid. But she was relieved to find someone to converse with in her native tongue. 'However, I must learn English first. Do you speak any English, Mademoiselle?'

'I should hope so. I've been here for two years, Madame,' said Marie-Anne; then she added: 'You need not worry. Just get mingling with the ladies here. It'll soon rub off on you. Some of them prattle on whether you understand them or not. You'll soon pick up the lingo.'

'You must be very clever,' said Jeanne. Marie-Anne had never thought of herself as clever before; she grinned. Jeanne went on. 'If only I could get the first words to help me enter into conversation, it would help. But I still don't know how to give someone *good day*, let alone say *métier à tisser*. And how do they distinguish between the formal and the informal *you*?'

'Oh, they don't. They just say *you* as in *Good day to you, Madam*. So, no complications there. And the word for *métier à tisser* is *loom*. Loo-oo-oom.'

'Loo-oo-oome,' said Jeanne, finding the word funny, and was unable to resist a spurt of laughter.

'There, easy!' said Marie-Anne, laughing with her. As they walked together back towards the tenterground, Marie-Anne told her the English terms for such words as *yarn* and *cloth* and *bucket of water*, the last of which Jeanne already knew from her son, who had picked it up. If she could pick up patois while living in hiding in France, and some German when in Schaffhausen, then there was no reason why she could not learn the language here, especially if this was to be her son's new home and her place of work.

'Good day to you, Madam,' said Marie-Anne in English as they parted company at the tenterground.

'Good day too yoo, Mademoiselle,' said Jeanne.

The town was beginning to wake, and so would Paul. *Loom, yarn, water*, said Jeanne to herself, in cadence with her march past dogs barking at a cat, venders pushing handcarts, and masons carting bricks and mortar into the city. She felt lighter despite the gathering clouds overhead and the extra weight of the water pail, and she was resolute to learn the vernacular. She would write to Jacob to bid him to return, and she would find out the law regarding weavers. She did not want to pay for a loom for it only to be smashed. But perhaps the guilds were not as stringent here as in Geneva. Perhaps the demand, given the size of the population, was much greater.

*

She tried to step lightly as she climbed the rickety staircase of the tenement house. Not that it would have made any difference. For the landlady had been keeping an ear out for her and opened her door as Jeanne set foot on the landing.

Mrs Smythe had been thinking. In fact, all night she had been tossing and turning, as much because of the new lodger as because of the prickly heat. She had a profound sense of duty, did Mrs Smythe, drilled into her from an early age by her father, a corporal who had served under Cromwell. She was now faced with the duty to report potentially unlawful activity under her roof. Spinning for home use was one thing, but what if the lady was planning on spinning as a business? There again, the French lady seemed well-to-do, her French husband had gone off to fight in William's war in Ireland (she had checked the uniform), and she did not offer superfluous smiles like some of the desperate wretches just over from France, who then stole her clientele. But a French woman potentially spinning for money in her rooms—whatever next? A loom, perhaps?

But Mrs Smythe also had a head for business. So she had thought up a line of attack that would satisfy her sense of duty and perhaps revive her enterprise. The question was, did the woman even know how to weave? She had decided to find out.

The French lady returned her nod as she stood on her threshold, trying to crack a smile, which she knew did not become her, so she did not try to push it too far. 'Madame,' she said. 'I see you have purchased a spinning wheel.'

'Madame?' said Jeanne with a guarded smile at the landlady, who looked perfectly insincere. 'Sorry?' she added. It was one of a dozen words she had picked up since her arrival.

'A spinning wheel! You are a spinner!' said Mrs Smythe, trying her best to get through to her. But visibly, the woman couldn't understand her arse from her elbow. 'A spin-ner. You

. . . spinning wheel,' she said more loudly while drawing a wheel in the air.

'Ah,' said Jeanne. 'Ze spinning veel.' She could hardly pretend she did not have one. And she saw her hopes suddenly evaporating. No matter, she thought; she would use the money she had set aside for the loom to find other lodgings where she could keep her wheel and retain her meagre independence until Jacob returned. 'And . . . vat . . . ze spinning wheel?' she continued, failing miserably to make a proper sentence. She could not help feeling a fool, unable as she was to construct the simplest of questions. So she rinsed her mouth with a spluttering of French in an attempt to recover some form of dignity.

'No, dear, in England we speak English!' said Mrs Smythe.

Jeanne put down her pail and crossed her arms. She was not going to be bullied by a lowly English matron. 'Vat you want? Madame?' she said curtly.

But Mrs Smythe cracked another smile, wider this time so that it frankly pleated the corners of her mouth. Then more gently, she said: 'Come, Madame. Please, come with me.' She closed her door behind her and stepped across the landing. *I'm not gonna blimmin' eat you, my dear*, she thought to herself on seeing the French lady's eye of defiance. 'Come, Madame, have no fear, leave the water here. No one will take it.'

Jeanne wondered what on earth she wanted. The landlady beckoned her to follow her down the rickety staircase. She was evidently making an attempt to be civil, so

Jeanne followed on down to the ground floor, where Mrs Smythe showed her into a weaver's workshop. It was full of labelled shelves of reels of yard, patterned fabric draped along the back wall, a great loom that took up a quarter of the space, and a dressmaker's workspace with bowls of buttons and reels of ribbon arranged by colour. The landlady pointed next to the loom. 'Spinning wheel,' she said.

Jeanne nodded. She wasn't stupid; she understood the first time. But she was nonetheless surprised to see the set-up and could now understand why the woman might be concerned about the potential competition. Too bad, thought Jeanne; she would find new lodgings. 'Yes, and loom!' she said, pointing to the large machine.

'Do you know how to work it?' said the landlady, forgetting her gesturing. Then she raised her voice while doing invisible actions with her hands. 'Can. You. Work. Loom?'

'Me work loom?' said Jeanne, cottoning on at last. 'Yes. I do loom and . . . er . . .' Jeanne stopped short of saying she would move on because she did not know how to say it. But then, Mrs Smythe's mouth broadened into an uncommon smile as she clapped her hands together under her chin.

'Good. Madame Delpech, you work here on this loom? For me, yes?' Was the woman offering her a job? 'You work your spinning wheel afternoons. And here in mornings, you work the loom, yes?' said the landlady, gesturing to the loom, then to the ceiling as she spoke.

With further insistence from Mrs Smythe, Jeanne at last gathered the deal. She would be able to keep her spinning wheel to spin yarn in the afternoons and work mornings on the loom at the workshop. At least it would keep her within the bounds of legality while she learnt the language, and she would not have to pay for a loom which might end up smashed anyway.

To Mrs Smythe's joy and relief, the French lady gave a short, definite nod of acceptance.

Mrs Smythe had her French fineries. The Smythe workshop was back in business!

Jeanne had only been in England over a week, and already she had a job. But how much would she be paid? She would ask Marie-Anne the going rates. But more worryingly, what would it be like to work under her landlady?

SEVENTEEN

IT SOON BECAME clear to Jacob that the army would not be pushing directly to Dublin as Isaac de Bostaquet had first suggested.

'Apparently, the supply ships that were supposed to put in at Carlingford Lough are encountering contrary winds,' said Isaac to Jacob and Philippe the morning after their arrival. He had just walked back up to camp from the town where the old marshal had set up his headquarters. The three Huguenot cavaliers were standing outside their mess tent, where de Bostaquet's valet was hammering home pegs. Jacob had advised that the tent stand in the sea breeze to chase away bad air whenever the sky hung low.

'I only hope we don't dig in for long here,' said Jacob, scanning the marshland to the east and the swollen river to the west. 'We might be well-protected from enemy attack, but there is little defence against the bane of bad air!'

Not only lack of provisions plagued the Williamite army. The outbreak of disease en route was growing worse, and already, numerous deaths had been registered.

The next day, parties of cavaliers were sent to scour the

countryside for food. Jacob rode with Philippe and de Bostaquet to Carlingford, an hour away in the saddle at a good pace, in search of reserves and for news of the supply vessels from Belfast. The morning was clement, the tide was out, and the bay lay placid as they set out along the damp track that ran through heathland, gorse, and heather. 'I had no idea there were so many,' said de Sève as they cantered along half a dozen flatbed carts carrying the deceased and the sick. The sick carts were also headed for Carlingford, where a hospital had been set up inside the stone castle by the lough.

Once in open country, they could have been anywhere, far away from disease and conflict, thought Jacob as they cantered on at an even pace. 'Don't know about you, Delpech, my good fellow, but the less time I spend in camp, the better,' said Philippe, letting out a chuckle. His spirits had lifted now that they had removed themselves from the dingy scenes of camp squalor and strife.

As Jacob nodded in agreement, his eye caught a puff of smoke in the distant foliage past Philippe's right ear. It was instantly followed by a crackle of shot. Philippe's mount let out a horrific squeal of agony as its legs gave way in full canter. 'Enemy attack!' roared Jacob, shortening the reins to regain control of his frightened steed.

'Over there!' trumpeted Isaac up ahead. He pointed to the higher ground to the left, where a flash of Jacobite redcoats had launched their mounts into full gallop. 'After them, gents!' hollered Isaac. 'We have the advantage of loaded pistols!'

'Philippe's down!' shouted Jacob, but Isaac had pushed his horse into a thundering gallop in the direction of the fleeing Jacobite vedette of three dragoons. Now riding close to his horse's mane, a primal instinct suddenly took hold of Delpech, overwhelming his initial desire to ride back to his fallen friend.

Pistol in hand, Delpech charged ahead like the wind, pushing his horse in the mud-splattered tracks of de Bostaquet's mount. But the enemy had a head start. And visibly more familiar with the mountain terrain, they knew where exactly to pass through the boggy patches and increased the distance that separated them from their pursuers.

Isaac led the chase for a minute more. But after losing eye contact, he then raised a hand, and with the other pulled on his reins to halt.

They gave a mutual nod, and then swiftly doubled back to the ambush point, where they found de Sève's horse lying panting, frightened, and helplessly in pain on the ground. Philippe was sitting, one leg stretched out, by the animal's head. He lowered his pistol on the party's approach and placed his hand on the horse's neck, now uttering sounds of comfort in an effort to calm the horse down.

Jacob dismounted and handed his reins to Isaac, who remained in his saddle to keep a lookout.

A cavalier's horse is more than a steed. It is an ally, a loyal friend that will run through hell, carry you despite hunger and fatigue until it drops. Philippe's feeling for his mare was no different. She had carried him when he was fatigued, had taken him through the mountains, across rivers, through mud and rain. He continued to speak to her, calming her nerves, until she laid her head flat on the ground, blood streaming from her eye, her leg clearly fractured. He passed his loaded pistol to Jacob. Jacob knew it would take a hard heart to kill one's own horse. Delpech returned a solemn nod. He took position near the mare's head, Philippe's pistol in one hand, his own in the other. 'All right, Rosy, girl, all right,' said Philippe, then gave Jacob the nod. Jacob fired twice into her skull.

'Better make tracks out of here!' said Isaac, breaking the short silence after the birds had flown and the horrible echo had died down. Struggling with his leg, Philippe managed to climb behind Jacob to finish the run around the mountain to Carlingford Town.

*

The seaside market town had suffered the same fate as Newry. Sacked, torched, and deserted, it provided no sustenance except for some oatcakes that they took from a few breadless inhabitants. In return, Jacob gave them the whereabouts of Philippe's dead horse, which they could cart back to Dundalk camp for a handsome reward and food.

'We will catch up with you on the road to Dundalk, once we have taken our fellow to the castle hospital,' said Jacob, translating for Isaac.

The three Huguenots proceeded to the waterfront where there was still no sign of supply ships. Philippe by now was unable to walk on his swollen ankle, which Delpech, after a brief diagnosis, suspected to be fractured. So the next stop was Carlingford Castle, where they could leave Philippe in the qualified hands of the medical staff.

The great room where medieval banquets were once held by day and where castle dwellers used to sleep by night was now occupied by the battle-wounded from Carrickfergus and, since yesterday, by the first casualties of the fever from Dundalk.

'Straw, blankets, and two bowls of gruel a day,' said Jacob, once Philippe had been given a spot among other French patients.

'Wonderful, I shall be living it up!' quipped Philippe, who spluttered into a cough.

Isaac stood shuffling from foot to foot, impatient to hit the road. For one, he detested hospitals; it was after all where most men died. Secondly, he was anxious to return to camp to warn the approaching sick convoy of roaming enemy vedettes. Although now with hindsight, he suspected the musket attack to be an opportunist strike by a straggling patrol.

'Cheer up. This could mean the end of the war for you, my dear fellow,' said Jacob to Philippe. 'There's a good chance they will send you back to England!'

'What for?' said Philippe. 'No one awaits me in England, except Mrs Smythe for her rent,' he joked. 'I shall stay here until I can walk. Then I shall hitch a ride back to Dundalk on a cart.'

'That's the spirit,' said Isaac. 'I will send you some moor rabbit. The soldiers eat them; not much meat but tasty all the same.' Then he stepped forward with bonhomie and gave Philippe a farewell pat on the arm to prompt their departure. They were yet to catch up with the local folk sent to recover Philippe's horse before the bloat set in.

*

Over the next couple of weeks, Jacob took part with Isaac and other officers in foraging missions, escorting dragoons into the surrounding fields to harvest hay and corn, which they rolled up and tied to their mounts. There had been brief visual encounters with Jacobite vedettes who, though they sometimes harried them in their toil, as yet had not ventured into armed conflict.

Every day Jacob returned from the field, he noticed a new development in the construction of the camp. Still unsure of his officers' true alliances and of the ill-trained Williamite army, Schomberg had decided not to advance on Dublin straight away but to dig in at Dundalk until his supply chain was secured and his army better trained. Earthworks were built, entrenchments dug, and batteries established at strategical points from the southern tip of the main street to the northern encampment on the other side of the Kilcurry River. Tents were gradually replaced by huts and barracks built from felled trees. And on each return, Jacob noticed the fever spreading with increasing ferocity.

One day, having harvested as much as their allotted field had to yield, they rode back into camp earlier than usual. Jacob was struck by the sight of tens of carts heading out on the road to Belfast, each transporting a grim load of dead soldiers. He cast a look of incomprehension to Isaac, who looked equally dumbfounded and sickened. Surely, had there been an assault, they would have heard the cannon fire that sounded the alert and bade their urgent return. But Jacob concluded that the guns had remained silent, for there was no hint of the acrid smell of gunpowder in the air. The entrenchments presented no damage, men around the camp yonder were being drilled as usual in the techniques of battle, and most of the horses were still in pasture, some sheltered in their newly made huts.

'What has happened here?' called out Jacob on approaching a cart driver.

'Camp fever, Sir,' replied the Irishman glumly. 'Dropping like sheep, they are. At this rate, ol' James won't even need to attack.'

The unhealthy spot, the atrocious weather conditions, and weeks of undernourishment had leagued in a tripartite force to assail the Williamite army, bringing not the bane of war's hellfire, but the scourge of disease. Soon, hundreds of men were dying weekly, hundreds more falling ill, while every day, Schomberg said his prayers in the local church. And in his indecision, he delayed any move forward. Needless to say, Jacob was glad to be in the saddle, and glad too that he had left Philippe in the healthier sea air of the castle by the lough.

*

The camp was divided by regiment and nationality. But old animosities rankled and tensions still grew, exacerbated by the rumour of a Catholic conspiracy within the ranks. And what put more oil on the fire was James Stewart's offer of a pardon to Williamites willing to defect to the Jacobite army—an army well fed, paid in real money, and provided with bedding and shelter from the oncoming sickly season.

Damon Laverty had grown ill. Even so, if there was a way to get back to his regiment and then be sent home without the risk of execution, he would have jumped at the chance. But Schomberg gave the order for no unauthorized soldier to venture out of camp upon pain of death. And he rewarded with money for every deserter or spy apprehended dead or alive.

One afternoon, Sergeant Tatlock came to Laverty's tent and ordered the private to get his carcass down to the bridge, where carts would be waiting to take the sick out of the godforsaken camp. Damon wondered if he could make it without shitting himself again as he laboriously pulled on his knapsack. Off he trudged with a horde of walking sick, withered and sallow. 'Jesus,' he thought, 'if the boys attacked now, we'd be done for!' But lacking the energy to carry the thought any further, he plunged his hand into his pocket and fingered his rosary beads.

*

The late September sky had opened up, offering a respite from the previous weeks of dismal weather. Jacob had been in the saddle since daybreak. His foraging party had been sent into the Carlingford-Newry mountains, the land south of Dundalk being now out of bounds, with the Jacobite army having seized the bridge over the Fane.

Delpech was standing in a field where his party of twelve were harvesting corn. He had advised that they cut from the top of the slope, the dominant side, where it was drier and easier to hack the stalks that grew in little mounds in sets of three or four. But even in the rare sunshine, it was still a hard graft. The razor-edged leaves could slice bare skin, so it was wise to keep covered all over, right up to the chin. But no one complained, really; at least they were being useful, and were out of the cursed camp. And there were perks to the job too. They had just had lunch, a proper lunch of cooked corn on the cob and fresh rabbit roasted on the spit, dowsed with a skinful of ale.

The men had risen from their meal and, under Isaac's

command, had scattered across the field to their allotted patch. Jacob could now hear the rhythmic sound of the chopping of corn stems that punctuated the song of swallows, catching insects fleeing the massacre.

'Another hour, lads!' Jacob heard Isaac call out.

He continued to cast his eyes over the valley from the south-facing mountainside while peeing against a tree, one of a cluster that flanked the cornfield. From here, he had a clearer view over the valley and distant hills, not unlike the view from the Quercy ridge of his homeland, where the great plain stretched to the foothills of the Pyrenees. These Irish folk certainly knew how to work their land, he mused as he contemplated the patchwork of fields, some divided by low stone walls. It was all predominantly of deep greens, beautiful under the patchy blue sky, which made it all the more difficult to believe how men could confine themselves to the squalor and damp of an unhealthy encampment. But such was the madness of man in his folly for war. Jacob's horse nickered as if to agree with his wandering thoughts.

During his lunch break, Delpech had read the letter again from Jeanne asking him to return to England. It had put the spring back into his step and restored his hope, knowing she had made it to London. According to Isaac, there would likely be nothing more than a standoff between the two armies before the bad season prevented military manoeuvres. The ground between them offered no firm battlefield, only marshland which would bog down man and horse.

'If we go into winter quarters, you might get winter leave,' Isaac had said.

Jacob finished peeing while his horse, holding its head

high, snorted its unrest more loudly. 'Easy, boy,' said Jacob, patting him on the neck. 'What's the matter . . .'

Then the source of his steed's fright came into earshot. A dull drumming quickly grew into a thunderous rumbling of hooves.

'Enemy attaaack!' he heard someone cry out from across the field.

Jacob's foot was in the stirrup when the first shots were fired, closely followed by more musket shots and the cries of men.

Now in his saddle, Jacob could see a dozen Jacobite attackers bearing down onto the harvested part of the cornfield. Their brandished sabres now shimmered like scythes in the late-summer sun. They had already emptied their pistols into the furthermost foragers caught by surprise.

With his loaded pistol at the ready, Delpech quickly pushed on to the field where his fellow cavaliers were mustering. Some were only just mounting, having run to their horses tethered in the shade of the trees.

They cried out in unison: 'A l'attaque!'

Jacob pushed forward with half a dozen Huguenot cavaliers to meet the assailants, who were mercilessly swiping at the men still running back from midfield. Isaac, who should normally have been in his saddle, had two enemy horses on his tail. Jacob broke from the pack, brandishing his pistol. He steadied his posture, held his breath, and gave fire. On the impact of the ball, his target fell from his horse. Isaac, meanwhile, dived to one side, narrowly escaping a beheading.

All about, the foraging party were retaliating, many of the attackers now fleeing under fire, having spent their shot.

Bearing in mind his poor performance when wielding his sabre during his brief training, Jacob decided to dismount. Besides, his first-ever encounter on a battlefield had been on foot with buccaneers in Cuba, and, having seen them annihilate a Spanish cavalry unit, he had more faith in their ways than in those of the army.

'Stay on your horse!' shouted Isaac. But Jacob had already swung his leg over.

The fallen Jacobite was already on his feet, blood seeping from the musket ball Jacob had planted into his left shoulder. But with the adrenaline of conflict now pumping through his veins, Delpech no longer envisaged the man. He now only saw the target. The choice was clear, kill or be killed.

The Jacobite, a burly veteran, visibly felt the same way. He charged. Jacob parried. After crossing swords three times, Jacob could now feel his strength ebbing away under the weight of each clash, the last of which resulted in a cut to his cheek. Again the Jacobite thrust forward; again Jacob parried. But this time, recalling his buccaneer training on the deck of a ship, he stuck out a foot as his assailant passed, knocking him off balance. The Jacobite swung round erratically, too widely. Jacob deflected the blow, leaving the adversary's guard momentarily open. With no time to think, Delpech thrust his curved sword deep into the belly. He pulled out his blade. Blood streamed out, the man went down—it was horrible. But there was no time to dwell.

'Your back, Delpech!' cried out Isaac on the approach of hooves to Jacob's rear.

As he instinctively crouched, he felt a sharp thud cut into his left collarbone. Then he rolled to the ground in a muddy pool as the horseman's blade swished an inch over his hatless head.

Glancing around to take stock, Jacob managed to get to his knees as the horseman manoeuvred for another attack. But for the life of him, in the slippery mud, Jacob could not get to his feet. Facing the charging horse, he would certainly be hacked, if not trampled, to death. But then he heard a loud blast behind his right ear. Looking round, he saw Isaac holding a smoking pistol.

'I knew I had it somewhere,' he said as the wounded cavalier veered off his trajectory.

Isaac hurried to Jacob's flank and gave him a hand to help him to his feet. But the horseman had visibly not had enough. He pulled his horse around for another charge.

Recalling how the buccaneers had retreated into a thicket in Cuba when faced with a mounted attack, Jacob hurled out: 'Back to the corn!'

'The stalks won't stop a horse,' shouted Isaac as they backtracked to the uncut corn a dozen yards further down.

'No, but they will break its course!'

Their backs were against the corn stems when the cavalier came coursing upon them at full gallop, holding out his sabre with his right hand. Jacob knew that, if held with a firm wrist, at this speed it could slice through a man's neck cleaner than a falling axe. But the cavalier had no choice but to pull on his reins as he approached the corn stems, breaking his steed's momentum.

Unable to use his left hand to pull the cavalier off, instead Jacob slashed at the enemy's left leg while Isaac deflected the horseman's sabre strike. The Jacobite let out a roar of sudden pain. Isaac swiftly pulled the man down to the ground and put him to death.

*

The skirmish had finished as quickly as it had begun. While Isaac searched the dead cavalier, Jacob staggered up the slope, where his previous victim lay crumpled in a pool of blood and mud. On the far side of the cut field, dead foragers lay by their shocks of corn. The wounded were being tended to.

Exhausted and clutching his left shoulder, Delpech fell to his knees, his thoughts numbed as he looked into the sky. The power to muster a prayer escaped him. So he simply watched the sun shimmering between the clouds.

After a few minutes, he felt the warm muzzle of his horse at his left cheek. As he fingered the trailing reins with his left hand, he glanced down at his red jacket, sopping wet and brown with mud. He removed his right hand from his hacked shoulder, undid two upper brass buttons, and found his white shirt sopping and crimson. 'Dear God,' he said. He had lost a lot of blood, but somehow he felt appeased in the sun, and he did not feel like paying attention to it.

But Isaac soon arrived to bring him round from the shock. Professional and efficient, he fastened Jacob's shoulder and left arm with the sash of the dead Jacobite. 'It'll keep your arm still. You don't want to be losing any more blood,' he said.

'How many?' said Jacob, nodding to the bodies on the far side of the field. They were now being loaded onto their mounts.

'At least five good men,' said Isaac. 'Come on, we'll get you properly strapped up at camp first . . . then off to the hospital.' Isaac gave Jacob a leg up so he could hoist himself into the saddle.

The dead foragers were attached to their horses along

with their day's shocks of corn, and the party rode into the valley back to camp.

*

Upon their arrival, a convoy of merchant carts was rolling out with their daily quota of dead from disease.

The sick were climbing unsteadily onto more carts that Jacob assumed were to take them to Carlingford hospital, where he too would be headed once he had recovered his effects. But first, he needed his wound to be properly bound, the ride back having loosened the sash and caused more blood loss.

On passing the line of sick soldiers, he picked out a familiar face, youthful but pasty and sickly. It was plain to see that Private Laverty was beset with fever.

'Come on, come on, a warm place and some grub await youse at the hospital, lads!' shouted the sergeant, to encourage the men to climb aboard the carts faster.

As Damon heaved his aching body into the flatbed cart, he lost his grip and slipped. He instinctively brought his other hand from his pocket to catch himself. As he did so, his rosary tumbled out and landed in the mud. Suddenly awakened by his inattention, Damon glared round quickly, then made for his communion beads, the beads that had kept him attached to God amid this inhumanity, to the Virgin Mary in the absence of his mother, to his home amid the squalor.

Behind him, Private Davies looked twice. In his delirious state, he could hardly believe his eyes. What should he do? All Catholics had been ordered to show themselves following the foiled conspiracy to infiltrate the Williamite camp. He had been warned there might still be Catholic spies among them. Davies remembered the marshal's orders: those who did not show themselves would be treated as spies and executed.

If he called the sergeant, Laverty could be hanged. Davies did not want his mess mate to be hanged, and he did not think he could be a spy either. So what should he do? He turned with his lips pursed as Sergeant Tatlock came marching down the line. But as he did so, Davies saw the barrel of a pistol in the corner of his eye suddenly being thrust forward. It belonged to the Dutch soldier behind him.

Jacob saw it too. As Laverty reached for his beads, he looked up and caught the French lieutenant's alarmed eyes.

'NOOOO!' blasted Jacob.

There was a loud detonation that covered Jacob's cry. Damon fell to the ground, clutching the item that had helped him bear up to the inhumane conditions. It would now be the item that would condemn him as a spy after death and declare innocent the puller of the trigger. But Jacob knew Laverty was no spy. He was just a homesick lad.

'Dear God,' said Delpech, 'this is madness . . .' Then he blacked out and fell from his horse to the ground.

EIGHTEEN

DELPECH HAD BEEN meaning to get to Carlingford Castle to see Philippe, but foraging duties had taken up all his waking hours, and the weeks had passed.

Jacob, of course, encountered no good Catholic nuns to cater for the sick at the castle, as he would have in his native France. The Protestant religion forbade them. It rejected the notion that wealthy men could gain God's grace by providing cash endowments to charitable institutions. However, the doctors and surgeons could at least count on female camp followers and a few wise women to dispense basic care.

With his prior knowledge and experience of battle wounds and despite the lack of laudanum, Jacob insisted that the deep slash to his shoulder be first investigated and thoroughly rid of any cloth drawn in by the blade before being cleansed in rose oil. After the harrowing and painful experience of being stitched while held to a chair, a carer dressed the wound. She then bound the arm so that the catgut suture would not come loose.

He felt calmed as the body's natural painkillers kicked in

and the carer finished working around him. He was sitting, eyes half closed, when an older matronly carer stepped into his field of vision.

'Monsieur Delpech, your friend is still here,' she said as the younger carer finalised her knot to secure his sling. Jacob looked up and nodded curtly to shake the sleepiness from his mind. The lady continued. 'I will show you to his place.'

'Thank you,' said Jacob. 'I think I know where he—'

'He has been . . . moved,' she said with solemnity.

A few minutes later, the matron was leading the way through the great room along an alley of hundreds of ailing men lying on straw ticks. Jacob slung his bag over his good shoulder as he passed the soldiers in various stages of the contagion. Its onslaught had already taken more lives than the whole of the Irish campaign put together.

With his free hand, he instinctively covered his nose from the stench of human faeces, and thought to himself that at least Private Laverty had been spared agonising in this foul place. It was small consolation, which nonetheless helped him stave off his raw feelings of injustice. But there was nothing to ward off the guilt he felt at the death of his five comrades in the field. If he had told them to start cutting the corn from the bottom rather than from the top of the slope, the assailants might have thought twice about attacking. For they would not have had the advantage of the downward slope.

'Monsieur Delpech,' said the matron in a discreet tone, after turning towards Jacob as they walked on. 'I must warn you, he has been very sick.'

'Sick? He came here for a broken ankle!'

'We believe he had already contracted the flux before his

arrival. For it took hold the day after you left him here.'

'But that was over two weeks ago, Madam. Why was I not informed?'

She explained that, besieged by the illness, they lacked time, resources, and space.

There was no point in discussing it further. He knew he would have been hard-pushed to make time for a ride to the hospital anyway.

'How is he now?'

'Very poorly.'

'Oh,' said Jacob, alarmed at the gravity in her face.

'Frankly, each day, we are never sure if he will make it through the night . . .'

She then stopped at the end of a line of sick soldiers. She gestured with her hand to an inert form lying on the floor and covered over with a blanket. They exchanged discreet nods. Then she left Jacob to it.

'Philippe,' said Jacob. The body beneath the blanket moved when Jacob bent down and gently nudged the shoulder with his free hand, the other being bound up under his frock coat. Delpech pushed aside a bowl of untouched gruel, got down to his knees, and sat back on his heels. The patient's limp hand slowly pulled back the blanket.

'Philippe?' said Jacob softly, barely able to hide his horror and grief. It was a rat-faced, beady-eyed man with a scraggly beard that glared back at him.

'Jacob, my good fellow,' said Philippe, his voice faint and hoarse. He had lost a lot of weight. His complexion was sallow, his skin sagging, and his eyes were sunken in their sockets. When he pushed aside the blanket revealing his upper body, Jacob saw he was but a pale reflection of the fine-looking man he had been in London. 'You . . . you should not have come,' he said, barely louder than a whisper.

Jacob said nothing of the wound that had forced him to visit the hospital, and he felt a pang of guilt. 'I would have come sooner,' he said, 'had I known you had been taken so poorly.'

Philippe went on. 'I am glad to see you, though, my friend.'

For want of anything better to say, Delpech gave news of the stalemate in Dundalk and the supply ships that were at last arriving from Belfast. But Philippe's misty gaze seemed to register no engagement. He just stared vacantly back at Jacob.

'Are you drinking? You must drink,' said Jacob.

Philippe shook his head once. 'Can't. All goes straight through . . .' He swallowed with difficulty, then continued. 'Listen, Jacob . . . I . . . I will not have made much of an impression on this earth . . . I fear my tracks will soon be erased. But you, my friend . . . you have a wife and family. Get out, Jacob . . . Leave this godforsaken place . . .' Philippe's voice was drying out. He paused again to muster more breath and gulped in an effort to lubricate his vocal cords.

'We shall both leave here,' said Jacob. 'Messieurs Delpech and de Sève, Merchants of London, remember?' But Philippe, not listening, went on with his discourse.

'I was wrong to bring you here . . .'

'We both came to earn a living and to fight for our beliefs, Philippe. And to prevent the spread of religious intolerance.' Jacob could not help feeling that his voice lacked conviction.

Philippe held up a feeble hand: 'Promise you will leave here, and I will die a peaceful man, Jacob.'

'You are not going to die, Philippe . . .' said Jacob. But Philippe looked desperate, and Jacob suddenly realised that a miracle was unlikely.

'No, listen . . .' said Philippe. 'My only solace now is in heaven . . . with my dear wife . . . and our infant.' Philippe struggled to swallow. Jacob suddenly feared the worst. He took his friend's hand. Philippe went on. 'But I don't know what . . . what heaven will look like. Do you know, Jacob?'

For a moment, Jacob was lost. Then he remembered his Bible. He let go of Philippe's hand, then brought out his Bible from his sack. He opened it at Revelation. He read: 'Then the angel showed me the river of the water of life, bright as crystal, flowing from the throne of God and of the Lamb through the middle of the street of the city; also, on either side of the river, the tree of life with its twelve kinds of fruit, yielding its fruit each month. The leaves of the tree were for the healing of the nations. No longer will there be anything accursed, but the throne of God and of the Lamb will be in it, and his servants will worship him. They will see his face, and his name will be on their foreheads. And night will be no more. They will need no light of lamp or sun, for the Lord God will be their light, and they will reign forever and ever.'

Philippe reached out a hand. Jacob clasped it. Philippe said: 'Read it again, Jacob.'

*

The epidemic in Dundalk claimed the lives of over six thousand men, one-quarter of the Williamite army posted there. Philippe de Sève was buried at a Protestant church, like many Huguenots whose French names were chiselled into headstones planted in the Protestant graveyards of Ireland.

Jacob was not given immediate leave. Even a soldier with one good hand could be part of a cannon crew should the need arise, and resources were running desperately low. But Schomberg's battle plan was still not on the table. So Delpech, against his friend's advice, put his medical experience to good use in the castle hospital that desperately lacked hands to help relieve the sick and the wounded.

NINETEEN

MRS SMYTHE WAS sure that if her first husband were still alive, she would be at the head of a house of half a dozen looms by now.

What he lacked in business acumen, he made up for in know-how. They had made a good team, for he had the talent to learn quickly and would have nailed the French techniques if someone had shown him. If only he had not slipped off a wherry and drowned, drunk as a lord, in the River Thames.

Since that fateful day, she had managed to navigate many a rough passage without him. More recently, she had weathered the French invasion of weavers by letting out her upper-floor rooms. She had survived the storm, and now she was raring to fight back.

Her new French employee was stringing whole sentences together. Nelly, her seamstress and second niece once removed, was learning how to set up a loom in the French fashion. And the weather was not likely to get any warmer—last night had been the coldest in November so far—which was all the better for business. Ladies would be requiring those new overcoats and suchlike they had been putting off due to a hitherto clement autumn.

But since yesterday, the leaves had fallen from trees in Spittle Fields and the old artillery garden. The freezing chill now had London firmly in its grip. By consequence, the tailors that Mrs Smythe supplied would be confirming their orders at long last. But not content to sell woollen, linen, and felt fabrics, she now wanted to get on to the fineries she had secretly dreamed of producing in the Smythe weave room, ever since the French invasion began. Her plan was to offer her clientele what they craved. In other words, the finest that Lyons could offer, and at very attractive prices.

It was early Monday morning and still pitch-black outside. She had prepared her workshop the day before so that her workers could not resist embracing her plan. She had purchased end reels of silk at a good price to use as a trial run. It would be pointless spending out on thread if no one could turn it into brocade, velvet, satin, or *peau de soie* . . .

If her plan worked, in time her deft little seamstress would take on the heavier cloth, leaving Madame Delpech to take the beam of a new loom.

The place was all aglow. She had lit a few extra lamps, which made the silk thread shimmer even more beautifully. And she had got the wood burner crackling earlier than usual so that the chill would be chased from the room come daylight.

The seamstress entered first as per her habit, for Mrs Smythe detested a late start. She allowed an exception to the rule, however, for the French lady who would invariably sail through the door like a breeze without so much as a word of excuse. But Mrs Smythe had learnt to keep the peace for the sake of good working relations, and generally made an extra effort to force her pout into a thin smile. But this morning, Madame was even later than usual, and pushed the door a full hour after sunrise.

Jeanne thought it pointless to sit down at the loom until it was light enough for her to see properly. And sometimes, the London sky was so dingy, she could hardly see properly even at midday. On those days, she would have to get the girl Nelly to do all the setting. With such a lack of bright light here, was it any wonder that weavers in France had the edge over the English when it came to colour? Not to mention that the windows here should be bigger, not smaller, to let in more light. Nevertheless, she was becoming used to the changes of life and the gloomy London sky. She had purchased warm second-hand clothes at the rag market at Petticoat Lane, and had managed to get Paul into the school at the Huguenot Church on Artillery Lane, a ten-minute walk from their rooms.

But she still had not gotten any news from her husband since early autumn, when she received a letter from him that spoke of his wound. As an enlisted officer, he had been obliged to remain at a place called Lurgan until the decision was given to end the season's war campaign and go into winter quarters. He had hoped this would mean getting leave to winter in England. She had written back to him, bidding him again to quit the army. She would rather live frugally with her gentleman merchant than receive a widow's pension. She had refrained, however, from mentioning that her daughters were still not with her.

The only news she had received since that last letter was through Mrs Smythe. She had been informed by the army that Monsieur de Sève would not be returning to her lodging house.

Jeanne had kept going, living on her meagre revenue, which she knew through Marie-Anne she could greatly increase if she offered her services to another employer. But working in the same building meant she would at least be accessible for Paul should he need her, and be there when he returned after schooling. And this morning, she had remained at his bedside, stroking his forehead, for he had come down with a nasty cold.

'Ladies,' said Jeanne in greeting as she entered the room that was noticeably warmer than usual. 'It is so cold this morning. I cannot believe it!'

Mrs Smythe struggled not to mention the lateness of the hour. She must retain her superior calmness, for Madame Delpech had already shown an ugly turn of temper on a number of occasions. Especially on one occasion, when Mrs Smythe tried to impose an extra hour of work during lunch. Jeanne had stormed off in a huff and would not return to work until two days later, narrowly averting a commercial catastrophe with one of the clients.

'Ah, Madame Delpech, have you noticed anything— apart from the lateness of the hour?' she said, which she immediately regretted, and tried to cover up the slip of the tongue with a benevolent smile.

'My son vas poorly zis night,' returned Jeanne as she scoured the room, smiled to Nelly, and noticed the shiny columns of silk thread. She took her seat at the loom.

'Well, I hope he gets better quick. Now, Madame Delpech, I have purchased the silk we spoke about last week so that you may start practicing on small items such as—'

'But I am sorry, Madam, I told you. I do not know about ze silk.'

Of course you don't, my sweetie, thought Mrs Smythe. She cracked another smile and went on: 'But you can learn, can't you?'

'How I learn?' said Jeanne, who never asked to become a silk weaver in the first place. 'I do not want.'

'Come, Madame Delpech, you are French. You must know something of silk. I suspect you are hiding your true colours again . . .'

'I do not do silk,' said Jeanne, more insistently. But her limited command of the English language turned her insistence into something bordering on rancour.

'While you are in my employ, Madame, you will have to learn!' said Mrs Smythe. She would not be talked down to by an employee who, what was more, lived virtually free of charge under her roof.

Jeanne's English had come along to allow her to express the bare necessities, but it left her without linguistic defence when it came to a verbal battle. Moreover, she now found herself physically trapped. For it would be unwise to move at the beginning of winter. 'I am not a silk weaver, Madam!' she said as her only defence.

Mrs Smythe's plan was going awry. She had hoped her good humour and the effort to purchase the beautiful silk thread would have incited the French woman to go the extra mile to satisfy her employer. Did the woman not have any professional pride? Nevertheless, Mrs Smythe was not done yet. 'Madame,' she said, trying to calm the tense atmosphere, 'I am prepared to increase your hours and pay.'

'It will make not difference,' said Jeanne. 'I am not qualified to do silk!'

'Ah, but if it is the London guild you are worried about, Madame, we are outside their jurisdiction. Why else do you think your countrymen have settled here outside the city walls?'

That was interesting to know, thought Jeanne. But even so, she would not be whipped into doing something she could not do properly. 'No, I say, Madam!' said Jeanne with finality. 'Now, I must go to my son!' She got to her feet and sailed out, head poised, into the half light of the freezing cold staircase.

*

Paul was sleeping open-mouthed. Jeanne wondered what she would do were she without him. He opened his eyes.

'Don't worry, Paul. We shall be out of here once I have found somewhere. We shall move to a nicer place.'

The boy sniffed and wiped his nose on his cuff. 'We don't have any money,' he said in his indomitable voice of reason. Then he sneezed.

Jeanne sat down on the four-poster rope bed; then she lay her head down beside him. She decided she would not return to the workshop. She would not work in any workshop. She closed her eyes, and fell into a comforting sleep.

*

There was a knock at the door.

Jeanne awoke to a glacial room, the wood burner having consumed its fuel. The tip of her nose was cold, but it was warm as toast in bed with her son, snuggled under the covers. She got up and covered over Paul, who groaned and sneezed.

'Yes, I am coming!' she called out in French in answer to a more insistent knock. She straightened her shawl and pinned back her hair, then opened the door.

'Madame,' said Mrs Smythe, standing on the landing with her big overcoat on.

'Madam?' Jeanne returned.

'I fear there has been a misunderstanding.'

Jeanne let the landlady stand on the threshold and looked levelly into her eyes, her head slightly held back. 'You mean?'

'I mean I would be much obliged if you returned to work. There is an order for your woollen fabrics. I am willing to overlook the silk until I find someone qualified to weave it, which should not be difficult as I will be offering lodgings with the job.'

'Ah,' said Jeanne, who guessed where the landlady was leading. It was surely a preamble to her eviction, was it not?

'Now, concerning your rent. Knowing your current circumstances, I have refrained from bringing it up.'

'Rent?'

'Yes, Madame. Your husband only paid for your first three months of accommodation here. So from August to the end of October. He said the money would be sent to you as part of his pay.'

Jeanne recalled the letter from Jacob, in which he briefly explained that his pay was in arrears, but that he had been told it would arrive shortly, and that money would be sent over to her.

The truth was that the Huguenot soldiers had not been paid for months. It was not considered urgent. They would hardly abscond; they had nowhere to go. Jacob had been able to borrow money for his own needs, but had no means to get any monies to his wife.

Mrs Smythe went on. 'In a letter from your husband, he asked me to allow him extra time to pay the rent. Well, I have kept my word, but the fact remains . . . your husband is in a dangerous line of work, is he not? All the newsletter reports are not good, and dare I say it, for all I know, he may even have gone the same way as Monsieur de Sève. For all I know, I may well get a message from the army like the one I got for Monsieur de Sève. Then what?'

Jeanne remained proud, unmoved, and dignified despite the turmoil inside and the freezing cold draft whirling up the stairwell.

Mrs Smythe went on. 'I am sure you are aware there has been a massacre due to camp fever. Now, you are six weeks in arrears, Madame. But, I am prepared for you to pay it back in instalments. That is, as long as I am able to count on your continued services to cover all the incoming orders. At least, until I have found a replacement for you.'

Jeanne realised Mrs Smythe was playing her trump card. But Jeanne also knew that Mrs Smythe was desperate to complete the orders, so she remained silent and let her suffer a little bit more.

'What do you say, Madame?'

'I say it is unfair,' said Jeanne at last.

'On the contrary, I have been very fair in saving you from the burden and strain of this debt. However, you will understand, I have a business to run, and a lodging house in high demand. Why, rents in the neighbourhood are going sky-high; the lands are being snapped up for building. You will not find a more spacious set of rooms for the price! Put yourself in my shoes, Madame.'

'I say it is unfair because you pay under the market rate!'

'Oh, so have I not been fair in employing you despite your lack of knowledge in silk? Weave silk, my fair lady, and I will pay you more!' Jeanne, putting her fist on her waist, was about to reply, but, holding up her hand, Mrs Smythe forestalled her. 'Nonetheless, Madame . . . Nonetheless, I will up your rate by a penny.' Mrs Smythe then pulled out a slip of paper from her pocket and handed it to Jeanne. 'Here, Madame Delpech,' she said affably, 'here are the details of the rent in arrears.' Jeanne took the slip. Mrs Smythe continued. 'May I leave it with you, Madame? I hope I can expect you downstairs tomorrow morning to fulfil the orders.'

The landlady turned to leave, then checked herself. 'Oh, and how is your son?'

'Recovering, thank you, Madam,' said Jeanne. Then she slammed the door shut, harder than she had intended.

*

Jeanne would not be walked over and exploited by a lowly workshop keeper, she thought, quite snobbishly, a trait that had nonetheless carried her above the lowly emotion of self-pity.

Through her church contacts, she told herself she was bound to find her own clientele. She had heard stories of Huguenots, from silversmiths to weavers, finding their feet and excelling in their endeavours, so why couldn't she? The London population was clearly open to the fashion and techniques brought from France, despite the war. And now she knew that being outside the city walls meant she would not be subject to London guild rules.

But what to do about the rent in arrears? She simply did

not have the ready cash to release herself from Mrs Smythe's debt. She was not alone, though. She would go to the church. She would seek advice from Pastor Daniel. If he had no answer regarding the legality of Mrs Smythe's proposition, at least he could put her in touch with someone who could help her.

It was bitter cold, and a flurry of snow covered the walk to the church on Threadneedle Street. This was the mother of Huguenot churches in and around London, where, like all Huguenots in the area, Jeanne had been registered, and through which Jacob sent his correspondence. It was also where she felt most in phase with her true nature, which made her suspect what a snob she really must be. For the Huguenots in this Soho district belonged mostly to a higher class of craftsmen than those of the church on Artillery Lane, who were mostly cloth workers.

At every turn of a corner, Jeanne never ceased to marvel at the maze of endless lanes and streets, not to mention the array of means of transport that conveyed people through them. The moment she stepped through the city gate, it all felt both grandiose and belittling. And it made her realise that she was really a country girl at heart after all.

Catholic and Protestant bells rang out in unison as they had once done in France. Jeanne had long since noticed that people did their business whatever your creed or confession here, unlike in today's France, where a foreigner was a stranger and being a non-Catholic was a crime punishable by death or a life at the oar. And to think, Jeanne used to believe that this kind of intolerance belonged to a time when people still wondered whether God had made the world flat or round. But it was happening today in her home country, whereas here, in this city of business par excellence, the religious freedom transcended the society, opening avenues and offering opportunities.

The south-facing church steps were glistening in a pool of sunshine that had melted away the night's frost. She pushed the small side door into the church, where a choir was practicing. She said a prayer and then marched to the sacristy, where she gave good day to Samuel Clement, the warden.

'I fear Pastor Daniel is out, Madame Delpech,' said Mr Clement affably. 'But if you have come about the letter, I can give it to you.'

'A letter?'

'Yes, from the army, I believe,' said Mr Clement, turning to a neatly placed pile of correspondence.

The mention of a letter from the army wiped away Jeanne's thoughts of her present dilemma as she feared the worst. A moment later, Mr Clement handed her the letter in question, sealed with the stamp of the army. She took it with solemn thanks and said she would open it later. She could not take another setback just now.

'Are you all right, Madame Delpech?' said Mr Clement.

Jeanne assured him she was fine. She thanked him again, told him to give her regards to his good wife, and walked out of the house of God. It was not a place to face her disillusionment.

Numbed by the shock, she took to walking the streets of London. A thin film of ice had formed over puddles in shaded streets where the pavement was uneven. Her feet took her down towards the river, where no tall buildings would oppress her. How she longed for open fields; how she missed the great sun-filled plain where she was born, where she had been so happy. Why is happiness such a perishable thing, she wondered, and so difficult to preserve?

She soon found herself at the riverside by Dowgate Dock, near Three Cranes Stairs. Only the buildings on London Bridge to her left blocked her view. She felt faint for lack of something inside her. She sat down on a bench and watched the boats and wherries carrying passengers wrapped up for the cold, back and forth across the Thames. She sat with her thoughts amid distant cries from stevedores and dockhands, fish wives and merchants as the old river continued its course before her under the leaden sky.

What should she do now? she wondered. How could she go on if the letter she was holding announced that Jacob had succumbed to his wounds or had contracted the terrible camp fever? Either way, crying about it would not help her situation. So she just sat there, gathering her thoughts.

'Madam. Nice day, innit?' said a cheery male voice beside her.

It was a warm voice, and a word of kindness would not go amiss right now. She glanced to her right and gave good day and a guarded smile to the gruff-looking gent, who had taken it upon himself to take a seat beside her. She did not want to appear a snob.

'French?'

'Yes, Sir.'

'I like a bit o' French,' said the man, with a crafty leer. Jeanne was not sure she understood right. He continued. 'How much then, eh?' Jeanne then looked at him in shock and horror. 'Come on, my lovely,' coaxed the man, sliding closer. 'How's about sixpence for a grope and a suck?'

Jeanne stamped to her feet, but he grabbed her arm.

'Only askin', ain't I?' he said in banter. Jeanne shook her arm from his grasp and scurried away with his barking laugh in her ears.

God, she thought, had it all come to this? Prostitution or the life of a labourer in a weave room?

The bells of St Paul's rang out behind her as she turned eastward onto Thames Street. She reflected on the possible missed chances God had laid in her path. The chance to recant, for example. Had she done so, she would still be in her beloved Montauban. Had she abjured, she would still have her children about her now, warming themselves by a well-fuelled fire. She would have lived in disaccord with her convictions, but maybe that was the price to pay.

Had she refused the path of abjuration out of pure selfishness?

If not, then for what? For the sake of religious freedom? For the right of every man and woman to follow their beliefs and their intimate convictions? For the right to walk through the doors of the church of their choice? For the right to denounce the Catholic one-thought regime, appropriated by unworthy men who created chains of power and worshipped their moneymaking schemes? Who had immorally attached their laws and political aspirations to the teachings of Christ?

Jeanne slipped on a puddle on Fish Street but managed to recover her balance. She continued on her train of thought.

True, she would still be in Montauban, but the world would be condemned to a one-thought regime if she, Jacob, and people like them had not resisted the temptation of choosing the easy path. That was all very high and mighty, but what now?

She suddenly wondered if her outlook on life was all wrong.

'Madam. Madam!'

Jeanne turned around at the call of an approaching lady. She stopped walking to let the young woman catch up with her.

'You dropped this,' she said, handing Jeanne the sealed envelope.

'Oh, thank you, Madam.'

'I know how important they are,' said the woman, who was forthright and rosy-cheeked, neatly dressed but not expensively so. She went on. 'I had one myself. My husband's a military man, too, you see.'

'Oh, I . . .'

'Cheered me up no end, so I do know how you'd feel if you'd gone and lost it . . .'

'What do you mean?'

'Ah, have a look inside, and you'll find out, Madam! Go on, open it!'

Jeanne paused a moment. The woman had a friendly face. She had run after her with the letter. She had received one like it. And it had made her happy.

At the woman's insistence, Jeanne removed her gauntlet gloves, which she held under her armpits, then broke the seal. She found it hard to decipher the English handwriting at first. She then brought her cold fist to her mouth as her eyes glistened in the freezing air.

'There, see, payment for officer's wives!' said the lady, underlining the words with her gloved forefinger.

Jeanne could hardly speak. She suppressed the impulse to cry, brushed her eyes, crushed her cold, red nose with her palm.

'Thank you,' she said to the young lady. 'Thank you!'

'Don't thank me; thank your ole man, my love. You just have to take it to the payment desk, and then you'll get what's owing to you.'

TWENTY

JEANNE STOOD BY the warp frame in the workshop.

She was wearing her thick woollen shawl over her shoulders to keep the cold and damp from her aching back, and was showing the seamstress how to set the warp. But though the girl was helpful and pretty, Jeanne found her not very bright and sometimes impertinent.

'All right, Madame Jeanne! So it's over and under and up to the top,' said the seamstress, trailing her finger over the corresponding pegs.

'Yes,' said Jeanne, trying very hard to keep calm and patient. She had already explained this part ten times to her.

Jeanne had paid her rent in arrears and agreed to carry on weaving on Mrs Smythe's loom in her frugally heated workshop for a raise of a penny, although she still had not received it. And now, with the run-up to Christmas, the orders had increased to such an extent that she was obliged to forfeit her own spinning and work the loom in the afternoons too. She had been working full days for weeks now, only able to get to church on Sundays. She felt like her world was shrinking, now reduced to her rooms and the workshop. She had received no more news from Jacob, and neither had she heard from her sister in France, now that the war prevented correspondence between the two nations.

'Over and under in form of an eight, Nelly. It is not so difficult,' said Jeanne in her heavy accent. But at least she was making sentences.

'All right, Madame Jeanne,' said Nelly, 'keep your hair on. You don't have to shout about it!'

'I am not shouting. But you must open your eyes, Nelly. You make mistake, you start again!'

'Well, I can't help it if I'm no good with machines, can I?'

'But do you want to be a weaver or no?'

'I'd much rather marry one, if you don't mind me saying! And my feet are blimmin' freezing. Ain't yours?'

Jeanne was losing her patience, and Nelly was losing her concentration again and becoming saucy.

Nelly did not appreciate being told what to do by someone who did not even speak properly. She might have been someone where she came from, but they didn't want her, did they! 'Anyway, I've got these dresses to do . . .' said Nelly, who was fed up with the French lady's moods. She was nice at first, but now she just kept talking to her as if she were a dimwit, which she was not, because dimwits don't know what they want, do they? And she most certainly did, especially since she met the gentleman the other day, when Madame Jeanne had stomped off upstairs in another one of her fits as she often did.

He was a weaver in his mid-twenties, not very tall but good-looking with long, wavy hair, just like the dead soldier who used to live upstairs, and he had smiled at her.

Mrs Smythe had introduced him to the seamstress and shown him the loom where Jeanne normally sat.

'I am purchasing a newer one. It should be assembled by next week,' Mrs Smythe had told the young man slowly and deliberately. After repeating it, and using her hands to convey what she was getting at, he had returned an irresistible accented grunt of comprehension. 'Ah, bien, monté . . . la semaine prochaine,' he had said. He was French, too, and only spoke a little English, which, with hindsight, Mrs Smythe saw as an advantage. It meant that she would command any linguistic exchange.

This weaver was young, male, and attractive, and Nelly had got to dreaming of a possible romance, unless old Aunt Smythe got in before her. But she knew deep down it was only her sense of jealousy playing tricks on her. Besides, now past mothering years, Mrs Smythe had already been through three husbands. She was only concerned with her business.

Now that she had broken in one foreigner, Mrs Smythe was ready to take on another. In fact, it had become crucial that she do so, what with the French lady's high-flown attitude, not to mention her lack of silk weaving expertise. And besides, a rebellious element could put her whole business at risk, especially now that orders were coming in fast and furious. She could not allow the momentum to slack. If she delayed the Christmas orders, she would be roasted. No one would ever trust her again.

So she had decided to invest in a new loom. While enquiring about prices and delays at the loom maker's, she had bumped into this Monsieur Chausson, a weaver's apprentice from Tours, no less. It did not take much to imagine what the mere mention of a weaver from Tours could do for her good name and business.

She had been planning on purchasing the loom after the end-of-year festivities, once her suppliers had paid her. But sometimes, you had to think on your feet and know to snap up an opportunity when the good Lord put one in front of you, because they did not come often. So Mrs Smythe had been down to the loom maker's that morning and had left a down payment, which was not an easy thing for her to do, since parting with money was something Mrs Smythe hated more than anything.

'Afternoon, ladies,' she said on entering the workshop, which lacked the familiar rhythm of the loom, a music Mrs Smythe loved more than any other.

'I thought you'd have finished setting by now. C'mon, get a wiggle on, ladies, let's get beating!' she said in a sing-song voice, punctuating her order with a clap of the hands. It was the refrain Jeanne detested most, loaded as it was with patronising superiority.

How she could have kicked herself for letting the woman get the better of her. She suppressed the impulse to stamp her foot and turn on her heels, for there were orders to honour. Instead, she smiled wryly and said in the politest voice she could muster: 'It would be easier if we had not so cold, Madam. There needs more wood on the fire.' But after only four months in the English capital, she had not mastered intonation as well as she would have liked. It came out like a demand.

Mrs Smythe had just handed over the first part of a small fortune to the loom maker. She was not in the mood for self-restraint. 'Madame, no matter how much wood goes up in flames, if you are not active, then you will always feel the cold! And besides, too much heat makes one sleepy, and I cannot have you delaying further on the orders, or they will never get done, will they!'

'I give you more hours than we agreed, Madam,' said Jeanne. 'I have kept my word, but you not. You said my pay would go up!'

'I also said, Madame, that I would have to be paid myself before I can become extravagant with pay!'

'Extravagant? You pay a lower rate than everyone!'

'Huh! Weavers are ten to a penny nowadays, my dear. It would seem all the world would be a weaver!' said Mrs Smythe, leaving the rest of her thoughts implied. But she knew she must not push it too far, for there were orders to be completed by Christmas Eve, which was in little more than a week. 'Until then,' she continued in a more temperate tone of voice, 'I promised to keep the rent at the present rate, which works out the same as an increase in pay, does it not, Madame?'

'No,' said Jeanne, standing erect. 'It removes my freedom of choice! And that, Madam, is why I am here! And you did not say you increase the rent!'

'Offer and demand, Madame,' said Mrs Smythe with a winning smile. 'But look at it this way: if the demand went down, then so would the rent!'

Jeanne was fuming inside. Did this woman think she was dumb? She would not be condescended to, and all her pent-up anxiety and fury began to boil over, which brought out her accent even more when she said: 'In zat case, I shall return to my veel, Madam!'

'You shall do no such thing if you want to keep your job. You will resume your loom!' said Mrs Smythe, emboldened by the knowledge that she no longer had to walk on eggshells, for Monsieur Chausson could easily step in for the moody French tart.

Jeanne had had enough of being talked down to by a lowly penny-pincher. She had had enough of this cold, damp place, of having to slip out and rush through her market purchases instead of enjoying the friendly banter of the vendors. She had had enough of having to refuse invitations from church acquaintances. She had fled her country in the name of religious tolerance. She was not going to forfeit her liberty to act in the very country that was fighting a war in defence of that tolerance, a country that had renounced Catholic domination, torture, and burnings at the stake for the freedom to choose.

'Then do it yourself!' she said.

'Oh, I won't need to!' said Mrs Smythe as Jeanne stomped past her to the door, which she pulled hard behind her.

Mrs Smythe was momentarily tempted to run after her. But then she remembered she did not need to. She would find the young weaver that very morning. She would tell him he need not wait for the new loom, he could start tomorrow, and that the job came with a room.

TWENTY-ONE

JEANNE STOOD BACK and admired her son, dressed in his new suit.

She had dug out a blue velvet coat, waistcoat, breeches, blue stockings, and buckled shoes at the second-hand clothes market and had altered the garments to fit properly.

It was Christmas morning, and rare sunshine flooded the apartment, setting off the lively colours. She was pleased with her handiwork and her attempt at fitting him out in clothes she thought more in keeping with his lineage. She fastened his thick, black woollen travel cloak beneath his chin, kissed his forehead, and placed his tricorn hat on his little head.

Then she put on her own heavy cloak over her beautiful oxblood boned bodice and beige woollen skirts. Her white linen neckerchief protected her bosom from draughts, and she had attached white linen cuffs for the special occasion. Next, she pinned her wide-brimmed hat over her coif and pulled on her embroidered gauntlet gloves of soft beige lambskin.

'How do I look?' she said to Paul.

'Like a countess,' he returned approvingly. 'Shall I go first to check that the coast is clear?'

Over the past week, he had served as her stairwell scout. And so far, they had not bumped into the landlady. Jeanne did not want to be asked to work in the workshop again. She had felt guilty at first about abandoning her post, but then was shocked at how quickly Mrs Smythe had replaced her, almost as if she had set her up to leave so the new weaver could make a start.

Jeanne did not want to stir up tensions, for, though she could hardly bear being under the same roof as Mrs Smythe, she knew she must wait until the cold snap was over to find new lodgings. In the meantime, she had kept mostly to her spinning wheel, venturing out to the market for provisions less frequently than before as, given the cold, she could conserve edibles in the larder for longer. Paul had been on hand to fetch up water and faggots for the wood burner.

'No, we shall go down together,' she said. She could not keep putting off an encounter. Anyway, the workshop would be closed.

As they descended the creaking stairway, they could hear the knocking of wood on the landing below. It could only be Mrs Smythe, sweeping before her door. Jeanne could hardly turn back, and besides, she would have to confront her at some stage.

'Madam,' said Jeanne as the landlady looked up from her sweeping. 'Happy Christmas, Mrs Smythe.'

Mrs Smythe cracked a smile which contrasted with her frosty frown, and returned her lodger's season's greetings. She sniffed and feigned not to notice their high-class garb.

'By the way, Madame Delpech,' she said, standing prim

and proper behind her broom. 'I should inform you that the new weaver will be moving in shortly now that the previous lodger, the northerner, has moved on.' She was talking about a discreet northern man who had rented the room above Jeanne's while he was in London. Jeanne had only ever seen him once, busy as she was at the time in the workshop downstairs.

'Thank you,' said Jeanne, who longed for the day when she would announce her move to another abode.

'So he'll be settling in Monsieur de Sève's old room. That poor friend of your husband's who died. Have you any news, by the way?'

'No, I have not.'

'May the Lord help him in his plight,' said Mrs Smythe, trying to be nice.

'Thank you,' said Jeanne, guardedly. Jeanne sensed the woman was leading up to something. It was clear she had deliberately formulated her chat to bring it round to Jacob so she could fish for news.

'I should also let you know,' continued Mrs Smythe, 'I have purchased another loom, better for silk. The other one will be needing a weaver, though, should you be inclined . . .'

'Thank you, Mrs Smythe, but I am sure you will find someone to work it for you,' said Jeanne, desirous to curtail the conversation. By saying it out loud, she had at last made intellectual and psychological closure. She was relieved to imply that she would never work for the landlady again. She felt better, suddenly serene for it.

'I am sure I will,' said Mrs Smythe as Jeanne stepped across the landing. 'Especially as the job comes with rooms!'

Jeanne gave Mrs Smythe good day while pushing Paul onwards to continue down the last flight of stairs.

It was a beautiful and frosty morning. Bells were ringing out across London as they directed their steps to the Huguenot church on Threadneedle Street. They had set out earlier than usual to make sure they would get a place in a pew, although Mrs Clement, the warden's wife, did say she would save them places next to her and her husband.

Jeanne exchanged nods, bows, and Christmas greetings to acquaintances as they entered the church, already two-thirds full of finely yet soberly dressed Protestants. A far cry, thought Jeanne, from the gaudy fashions in France. Mrs Clement gave a sign, and Jeanne and Paul took their places.

The minister preached most excellently on Luke 3, she thought. But Jeanne soon let her attention drift and her thoughts ramble, and prayed for her husband's safe return should that please Almighty God. Then she got to pondering over Mrs Smythe's remark. She had said that the weaver job came with accommodation, but there were no other rooms available if the new weaver was taking the one recently made vacant. Jeanne concluded that it was a thinly veiled threat. Either she resumed her work at Mrs Smythe's loom, or she would be thrown out on her ear. Whatever the legality of the situation, it meant Jeanne would have to act quickly. For she was adamant this time: she would never set foot in Smythe's workshop again. It was bad enough knowing that the woman slept in the room beneath hers, let alone sharing the same air under her haughty stare.

After the service, she and Paul joined Mr and Mrs Clement along with Pastor Daniel and half a dozen other acquaintances for Christmas dinner at their house in neighbouring Soho. Jeanne was surprised to find a handsome neoclassic town house, three windows wide and three storeys tall. It was set back from the street and entered through an elegant white portico. Decidedly, Mr and Mrs Clement had done well to have fled France with their fortune intact before the troubles in France had begun. Jeanne felt a pinch in her heart at realising she could well have done the same, and been in a similar situation now with her husband and children around her at this Christmastime.

A gentleman who Jeanne knew by sight but had never officially met was introduced to her as Monsieur Jacques Rulland. An English gentleman of French ancestry, his father had moved his English wife and their family to London from La Rochelle back in '48 after Cardinal Mazarin, in an effort to curb Protestantism in the port city, founded the bishopric of La Rochelle. A mature and prosperous man in his early fifties, Monsieur Rulland possessed a weaving house and had been a widower since the previous year, when his wife succumbed to scarlet fever. He had the rigid allure of an Englishman, and spoke French with a slight English accent, pleasing to a French ear. It occurred to Jeanne that this was how Paul might sound and appear in years to come, the gentleman having left France at the same age as her son.

After the usual badinage, the topic of conversation at table inevitably turned to the Irish campaign, the fear of James Stuart's return to the throne, and the determination of the new Dutch king and the English people to retain their freedom to practice the religion of their choice. It was common knowledge that Jeanne's husband was fighting in Ireland, and she appreciated that they had not limited the conversation on her account. After the mention that there would be no more advancements made during the months of winter, in her calm and poised voice, Jeanne said: 'I only hope and pray I get my husband back. Though I am proud he has embarked on the fight to stave off intolerance.'

'And so you should be, dear Madame Delpech, and so should we all!' said Mr Rulland quite spiritedly in his quaint English accent. 'And so should his son, my word!' he continued, placing a benevolent but frank eye on Paul, a cue for the boy to speak.

'I am, Sir,' said the lad forthrightly. 'And I hope to follow in his footsteps.' This took everyone by surprise, coming as it did from an eleven-year-old, and no one less so than his mother. There had been no soldiers in her family, and she secretly hoped there never would be. But not wanting to belittle him, she held her tongue.

'And whose side would you fight on, my lad?' said Mr Clement.

Paul sensed this was an important question, especially as it was asked by none other than one of the men who let people into church. 'Why, that of freedom of conscience, of course!' Mr Clement gave a thin-lipped smile of appreciation while the table gave a round of hear-hears.

Mr Rulland raised his glass. 'To the birth of our Lord Jesus and freedom of conscience!'

After dessert, they retired to the spacious, high-ceilinged parlour with crystal chandeliers, where Mrs Clement and her daughters led the singing. Then they merrily played blind man's buff. Jeanne laughed so hard, it brought tears to her eyes and made her cheeks hurt. It surprised Paul to see her so merry. In fact, he did not recall ever seeing her in such a frivolous state.

After the fun and games, a collation was served.

'Madame Delpech,' said Mr Rulland, who was sitting opposite her in a wide-winged armchair. Jeanne was seated on a canapé. There was a low table between them with a tray of mince pies, and Mrs Clement sat in her poised and affable way next to her. 'I have been given to understand you have a talent for the loom. Surprising of so fair a lady, if I may say so.'

Both piqued and flattered at the suggestion that weaving was below her, Jeanne said: 'Surprising, perhaps, but it has stood me well, Sir, and helped me pay my own way.'

'I see. If I may be so bold as to ask, who do you weave for?'

'Actually, I am contemplating acquiring a loom of my own, for the wage I earned at my previous employer was ridiculously low compared to the going rate.'

'I see. So you are without a loom for the moment?'

'I am, Sir. But I have my spinning wheel to keep me going. I should have to move to new lodgings before I install a loom.'

'Madame Delpech says she would very much like to learn silk weaving,' prompted Madame Clement.

Jeanne explained: 'I have been given to understand there is a more lucrative market in silk cloth.'

'Indeed, there is, Madame,' said Jacques Rulland. Then, licking his lips as though turning over words in his mouth, he inched forward in his seat and said: 'As a matter of fact, Madame Delpech, silk is one of my workshop's specialties. Should you be seeking employment, albeit temporary, I should be glad to have you aboard. If you know how to use a loom, then you will learn silk weaving quickly enough.'

'Oh. That is most kind of you, Monsieur Rulland. However—'

'Please,' said Rulland, sensing the prelude to a rebuff, 'there is no hurry for an answer. But please, do dwell upon it, Madame.' He brought out a visiting card and handed it to her. Jeanne thanked him kindly and promised she would.

From the other side of the room, Mr Clement stood up and suggested a last game of blind man's buff, to everyone's delight.

Rising with her counterparts, Jeanne felt a warmth in her heart with the assurance that should Jacob, alas, not return from Ireland, she need not remain a lonely widow for very long. And then, as the very thought of becoming Jacob's widow sunk into her slightly fuddled mind, she clasped Paul's hand and inwardly prayed her husband would return to her, that they would live again as a family.

*

Jeanne had had a delightful day in the bourgeois comfort at the Clements' house in Soho.

Now she felt like a countess as she was driven through the streets of London, through Bishop's Gate, up the busy thoroughfare, and through the narrow streets past Spittle Field. How easy it was to fall back into manners of old, she thought. It felt right. She was once a wealthy countess, after all.

But of course, it was all a sham. Tomorrow, she would be dressed in her common grey petticoats and bodice. Tomorrow, she would be carrying water to her rooms. Tomorrow, she would be lighting faggots, opening windows to let out the smoke, and stuffing rags into gaps to stop up the cracks in the wood burner. If it was sunny, she would be spinning at the window; if it was overcast, she would be spinning by the stove, in spite of the dim light. But that was tomorrow.

Today, she was a French countess, dressed in elegant simplicity, wrapped in her warm travel cloak, riding through the streets of London in a carriage paid for by a gentleman acquaintance. Mr Rulland in his enthusiasm had even promised to take her for a bucolic ride into rural Hackney, come springtime. Naturally, she had declined; it would not be correct to accept to go on such an outing with a gentleman unless they were accompanied. But she noted that he had not been put out and suspected that he would arrange something with the Clements.

People glanced up at her as the carriage trundled through the crowded poor districts. Paul was gripped by the view out the opposite window; how strange it was to look at his play area from the height of the carriage. It looked shabby, and he felt ridiculous in his best bourgeois clothes. What would his street mates think?

They turned left onto Brick Lane, where the road was bumpy, frozen solid into furrows. A knock on the roof interrupted Jeanne's sumptuous thoughts. It was accompanied by the jangle of harness bells as the carriage came to a halt.

'Maman, we are here,' said Paul.

'Brick Lane, Madam,' called the driver.

Jeanne asked the driver to pull up past Brown's Lane. He did not need to see where they lived. After descending, she felt the shock of passing from Soho to Brick Lane, and suddenly worried she would be taken for a wealthy bourgeois who had lost her way. She clenched her cloak around her and hurried along with Paul to the tenement building.

But a few minutes later, they were thankfully climbing the stairs to their rooms. It was getting dark already, and there was a warm glow coming from the door ajar on the landing above. It was accompanied by the sound of scraping, as if furniture was being moved.

As Jeanne turned the key in the lock, someone came bounding down the stairs. It must be the owner of the pile of linen that had been left on her landing, she thought.

'Oh,' said a male voice as Jeanne half turned to face the stairs. She saw a young man with cavalier curls. He bowed. 'Er, I am . . . Monsieur Chausson,' he said, fumbling for words in English.

'You can speak in French,' said Jeanne levelly.

'Ah, good, that's a relief,' he continued. 'I am the new weaver, Madame . . .'

'I see. And I am the old one,' returned Jeanne, unable to keep a sardonic twitch from creasing her brow.

'Oh, I would never have guessed,' said Chausson, with a fleeting glance at her attire. 'I . . . I have been admiring your work, Madame. But if you don't mind me asking, why did you stop?'

'Shall we say . . . discordance,' returned Jeanne. The word just popped out of her mouth; she did not mean it to refer to any difference of social class, but it seemed so apt for many aspects of her life now.

'I can well understand that,' said the young weaver. He then explained he had been a journeyman since his arrival from Holland, though he was originally from Tours, where he had been an apprentice. 'I shan't be here long, though, a stopgap until I get to grips with the language. Then I'll get my own premises and a loom of my own,' he said. Jeanne wondered if Mrs Smythe and the seamstress would let him get away so easily. Without further discussion, he picked up his pile of linen and bid her and the boy season's greetings and a good evening.

A few moments later, she sat down on her bed, her dress discordant with her surroundings, her education discordant with her situation, and stared at her spinning wheel, discordant with her breeding. But had she any other choice than to be what she was not? At least she had not betrayed her faith and deepest convictions. Paul came and sat on the bed beside her.

'Mother,' he said, 'what will you do if Papa does not come back, like the gentleman implied?' She looked at him as his eyes welled.

*

Jeanne worked through Christmastide and into the New Year, her orders keeping her busy, keeping her mind from becoming wayward. For she had been thinking of her future options, whether Jacob returned or not.

She could take up Mr Rulland's job offer, or wait to purchase a loom once the cold snap was over and she had found new accommodations. The second option would give her freedom from subordination. However, it would also mean living life to the rhythm of the loom beater. But the encounter with the French-born English gentleman and the ride in the carriage also allowed her to realise that she was not as old as she sometimes felt. She still had her breeding and could still attract a husband of quality. And she still had a good few childbearing years ahead of her yet. Should she have to remarry, she knew it would be hard to build an unbreakable bond of love such as the one she had enjoyed with Jacob. She would have to build instead a strategic alliance for the sake of her future, to save herself from the loom and to give her children a station in life that she had forfeited by not recanting her faith in France. Someone like Monsieur Rulland, who had known true love and would have more pragmatic expectations, might be a prime choice.

Sitting at her wheel, she gazed out at the barren yards lit up by rare winter sunshine, as her ears pricked to the sound of heavy masculine footsteps on the stairway. The new weaver returned to his room every day at lunchtime. No doubt to escape the oppression of Mrs Smythe, thought Jeanne. She had left him to his own devices, had exchanged neighbourly greetings whenever they crossed on the landing. He looked the part and seemed to be getting on well, especially with the girl. On returning from the market, Jeanne often heard gales of laughter coming from the workshop and overheard the seamstress correcting his English. The girl was apparently showing a better frame of mind with him than she had done with her. And Jeanne had once heard a soft giggle and two sets of footsteps creeping up to his room. It was looking as though young Nelly would catch herself a weaver after all. And why not? She was pretty; she would teach him English; they would make a complementary team when setting up business.

Their alliance made sense, as had hers with Jacob. Jeanne born into a noble family, he a wealthy notary, and they had made a beautiful family, shattered by the folly and intolerance of the Catholic Church and a king.

The steps halted outside her door. She turned on her stool with sudden alarm on the second rap. 'I'm coming . . .' she called out as she stood up. Crossing the room, she tucked her fringe beneath her bonnet. Dear God, she said to herself, closing her eyes, bracing herself for the dreaded news she had been half expecting. But as she stepped forward, the doorknob was turned. The door flung open. There stood not one but two people. Paul in the arms of his father!

Jacob stood wordless on the threshold as Paul scrambled to the ground.

Dumbfounded, Jeanne stopped in her tracks, four yards from the door, and let her hands drop to her sides. Jacob, thinner, rugged, and dressed in a grey military overcoat, was barely recognisable as the middle-aged, portly merchant-planter she last saw nigh on four yours ago. Attired in a simple grey dress, wisps of hair escaping from beneath a white bonnet, Jeanne stared intently with her pale blue eyes.

'Jeanne?' said Jacob. She realised how she must look to him; he had never seen her in a cloth maker's garb. 'My dear Jeanne,' he continued. Her eyes studied the soldier's uniform, then his face. He had a scar on his right cheek, half covered by his beard of two weeks.

Paul tugged on his father's thumb, and Jacob stepped into the room. 'I expect you are hungry,' said Jeanne.

'I expect you are angry,' said Jacob.

Jeanne shook her head. His eyes conveyed to her his deepest regret and told her he realised all she had suffered. She bowed her head into her knuckle; then she lunged towards him. He took a step forward and met her grasp with his embrace.

'I am here now,' he said, kissing her forehead, then her cheek, then her lips.

Paul said: 'I will go and fetch some more wood.'

'And some beef!' said Jeanne, cheerily, wiping away her tears of joy as the boy flew out, closing the front door behind him.

She turned back to Jacob. 'Our daughters . . .' she began. But he put a finger on her lips.

'I know. Paul told me.'

She guided him to the room next door, removed his greatcoat, then his jacket, his smell invading her senses. 'Does it still hurt a lot?' she said, on sensing him flinch at the touch of his left shoulder.

'Not anymore,' he said. He scooped her up like a newlywed and carried her to the rope bed, where he had thrown his hat.

*

Jeanne caressed his bosom with her palm, then ran her fingers lightly over his left shoulder, softly exploring the deep red scar in his flesh.

'It still hurts.'

'It twinges. Still cannot raise it above my head, but I should rather count myself lucky. Half a span further, and it would have been my neck . . .'

She placed an ear to his chest so she could listen to his beating heart. 'I missed you. I missed us, Jacob,' she said as he caressed her hair. Then she raised her head as a sudden thought pierced her mind. She said: 'You are not going back.' He touched her temple lightly with his right hand but remained wordless. 'Jacob . . . Jacob?'

'The war is not over, my Jeanne. I must return when the campaign resumes. But we'll have time to work things out.'

Jeanne sat bolt upright, her steely eyes glaring at him with indignation. 'Jacob, don't you dare! I have been through hellfire and heartache to follow you here. We have to get our children back and build a home. For the love of Christ, you will not leave me again, Jacob Delpech!'

Jacob was both moved and reassured by her passionate outburst. She loved him, and he felt it in his heart. Nevertheless, trying to reason with her, he said: 'Jeanne, my dear beloved wife, I have thought of nothing else since I left Belfast. All the way, I have been tossing it over in my mind. But—'

'No, Jacob, no excuses! You will not leave me here in this horrid place! I can't anymore . . .'

'Wait, Jeanne, hear me out,' said Jacob, gently catching hold of her hands. 'You are right, and we have much to do. But the truth of the matter is . . . I need a wage.'

'I have heard it said at church that some soldiers will be allowed indefinite leave with a pension equivalent to half their normal pay. We shall move away to somewhere cheaper. We have never been city people, Jacob. We shall find a place in the country, near a port.'

Jeanne sat up straight, her ample breasts moving freely under her shift. She was still a beautiful woman; her hips were wider than when they first met, but she had maintained her figure.

He reached over for his jacket, slumped on the chair, and pulled out a pouch from his inner pocket.

'The truth is, my pay is in arrears. My partner is dead. This is my only treasure, my dear wife.'

Jacob reached then for the tray on which Jeanne had served him bread and cheese. He placed it upon the bed between them and rolled five acorn faces from the pouch onto it.

'These are what have kept me going, and they are frankly all I have left. I shall not stop until we are all together, Jeanne! Even if it means going back to war!'

Jeanne locked eyes with her husband. She read desperation and determination. He read compassion and resolution as she said more softly: 'You will not have to go back to war, Jacob . . .'

She jumped off the bed. He watched her hips swaying gracefully as she moved across the room to fetch her great cloak. She then skipped back and sat on the edge of the bed with a knife and carefully began unstitching the cloak's lining, the chill in the air making her nipples point under her shift.

'What are you doing?'

'Wait, and you will see,' she said.

He was thinking to himself how he had missed her body when she pulled out her hand from the lining to reveal a small leather drawstring pouch, one which normally carried change. Without a word, she untied the mouth. Then she poured not loose change, but diamonds and pearls, rubies and emeralds next to Jacob's acorns. Amazed, he recognised the diamonds, the pearls, and the gemstones that had been set in her ancestry jewels, her diadem, the necklace he had bought her . . .

'Why, you clever, clever lady!' he said joyfully, his hand meeting hers.

Jeanne explained how she once nearly lost them, how she had constantly sewn them into her coat, her skirt, her bodice, changing places lest someone suspected their presence. She told him about the horrid pauper who stole her coat, thinking her jewels were inside the lining, then how he had followed her and stolen her bag, leaving her for dead. She spoke about her life in Geneva, her stay in Schaffhausen, and her escape with Paul through the war-torn region of the Palatinate.

'Now, Jacob. You shall not go back to war. We have both been through enough wars. And we have means to find a home for your acorn family!'

He placed the tray beside the bed and wrapped her in his arms as they heard footsteps, deliberately loud on the stairs. Jeanne quickly whipped her shawl around her shoulders as the latch was lifted and Paul entered the room next door.

He put down the basket of wood and placed the slab of beef on the table. Responding to his mother's call, he entered the bedroom where he looked coyly but contentedly at both his parents in the bed in the middle of the day. His bashful smile broadened when his gaze fell on the tray. Upon it, he saw the gemstones. Among them, he saw the acorn faces he had made all those years ago in the farmhouse where he stayed with his mother and sisters. He wished they could all be together now.

TWENTY-TWO

AMID THE SEETHING melee of fighting men, Jacob suddenly remembered to never leave his flank exposed. He swung round desperately, wildly clashing sabres as another determined assassin came upon him . . .

'Jacob. Jacob, darling. You were having one of your bad dreams . . .'

They came less frequently nowadays, but when they did, he felt drained of energy and at odds with himself, as if his soul had been scathed. Then, as always, he remembered he had killed a man. In fact, he had purposely killed twice. Once in the woods of a Cuban township when he shot an assailant in the chest, and once with his sword in a cornfield in the Carlingford mountain that overlooked Dundalk Bay.

He cracked open his eyes at the caress of a calming hand on his greying temple. Jeanne knew his nightmares came especially when he was agitated over something. She too had spent a wakeful night, unable to get to sleep under the weight of her regrets.

'It'll be all right,' she said as he held her hand an instant on the side of his face.

A few moments later, Jeanne jumped out of bed and threw on a brocaded robe over her nightgown. Jacob eased his legs over the edge of the bed while she folded back the interior wooden shutters, then pulled open the window that looked out onto the emerald hills south of Dublin. The deep green scenery always had a soothing effect on him, whatever the weather, especially after a nightmare. Jeanne enjoyed the view, too, for it was the colour of hope.

There came a soft knocking at their door.

'Come in, my boy,' called Jacob, having recognised his son's footsteps in the corridor. He told himself he must kick the habit of calling him *my boy*. He was a young man now, after all.

Paul pushed the door into the bedroom, where morning light flooded through the window that his mother was closing. She turned to face him with an anxious furrow on her brow. He was already dressed in his uniform, not grey as he had remembered his father's to have been, but Venetian red. 'Mother, Father,' he said. 'A messenger has come. The *Sapphire* is in the roadstead.'

'Thank you, thank you, dear Lord!' said Jeanne, clenching her hands.

'But the tide will be out, so might I suggest we head out for Ringsend?'

The village of Ringsend was located on the estuary of River Liffey, a mile from Dublin, and barely a couple of miles from their house. It was where ships could ferry urgent goods, messages, and passengers when faced with contrary winds, or if the tide was not favourable for an entry into Dublin harbour.

'Should I get the messenger to tell them to unload the barrels as well, Father?'

'No, Paul, the wine can wait, my boy,' said Jacob, slowly half turning with a hand on the base of his back. 'The barrels can be unloaded in Dublin. Ouch . . . I only wish I hadn't put my blasted back out.'

'Serves you right for trying to lift one on your own! Honestly!' said Jeanne, in mirthful rebuke. Jacob realised her playful tone was a vent for her deep relief. The ship was in!

'Oh, it wasn't so much the barrel as my blasted shoulder giving me gyp; that's what put my back out.'

Jacob had been laid up for two days already, but at least he was able to sit up and walk now.

'I can go on my own if you prefer, Father,' said Paul.

'Oh no, my boy, much better today. But I shall let you take the reins, though.'

Paul said he would have the carriage ready in half an hour. Then he took a step back into the corridor and closed the door behind him.

A robust young man of eighteen, bicultural and bilingual, Ireland was now his home. He had been schooled by a master in the new Huguenot town of Portarlington and was destined for a military career in the British army, albeit against his mother's wishes. But Jacob still hoped to bring him over to the family business.

It was May, the year 1698, twelve years after the dragoons invaded Montauban and ejected Jacob, Jeanne, and their children from their home. After William of Orange had chased James Stuart from Ireland, Jacob was among the loyal Huguenot officers who were awarded a pension which equated to half his normal pay. Like many Huguenots, he was invited by the English Crown to settle in Ireland, where the cost of living was cheaper. They had been settled in their new home since '92. Around the same time, he had also received an invitation from friends to settle in New Rochelle. But Ireland was closer to France, and Jeanne had never lost hope of seeing her daughters again. 'As long as there is a breath in me still, I shall hope,' she would say.

Jacob's pension was barely enough for a family to live on, even in Ireland. But from the proceeds of the sale of Jeanne's jewels, Jacob was able to build a house a mile south of Dublin from the ruins of an old farm. He had since managed to build up a small trading nexus with the help of his late brother-in-law, Robert Garrisson, and former business partners now settled in Amsterdam. There had been ups and downs with cargo lost to the French and rough weather, but Jacob had long since learnt to hedge his orders by not putting them all in the same ship. The small business had kept him going.

The house that they called *Les chênes*—translated as The Oaks—was a far cry from the château Jeanne and Jacob Delpech de Castonnet had left behind in the south of France. It was of simple construction, with large windows and spacious enough with five bedrooms, three good chimneys that also served the upper floor, flagstone flooring in the kitchen, and solid oak floorboards elsewhere.

Despite his back pain, Jacob was particularly joyful this morning, and pleased by the knowledge that the ship at anchor had brought his first delivery of barrels from France safely to port. Since the Treaty of Ryswick, signed the previous autumn, so bringing an end to the Nine Years' War, business was flourishing. The Channel had become a less dangerous place, now that trade had resumed with France.

However, trade was far from being his main concern today as he sat contemplating the early-morning sunshine breaking through the clouds, flooding the distant hills here and there in a golden sheen. It was not the warm, vibrant sunrise he used to love in his homeland of southern France, but it nonetheless brought him an inner peace.

'Are you sure you don't want to come to the landing stage?' he said to Jeanne, who was doing her toilette at her dressing table behind a three-fold screen.

'No, Jacob, there will need to be extra room for baggage, and besides, who will look after Pierre?' Of course, the maid could look after their youngest, but Jacob said nothing, suspecting that she wanted it to be like a homecoming.

*

The mackerel sky, strewn with longer rags of blue, brightened the deep greens here and there of the surrounding fields. Little Pierre, Paul's six-year-old brother, jumped off the swing attached to the oak tree upon the sound of an approaching carriage.

'Mother!' he called out from the front door. 'They're here!'

Having removed her apron and left her culinary preparations to her maid, Jeanne now stood, wringing her hands on the threshold.

How could she explain her flight from France, leaving her daughters for the sake of her faith? In their eyes, was she not the mother who had abandoned her children?

Paul pulled on the reins, and the open carriage slowed to a halt at the bottom of the garden, a stone's throw from the front door. Jacob climbed stiffly down, then gave his hand to his eldest daughter.

Elizabeth had felt overjoyed and strangely humbled to find her father waiting for her at the windswept landing stage, along with her brother Paul, a young man now, and so fine in his military frock coat and boots.

Neither she nor Jacob spoke about what had become of the townhouse, the château, the estate, and the farmland. Before his death the previous winter, Robert had made it clear in a letter to Jacob that there was no possibility for Protestants abroad of recovering confiscated land and property.

Neither did they speak of religion or of his daughters' forced Catholic upbringing. Instead, they spoke about the difficulty of leaving France, of the long voyage and how Aunt Suzanne had insisted on having her manservant, Antoine, chaperone them to the ship in Bordeaux.

'She has become more fretful since Uncle Robert passed,' Elizabeth had said. 'Thankfully, she still has Cousin Pierre, and us . . .' After an awkward pause, she had said: 'Father, you do know that I must return to Montauban?'

Jacob recognised the steely resolution of Jeanne in his daughter's eyes. He had said: 'Fear not, my dear daughter, I have not asked you to come here to deprive you of your free will.' She was contented, but what about her mother?

Isabelle, overawed at meeting her father and brother, sat with her hand in her sister's. Jacob let her get used to him in her own good time. He trusted the knotted threads of the past would all become untangled in due course.

But other long-harboured worries assailed Elizabeth as they had made their way between laboured fields and meadows with gambolling lambs to the house in the country. She had had her reasons for refusing to leave France all those years ago, for letting Paul go with the guide instead of herself. But was it really to remain with her sister? Or was it through self-interest and preferring the company of her friends in Montauban? She had nevertheless taken it upon herself to become her sister's surrogate mother, albeit not realising the role would last so long. It was one reason why, at twenty-five, she had so far refrained from marrying, even though she had not lacked suitors, especially with the Delpech patrimony thrown into the marriage portion. And would her mother forgive her for wanting to return to her hometown after this visit? Would she forgive her at all?

Jeanne recognised Elizabeth in the body of a poised, pretty, and refined young woman as Jacob helped her alight. Then she instinctively turned to take the little girl's hand in a motherly fashion.

It suddenly occurred to Jeanne that she must look a great deal older than the lady in the painting that the girl had grown up with.

After a moment of unblinking hesitation, Jeanne marched forward, her hand to her mouth. But then emotion got the better of her self-restraint, and she ran like the wind as Elizabeth burst into tears and opened her arms unreservedly. Mother and daughter fell into each other's arms.

Moments later, Jeanne was at last holding the baby, now a girl of eleven, snatched from her breast in one of France's darkest and cruellest periods of intolerance.

*

Half an hour later, while Elizabeth, Paul, Jacob, and Jeanne chatted excitedly in the lounge before dinner was served,

Isabelle played with her younger brother on the swing under the oak tree. She thought it all very strange, being an elder sister and having parents. Yet somehow it all seemed to fit, like a torn tapestry stitched back together.

Enjoy this book?
You can make a big difference

Thanks for reading *Land Of Hope*, I hope you enjoyed it.

Honest reviews of my books help bring them to the attention of other readers. If you've enjoyed this book I would be very grateful if you could spend just five minutes leaving a review on the book's retailer page.

Thank you very much.

Paul

ABOUT THE AUTHOR

Paul C.R. Monk is the author of the Huguenot Connection historical fiction trilogy and the Marcel Dassaud books. You can connect with Paul on Twitter at @pcrmonk, on Facebook at www.facebook.com/paulcrmonkauthor and you can send him an email at paulmonk@bloomtree.net should the mood take you.

ALSO BY PAUL C.R. MONK

In the HUGUENOT CONNECTION Trilogy

MERCHANTS OF VIRTUE (Book 1) France, 1685. Jeanne is the wife of a once-wealthy merchant, but now she risks losing everything. Louis XIV's soldiers will stop at nothing to forcibly convert the country's Huguenots to Catholicism. The men ransack Jeanne's belongings and threaten her children. If Jeanne can't find a way to evade the soldiers' clutches, her family will face a fate worse than poverty and imprisonment. They may never see each other again…

VOYAGE OF MALICE (Book 2)
Geneva, 1688. Jeanne dreams of her previous life as a wealthy merchant's wife before Louis XIV's soldiers ran her family out of France for refusing to renounce their faith. Jacob hopes his letters make it to Jeanne from the other side of the ocean. As he bides his time as an indentured servant on a Caribbean plantation, tragedy strikes in the form of shipwreck and pirates. If Jeanne and Jacob can't rise above a world that's closing all its doors, then they may never be reunited again…

Also in the The Huguenot Chronicles series

MAY STUART
Port-de-Paix, 1691. May Stuart is ready to start a new life with her young daughter. No longer content with her

role as an English spy and courtesan, she gains passage on a merchant vessel under a false identity. But her journey to collect her beloved child is thrown off course when ruthless corsairs raid their ship. Former French Lieutenant Didier Ducamp fears he's lost his moral compass. After the deaths of his wife and daughter, he sank to carrying out terrible deeds as a pirate. But when he spares a beautiful hostage from his bloody-minded fellow sailors, he never expected his noble act would become the catalyst for a rich new future.

Other works

STRANGE METAMORPHOSIS

When a boy faces a life-changing decision, a legendary tree sends him on a magical expedition. He soon has to vie with the bugs he once collected for sport! The journey is fraught with life-threatening dangers, and the more he finds out about himself, the more he undergoes a strange metamorphosis.

"A fable of love and life, of good and evil, of ambition and humility."

SUBTERRANEAN PERIL

Set in the story-world of Strange Metamorphosis, this action-packed novelette offers a thrilling episode of a boy's fabulous and scary adventure of self-discovery. When 14 year-old Marcel leads his crew out of a dark and disused snake tunnel in search of fresh air, little does he know he is entering the labyrinthic galleries of an ant nest.

CPSIA information can be obtained
at www.ICGtesting.com
Printed in the USA
BVHW031326301120
594518BV00025B/227